Readers love M. King's
Breaking Faith

"Sensual, moving … If you enjoyed *Brokeback Mountain*, you will love Breaking Faith."

—Renee Knowles, www.reneeknowles.com

"…brilliantly written, with stunningly well-drawn characters… superlative… I couldn't put it down…"

—Dear Author

"…a wonderfully written, intense story … an incredible honesty … This one will stay with you for a long time to come."

—5 Stars, Rainbow Reviews

BREAKING FAITH

M. KING

Dreamspinner Press

Published by
Dreamspinner Press
382 NE 191st Street #88329
Miami, FL 33179-3899, USA
http://www.dreamspinnerpress.com/

Breaking Faith

Cover Design by Mara McKennen

ISBN: 978-1-61372-119-3

Printed in the United States of America
Second Edition
October 2011

First edition published by Freya's Bower in 2008 under the same title.

eBook edition available
eBook ISBN: 978-1-61372-120-9

"In the South the traveler learns the idealism that makes all great causes possible. Idealism is a response of the heart to the beauty or ugliness in the world around us."

—from *The Sacred Tree*, Four Worlds Development Project

CHAPTER ONE

IF THERE'S one thing the Northwest does well, it's cold weather.

Halfway through the second week in January, the Montana winter had set in with teeth and claws of ice, and Brett Derwent was wondering why the hell he'd decided to take this job in the first place. Sure, he'd done the training, and "apprentice ski instructor" looked great on application forms, especially where it concerned kids' classes, youth leadership, and all that other total bull that colleges loved, but....

Right now, waiting on the lower slopes of Bear Paw Ski Bowl with a pack of twelve bored and fractious five- to seven-year-olds and windchill bringing the temperature to fourteen below, college applications just didn't seem like the best reason to be here. If Lisa, the certified instructor, didn't show up within the next ten minutes, Brett wasn't going to be responsible for his actions.

"I have to pee," one of the kids whined.

He sighed inwardly.

"There's a Porta-Potti behind the concession stand, Jenny."

The little girl screwed up her face in complaint.

"Unless you're not brave enough to go on your own," he said—a low blow, but he couldn't leave the group unsupervised.

Jenny scowled.

"I am so!"

"All right, then. Take your buddy and don't be long, okay?"

"'K," she said reluctantly.

Brett smiled as she stuck one gloved hand in that of her friend, Shannon, and started off toward the stand. Bear Paw had nothing like the bustle and chaos of a big resort, so he could keep tabs on all of the kids without leaving any of them really unattended, but that wasn't the point. If Lisa didn't get here soon, a riot might break out.

Cussing her under his breath, Brett broke up a rapidly escalating snowball fight at the back of the group and got the kids started on some warm-up exercises and positional practice. At least teaching them through games made it easier to keep them occupied.

It wasn't the group's first class, and even the most junior novices knew how to play "pizza and chips," so, within a couple of minutes, Brett had the kids moving in parallels and practicing how to balance their weight without even realizing it. Sneaky education, he thought, still scanning the horizon for Lisa.

Her affair with Doug, the under-tens' advanced coach, might be common knowledge, but it wasn't really spoken about in town. Havre, like a lot of the Hi-Line area, tended to be about as accepting as a place can be without genuine tolerance; that is, you could get away with a lot, so long as you kept your business to yourself.

A lot, but by no means everything.

Right now, Brett didn't give a damn about the sanctity or otherwise of Doug's marriage vows (or Lisa's, come to that), but he could do without her leaving him in charge of a class he wasn't yet fully certified to teach while she got her après-ski in the back of Doug's truck.

He spotted her coming to join them just as Jenny trekked back from the concession stand. Lisa, tall, blonde and—if you liked that kind of thing—really very attractive, looked radiant. Glowing. Well-fucked, Brett thought irritably, which was more than some people got the opportunity for around here.

"Hey," he said as she gave him an exaggerated little wave.

"Hi, Brett. You started without me!"

"Just a few warm-ups," he said, resisting the urge to smack her in her expensive Dragon goggles.

"Well, it looks like you've done a great job. Okay, guys, those are great 'chips'…. We all ready to go ski?"

A ragged chorus of cheers sounded, and the lesson moved up to the bunny hill, with Lisa reminding the kids to keep doing their stretches and warm-ups on the ascent. The stuff, Brett realized, that he had already told them, though he wasn't about to say anything. His pay might be pretty paltry, but he got free time on the trails and, if he could stick it out 'til the end of March when the season closed, his college fund would really benefit.

Brett was looking forward to college. High school graduation already seemed like a lifetime ago, and over the past few months, he'd been watching most of his friends segue straight into jobs in town. Fine, but not what he had in mind. He had the grades, he had the ability, he knew, and now he almost had the cash. With luck, this fall he'd be off to Washington State.

Sure, the Montana State University-Northern campus lay right here in Havre, but that felt a little too close to home. Washington would be just far enough to be off the radar, and Brett couldn't help thinking of it as an application to life. He'd be leaving home, leaving Havre, leaving everything that made it hard to, well, come out. Not that he planned on throwing a pride parade the first minute he got onto campus. No way. It would just give him some time to meet new people, do new things, maybe even figure out exactly what he wanted out of life... which was totally different from knowing what he planned.

Brett *planned* to get into a good pre-med program, study hard, and be a doctor. He'd enjoy the challenge, he knew that. Helping people, making a difference. But wanting.... Whole different ball game, and a challenge he wasn't enjoying; it taunted and poked at him until he felt six inches high and stupid with it.

He knew, in a way, what he did want. Same as anyone: love, respect, friendship. Passion, in an ideal world. Sex wasn't a—okay, sex *did* present a problem. He preferred girls, mostly, to going solo, but they didn't excite him. He'd dated Lynsey Schaeder for two years straight, no pun intended, because the thought of not doing so, of having to run the dating gauntlet over and over, scared the crap out of him. She'd been convenient—no, honestly, they had both been convenient for each other—but Brett'd had to try hard to be hurt when, barely a week after the senior prom, she dumped him for some guy on the wrestling team.

He still missed the release Lynsey could give him, her warmth and humor, but she'd never really moved him despite the times he'd told her he loved her. Brett knew just what kind of bastard that made him, and he'd hated doing it though he'd been too scared not to. However, the way she looked at him, now that she had a guy who really made her light up, felt much worse. Every time Brett saw her—and they still moved in the same social circles, still turned up at the same parties—she looked so happy, but when her eyes turned to him, Lynsey got awkward. Not with embarrassment, it wasn't that. Even embarrassment would have been better than pity.

Brett figured she might as well chop off his dick and give it back to him in a box; it couldn't make him any less of a man. He'd faced up to the fact that girls didn't do it for him, but it stung to know he couldn't do it for them. Brett knew what he needed, what he wanted, but that didn't make it something he could translate to everyday life. The Treasure State might be big country, but the towns still acted pretty small.

Now, he supervised the kids off the lift, and Lisa lined them up, checking positions and talking to them in her broad, clear voice. He didn't want to be the gay kid. He didn't want to have to play all those games of acceptance and politics when, well, when he'd never even been with a guy in the first place. It felt… fraudulent.

Brett hunkered down, showing Jenny how to bend her knee without tightening up.

"Like you're sitting in a chair, not hanging on a trapeze," he said, and she laughed.

When she isn't being irritating, she's a good kid.

Her left binding, joining her boot to the ski, squeaked a little.

"Did Lisa check this for you when you put your skis on?" he asked.

"Uh-huh."

"And did your mommy rent the skis, or are these yours, Jenny?"

"They're mine. They used to be Sarah's, but they're mine now."

Brett nodded. Sarah, Jenny's older sister, had been consistently highly placed in downhill races for her age group, leaving Jenny justly proud of her. Sarah had nearly eight years on her sister, though, so that meant the bindings were at least—

"Brett? Is there a problem? We don't want to hold the class up when we're already running late."

And whose fault is that, Lisa?

Brett straightened up and waved to her.

"Uh, Lisa? Has the DIN on Jenny's bindings been checked? I'm not sure that—"

"They're fine," she called, waving the next group of kids on. "Old, but fine. All right, that's very good, Kurt. Remember, big as a house, then small as a mouse on the end of the turn. And keep your elbows in! Okay!"

Jenny looked indignant. "They're not old!"

Brett patted her on the shoulder. "They're great," he said wearily. "But you be careful, all right?"

"Brett?" Lisa clapped her mitts together and pushed the next set of kids into action when she called to him. "Brett, could you just scoot down there and make sure we don't have any loose cannons at the bottom of the run, please? That's it, remember, everybody keeps together!"

"Sure. Uh. You might want to look at—"

"Okay, guys!" Lisa turned back to the class. "Keep it comin'!"

Brett pushed off and went to haul in the group of three boys who were already ranging over the slope. They might have energy to burn, but it would be nice if they managed to do it without wiping out any passersby.

He squinted up at the mountain through his goggles. There might even be time for a few runs to himself after the class. He liked the freedom and the tranquility of the slopes, especially on fresh powder. A nice way to relax after having to deal with Lisa, though the chance wasn't looking likely if World War Three broke out, the way it was threatening to do among the boys.

"Kurt! Quit that right now, or I swear I will tell your mother, and I know what she's like when she's angry."

The scuffling ceased, and pretty quickly. Kurt Anders, a small boy with strawberry-blond hair and very pale blue eyes, looked briefly terrified. No one, least of all Kurt, wanted to risk the wrath of his mother. Gina Anders—PTA queen and part-time desk officer at the Sheriff's department—knew the whole town's business and was popularly thought to have eyes in more than just the back of her head.

The lessons weren't long, only an hour and a half at most in consideration of the age of the kids and their beginners' ability level, and perhaps because of that Lisa let her attention slip. They'd neared the finish time, but she still had Jenny under her supervision at the top of the trail.

Brett heard her fall before he saw it.

The girl screamed and slid, out of control. Her left binding had pre-released, shooting the ski out from under her, and from where he stood, Brett could hear the crack as the board flew up behind and hit her helmet.

Gasps and tearful screams burst from some of the younger kids, and he was moving before he realized it. Jenny skidded on her stomach, her arms pulled up in front of her face, and though she wasn't sliding as fast as if she'd been traveling at real speed, she was still heading for a brush thicket. Brett got in between Jenny and the trees, stopping her from getting caught in the glade but landing heavily himself in a big, tangled wipeout.

There was a horrible, sickening crunch. Brett sat up in the snow, trying not to panic. Jenny started to cry loudly; more encouraging than the pale silence of a child who's really hurt herself. With a scrape on her cheek and a cut on her lip, she was clutching her left arm to her chest, but seemed to be all right. He'd broken her fall, at least.

Brett ran through the first-aid drill as Lisa came running with the medi-kit. After ten minutes or so, swabbed and patched, Jenny acted pretty brave about the whole ordeal.

"You saved my life," she told Brett very gravely.

He tried not to laugh at her pinched, white little face.

"Now you see why we ask everybody to wear helmets, right?" he said instead, smiling at her.

Though glad he'd been wearing one, he hadn't come out of the tumble completely unscathed. A mild throbbing pain plagued his ankle and one wrist, together with more bumps and bruises than he really needed. A deep scratch on his jaw stung in the cold. Brett took off his goggles to assess the damage and almost cussed at a huge crack that ran the length of the lens. That had been the crunch, then. *Really* sickening, given how much they cost.

"…and coulda smashed my head right open," Jenny was saying, with the ghoulish delight of small children. She was obviously feeling better.

"Ah-huh," Brett said absently, getting slowly to his feet. "You know, if you spill brains on the snow, they make you come back and clean it up."

Jenny gave him a disbelieving look, then grinned.

She's fine.

Brett glanced at Lisa. She was shepherding the kids through the collection of bags and rucksacks and looking rather nauseous. He felt kind of sorry for her she hadn't listened, but accidents did happen— and so he went to talk to Jenny's parents when they turned up at the collection point.

"Brett saved my life!" she said again, and he groaned.

It wasn't at all true; her helmet and pads would have saved her from serious harm, but she could have been badly scared, and for a six-year-old, that would last longer than any cut or scrape. He said the same thing to her father, Mr. Jaeger, while Jenny's mother hugged her daughter. Mr. Jaeger shook his hand, and Brett caught a glimpse of Lisa giving him an evil stare as she put her gear in the back of her truck.

"Really, it's nothing to, uh… really. Uh. Bindings can release unexpectedly, and that's all that happened. It might be worth getting the settings tuned up. The sports store in town can do that for you. Actually," he added, tucking the busted goggles in his back pocket, "I'm heading down there now, so if you'd like me to drop the skis in, it's no problem. I'll give Mr. Klass your number."

The parents jumped at the offer, and Brett hoped they didn't think he'd suggested, however obliquely, that Jenny's accident had somehow been their fault. Equipment aged, kids got bigger, and DIN settings depended on the height and weight of the skier. Even a tiny little one like Jenny.

Lisa had already driven off by the time Brett loaded Jenny's skis and his own gear into his elderly, decrepit, and pug-ugly '88 Ford Bronco, but he figured that might be for the best.

BRETT parked as close to the sports store as he could. Havre's wide and desolate streets gave plenty of room for biting winds to swipe at unguarded flesh. He grabbed Jenny's skis and made a dash for the store through a vicious gust that chilled him with the burn of liquid nitrogen.

The door swung shut behind him, the electric bell above it announcing his presence with a brief, flat buzz.

"Cold one, huh?"

Brett looked over at the cash register. The guy behind it definitely wasn't Mr. Klass. Younger, for a start. A lot younger, probably no more than twenty. He wore his black shoulder-length hair loose, and his skin was coppery though not that dark. Brett guessed at him maybe being half-Indian, though more than that, he found it hard to tell. Havre lay close to the Chippewa-Cree Rocky Boy reservation, but the Gros Ventre/Assiniboine Fort Belknap rez wasn't far away either.

Whatever the guy's heritage, he'd gotten damn good genes. Dark, expressive eyes, high cheekbones, and a very, very sexy mouth.... Brett quickly pushed those thoughts right out of his head. He'd grown used to doing that years ago.

Look, but don't touch. And look away pretty damn quick too.

Whatever you do, don't get caught.

"Sure is," he said, and damn it because, but for the two of them, the store appeared to be completely empty.

Shit, this is going to be worse than trying to get through football season.

Brett knew by the law of averages that he wasn't the only one. He couldn't be. There had been nearly seven hundred students at his high school, and although not everybody who got called a queer or a dyke could possibly be one, there had never seemed to be any proof. Certainly not among his own friends, or in any kind of visible community. He guessed there must *be* people who came out… but he didn't know any. Nobody ever seemed to make a dramatic gesture out of it, anyway. Not if they were smart. Havre might have been the biggest town on the Hi-Line, but there wasn't a lot to do except bowl, go to the movies, or pick through other people's lives. So far, no one had moved Brett to take what he saw as that kind of risk. He preferred the comfortable cowardice of secrecy, he supposed.

He cleared his throat awkwardly.

"I, uh, I'm looking for Mr. Klass. Need a DIN check on a kid's bindings and some replacement lenses for a pair of Oakley Crowbars. HI yellow, if you have 'em."

The vision in hotness at the register smiled. An easy, broad smile. He reached up and tucked his hair behind his ear, leaving Brett's stomach in a confused knot.

"He's out for an hour or so, but I can take a look," the guy said. "Shouldn't take long."

"Sure. Uh, thanks."

Brett passed him the skis and the portion of Jenny's registration form with her height and weight on it. The ski classes required all the kids to hand over those details in case their settings needed checking. The guy took the skis and went through to slap them on the torque test machine, leaving Brett to occupy himself looking at the bindings and boots on the display shelf. Some sweet pieces of gear, but in the winter the stores always stocked up with new issues, trying to tempt him or— even better—the tourists into parting with some hard-earned cash.

"So, what? These your little sister's?"

Brett blinked. He hadn't been expecting the guy to carry on a conversation with him from in back, but he'd left the door open and he was looking out from around the machine, one of Jenny's skis located on the plate. The board creaked as the machine's gauge started to move.

"Uh, no. Student's," Brett said. "I'm shadowing the instructor on a beginners' class for kids. One of the girls took a tumble when the left one pre-released, so I thought… y'know."

The guy smiled that smile again.

"Man, this is a Marker binding. Don't need a machine to tell you it's gonna pre-release. Old one, too."

"Yeah." Brett chuckled. "Turns out they belonged to her older sister. I figured it's worth checking the setting, but I wasn't sure if the spring needs replacing. What d'you think?"

The guy made a few notes from the DIN chart taped to the torque tester.

"We-ell," he said as he came back to the counter, "they could do with a tweak, but you're right. The spring's worn. Could do with a new one, especially for a kid. Accident waiting to happen." He peered at the scratch on Brett's jaw and arched one thick eyebrow. "Or maybe already happened."

Brett half-raised his hand and smiled.

"Oh. Yeah…. She's fine, though. I thought I could help, just completely wiped out. Go figure, huh?"

That smile appeared again.

Hell….

"No good deed goes unpunished," the guy agreed. "I'd do these for you now, only I'm supposed to wait for Mr. Klass so there's someone on the counter. Should have 'em done inside twenty-four hours, though, so maybe you could come back and pick 'em up? We're open for a couple hours tomorrow, or you could come by on Monday."

He tucked his hair behind his ear again, and Brett followed the action with his eyes. He had incredible hands, graced with long, slim fingers, yet they weren't at all feminine. His nails were short and blunt, one or two torn, and calluses marked his palms.

Slowly, Brett became aware that he'd been asked a question, but more than that, he felt the guy's dark brown eyes on him, trailing over him as if he liked what he saw. It couldn't just be his imagination, could it?

"Uh, sure. Monday's fine," he said and, blinking, he looked away.

What the hell are you doing? screamed a voice in his head. *You idiot... he's checking you out. He is! Freakin' smile or something, moron!*

Brett stared at the faded linoleum floor and gave himself a good, hard mental kick.

So stupid....

"Okay. I can do the lenses for you now, though. Be right back."

"Thanks."

Brett exhaled slowly and took another look at the rows of ski gear on the wall. He didn't mean for his eyes to slide sideways, but it wasn't really like he'd be checking out the guy's butt if he did happen to look. And he definitely wasn't disappointed that his fleece hung down so far. He focused on the kick-ass bindings on the second shelf instead.

"Anything you like?"

Brett nearly jumped out of his skin. The guy had reappeared at his elbow, mysterious as smoke. Brett's pulse thumped in his throat. He turned, taking a step away from him and almost bumping into the display. He put out a hand to catch himself, turning it into a dismissive gesture.

"Ah, you know... a lot. But I think I have a few extra hours to work first."

"I hear that."

"Yeah, it's the car, the college fund, and then the fun stuff. Kind of sucks, but...."

The guy leaned against the counter, legs out in front of him and hands resting on the wood behind him. A white crewneck peeked out from beneath his dark-blue fleece and a flash of brown skin beneath that. *Ouch.* The guy had shoulders, too. Serious ones. Not built, but clearly fit; broad where he ought to be, tapering down to slim hips and those long, long legs.

Brett tried not to let his gaze trail down his body, focusing instead on his face. Definitely not his neck. *Hell, that's a nice neck.*

"If you really wanna torture yourself, we've got Atomic FFG 14s," he said, all golden skin over fluid muscles and a voice like dark chocolate. "14-DIN, high elasticity. Adjustable toe wings, movable AFD; you'll never wrench another knee again."

"Oh, God… how much?"

"Three eighty-nine," the guy said with a grin. "Or we got Rossignol Axial 2 140 Ti Pros, as per the World Cup circuit. You like freestyle, you'll love 'em. Forty percent stiffer heelpiece than the old design, so you lose less power and get a more responsive ski. Titanium springs, superwide brakes… and they're, like, indestructible. Of course, for $350, you'd hope so."

Brett shook his head. "I'd love to say you'd convinced me, but there's no way… looks like I have to learn to love my old Salomons."

That smile danced over the guy's face again.

"Forget it, I'm just practicing the hard sell. This is only my first week."

"You working the ski season?"

"Uh-huh." He nodded. "Weekends and two days a week 'til March. When I'm not here I work fittin' stone counters and worktops with a kitchen company in Burnham. It's a living," he added with a shrug. "So, college boy, huh?"

Brett grimaced. "Maybe. Hoping to get into Washington on a pre-med. Kinda starting to wonder if it's going to be worth the effort."

"Aw, it will. I'm Tommy, by the way."

He held out his hand. Brett shook it, and a strange, sad kind of smile crossed Tommy's face. Brett's gut flip-flopped, pulling him between panic and excitement for the briefest of seconds.

"Brett," he said, praying his voice wouldn't shake.

"Well," Tommy said, brandishing the cloth lens case he'd brought out from overstock, "Brett. One pair HI yellow Oakley Crossbar lenses. Guaranteed to slay all low-light conditions and a steal at $70."

Brett winced. "Ouch. Okay, and the torque check…?"

"Nah, that's on the house."

"You sure?"

Tommy nodded, and Brett told himself sternly that he definitely wasn't staring at that little arrow of flesh at the base of his neck, which absolutely wasn't becoming more delicious by the second.

"Thanks, man."

"No problem. Y'know, for a hero an' all, saving little kids from tragic mountain doom."

Brett groaned and handed over his card. "Oh, come *on*...!"

He would have said something more as Tommy ran the purchase through, but the electric bell buzzed, the door opened, and a family of weekend skiers entered, looking to rent equipment.

"There you go. I'll see you around, Brett," Tommy said, nodding at him as the weekenders clustered up to the counter.

"Yeah," Brett said lamely. "See you."

Brett would have liked to say his name in the same easy, familiar way that his own had tripped off Tommy's tongue, but somehow it just wouldn't come out of his mouth. He didn't know why. All the same, a stupid smile washed over his face as he stepped out into the street.

It didn't last long, because the wind blew in like a razor, and Brett dived back into the safety of the Bronco, cursing and reaching for the heater. It clicked and crackled like it normally did, eventually giving out a weak warmth only just better than nothing. Brett gripped the wheel and exhaled slowly.

What in the hell had that been about? He wasn't sure, other than the fact that Tommy had totally knocked him out. *God.* Talk about gorgeous. Had he really...? Brett buckled up and drove home slower than he needed to, thinking over the thousand-and-one things in his head. Most of them involved that sneaking little glimpse of Tommy's chest.

Damn.

CHAPTER TWO

TOMMY HAWKS sat in his 1980 Chevrolet pick-up, staring at the house. He'd parked a little way down, as usual, so the engine noise didn't disturb anyone, but he wanted to put off the moment when he'd have to get out and walk up to the door. He glanced at his watch. Nearly six o'clock and already getting colder. The heavy sky threatened more snow, and murky clouds coiled overhead.

Tommy sighed, got out of the truck, and hunched his shoulders against the wind. As he got closer to the front door, he heard the TV blaring. To his left, his father's gray Pontiac, parked crooked on the driveway, took up the space that usually held his mother's red Taurus. Tommy frowned.

He pulled the key from his pocket, let himself in, and stood for a moment in the dark hallway. The flickering blue reflections from the TV screen played on the faded wallpaper, a panel of light from the living room doorway cast across the brown carpet. Tommy wrinkled his nose at the smell of stale tobacco and beer.

He passed the stairs and went straight through into the kitchen. Everything seemed strangely quiet apart from the noise of the TV. It sounded like a wildlife documentary. Bears, maybe.

A large pile of dishes sat in the sink, though not as many as there'd been that morning. A chunky plastic magnet held a yellow notelet to the refrigerator.

All out to dinner, it read in his mother's writing.

Tommy rinsed out the dishes in the sink, set the tap to run to hot while he opened the fridge, and snagged himself a beer and the makings of a cold bacon-and-tomato sandwich.

While he was slicing the tomatoes, a noise in the doorway startled him. He quickly wiped the knife on his sleeve and slipped it back into the drawer.

"Tommy?"

Martin Hawks's voice rasped thick and low in his throat.

"Hey, Dad." Tommy turned around with the sandwich in his hand. "You hungry?"

Martin shook his head. A stain marred the collar of his wrinkled shirt, and his chin sported a couple of days' beard growth. His loose face, settled into sagging, uneven folds, spoke of an afternoon spent sleeping on the couch. His hair clung greasily to his cheekbones, and his bloodshot eyes followed Tommy uneasily, as if he was having a hard time making the world stop spinning.

"Ain't you workin'?"

Tommy bit into his sandwich. "I've been at work, Dad. It's after six."

"Where is she?"

Martin blinked and leaned a hand on the doorframe. He looked around the kitchen, then behind him into the hall. The last dirty, crumpled third of a home-rolled cigarette smoldered in his fingers. He took a pull on it, wincing at the smoke's acrid tang.

"Mom took the kids out to eat. You, uh, probably weren't feeling too good. You know how she likes to make sure their noise doesn't upset you, right? She left a note."

Tommy swallowed. Right now, he wished he had the sense to be somewhere else too. Just about anywhere would do. He wasn't hungry anymore, but he took another bite of his sandwich anyway.

Martin licked his lips. The stale beer-sweat-tobacco smell rolled off him as he shambled toward the counter. He picked up Tommy's beer and folded into one of the breakfast chairs.

"Upset," he muttered indistinctly. "Wouldn't be no upset if she didn't spoil 'em. Bring 'em up wi' no respect. You don't have respect, you don't have anything. Right, Tommy?"

"Right, Dad," Tommy said, chewing. "Respect."

His gaze flicked to the door, the hallway, and beyond that, what had once been known as the family room.

Martin belched. "Yeah. Hey, where you goin'? Sit down. Sit down and have a damn beer with me, kid. Come on. I'm your fuckin' father."

Tommy grabbed another beer from the fridge and sat down. Doing what Martin told him usually worked out easier, sooner or later. He ate the rest of his sandwich in silence, one hand picking at the label on his beer.

"S'like you," Martin said genially, pointing a little to Tommy's left. "That's why you couldn't hack workin' at the auto shop. No respect. *Discipline*. Not willing to... to, uh, sacrifice for anything. Y'only learn that through hard work. No wonder you crapped out."

Tommy's fingers tightened on the neck of the bottle, but he said nothing and raised the beer to his lips instead. He finished the sandwich and wiped his hand on his jeans.

"Not your fault," Martin said. "Y'mother never taught ya that. I know. Your mother—and I love her, God knows—but she ain't no kind of woman to teach a kid anythin' about self-control. Behavior. All her nerves and her headaches.... S'no wonder you grow up like you do. Like your brother. I mean, you're a spineless little cocksucker, but he...!"

Martin laughed wheezily, a tar-stained chuckle from the base of his chest.

"Remember how he used to be? Damn near piss'n in his pants 'fore he'd stand up for hisself."

Tommy stared at the table. Scott wasn't just his brother but his nonidentical twin. That meant something, and at any other time, Tommy would have said something in his defense, maybe risked the backhander that would go with it. But not now. He knew this rambling, shambling, amiable mood of his father's. It turned sour quicker than some of the others. And meaner. He took another swig of his beer. Martin was still smiling hazily, as if pleased with some clever joke he'd made, some piece of remembered pride.

"Always like that," he said. "All them whiny apologies. 'Sorry, Daddy....' I used to tell him—I told you, didn't I?—yeah. Sorry ain't gonna cut it. Sorry is... is a sign o' weakness. Day you can stand up and say 'Yeah, I was wrong', *that's* the day you're a man. Not when you just crawl about on your ass sayin' sorry."

Tommy finished his beer. He'd drunk it too fast, he knew that; he still felt the bubbles burning. He saw Scott bleeding. Sorry and bleeding. He hoped that this memory of his father's had been long-buried, not freshly burned. Maybe Scott had gone with their mother. A Big Mac with extra ketchup wasn't fry-bread tacos like Gramma used to make, but it had to be better than this.

Martin reached out and grabbed his arm. Tommy flinched. Their gazes met, and it seemed to Tommy that his father looked hurt. Hurt? What in the hell right did he have to that? Tommy stared back at him. They looked alike, he knew that, though he hoped he wouldn't end up drinking his way to the ravages that Martin had.

"Whassa matter with you? Jumpy little faggot." Martin lifted the bottle to his lips, gave another wheezy half-laugh, and patted Tommy's sleeve. "Nah. Nah... you're my boy, Tommy. You're a good kid."

Tommy looked away, brushing the ash off his sleeve, torn between the slimy hatred of this moment and the truth and the hope of it; that he loved his father and that, maybe, there might be good times again. It hurt. He stood up from the chair and stumbled a little.

"I'll... I'll get you another beer, Dad."

"Good boy," Martin muttered vaguely, slipping back into whatever moment had been occupying his mind.

Tommy stood the bottle on the table and left the kitchen, unable to be in there anymore. He took three or four steps into the hall, and his father's voice whipped him around the back of the head.

"Where ya fuckin' going now? I'm talking to you, Tommy! What—what's so goddamn important you always gotta be runnin' out on me, huh?" His chair rasped on the floor. "I say you could fuckin' go? No! So, what? You can't stand to spend five minutes with your own fuckin' father? Ungrateful little bastard!"

Tommy tensed. Martin's hand landed on his shoulder, spinning him around. *Amazing just how fast he can move when he's drinking.* The half-curled weight of Martin's hand cuffed the side of Tommy's head. *Sure, he might look like he's fogged up so bad he ought to be holding onto the carpet to keep from falling off, but he can still swing.* Another blow landed on his cheek, and his neck jerked as his head snapped round with the force of it.

They'd been of almost equal heights since Tommy's sixteenth summer, but Martin still had an inch or so and a good forty pounds on him. He wasn't a huge guy, but big enough to throw his weight around.

"C'mon. Where else you got to be, huh?" he demanded and pushed Tommy in the chest until he backed, hard, into the wall. "What's so fuckin' important?"

The burn of the cigarette, crushed out unheeded, zipped straight through Tommy's shirt and bit into the skin just below his collarbone. He winced.

Fuck!

"Sor— no. Nothing. I—I don't have anywhere else to be, Dad."

"Damn right you don't!"

Tommy rubbed the sore spot on his head and waited for the air in front of his eyes to stop vibrating.

"I'm hungry. Where's your goddamn mother? I don't know what a man has to do to get somethin' to eat in this fuckin' house...."

"I got it. I'll make you something, Dad. Why don't you go and relax, huh?"

Martin looked at him, unfocused for a moment, then shambled off back to the couch and the TV, mumbling as he went. Tommy leaned against the wall, exhaled, then got out a skillet and started to make scrambled eggs.

He took the plate in to his father and left him eating while staring at some crappy cable game show, unsure if he was really watching it or not. From out front, the sound of a familiar engine hummed, and he slipped out of the side door in the kitchen just in time to see his mother's Taurus pull up.

"*Tommeeee!*"

He knelt and caught Lila as she barreled out of the car and into his arms. Since Katie's advent, Lila had moved up to being his biggest little sister, and in her winter woollies with her pink down jacket, stripy pink hat, and bright pink scarf, she looked like a shiny chokecherry. Tommy hugged her tight.

"Hey, Bear Bait."

"We had Big Macs!"

"Really? Cool. How many'd you eat? Four? Six? Did they have to close the kitchen? Get security to throw you out?"

She stuck out her tongue, and he bussed the top of her head.

"Go on inside. You be quiet, though. Daddy's not feeling too good."

"Still?"

He looked up and nodded wordlessly in reply to their mother. Mei got out of the Taurus with an armful of brown grocery bags. She handed them off to Tommy so she could undo the straps on Katie's booster seat.

"Robbie, don't just sit there; help your brother with the groceries."

Tommy's youngest brother sloped out of the back of the car.

"Hey, Robbie," Tommy tried, but the kid ignored him, traipsing past with his hands in his pockets and scowling at the ground.

Tommy looked at his mother as she straightened up, baby Katie on her hip. She glanced at him and shook her head.

"I don't know. Something at school, maybe. He's been difficult all day. The… the both of them."

"Where's Scott?"

Mei shrugged. "I don't know. Out. Probably with that girl he won't bring home."

"Did he and Dad—"

"Not so's you'd notice. Tommy, it's cold. Can we go inside? Please?"

He kicked the car door shut after her and followed on indoors with the groceries, lingering a little to look up at the moon. Pale light washed the snow, mud-streaked on the ground but bright on the trees and the roof. Further down the icy track, the scattered neighbors' houses lay under thick blankets of powder, glass-like crystals frosting their wire fences.

The sound of crockery smashing tore the air and, from inside the house, Katie's tiny lungs gave vent to an improbably loud wail.

"You see what you've done now?" Mei shouted as Tommy walked through the door and placed the groceries on the counter. "You happy?"

"Oh, an' what's this? More fucking money," Martin retorted, lunging at the bags Tommy had set down. "What the hell you buy all this for?"

"Well, that's the funny thing about food, Martin. You buy it, then you eat it, and then you have to buy more. Crazy, no?"

Martin rooted through the groceries, muttering about budgets and overspending. Tommy took in the shards of broken plate on the floor, the red flush in his mother's face, and decided it would be best if he took Katie upstairs. She squalled in Mei's arms, her cheeks balled up like little apples and her eyes screwed shut.

"Let me—" he started, reaching out.

The egg hit Tommy in the back of the neck, hard, but not as unpleasant as the wet, sticky, cold sensation of it dripping through his hair as it broke. He tensed for a moment, then took Katie, her pudgy fingers stretching to dandle in the mess as he carried her out of the room. Martin's laughter and Mei's litany of reproach continued as he climbed the stairs. The house wasn't large, and all the talk of moving or extending the property had stopped when Martin lost his last job with the construction firm in town.

Tommy paused to check in on Lila and Robbie, playing a video game in the back bedroom they shared. It wouldn't be long before something had to be figured out there; at nine, Robbie was already itching for his own space, while Lila, at seven, would soon reach the point where a curtain hung on an old broom handle between her and her brother's half of the room couldn't provide enough privacy.

He took Katie into the bathroom and set her down on the floor while he wiped the worst of the egg out of his hair. She gurgled inquisitively at him and tugged at his jeans, so Tommy made a goo-goo face and a silly noise for her, and she laughed.

It wasn't as if either he or Scott could move out. The room they shared would be useful, but not as much as the wages. Tommy flushed away the paper he'd used and picked Katie up.

"Yucky egg," he said seriously.

Katie wrinkled her small nose and poked him in the eye with one pink finger.

"Ow." Tommy seized the little starfish hand and blew against her palm. "C'mon. Let's get you changed."

CHAPTER
THREE

SUNDAY in the Derwent household wasn't so much a day of rest as one of blissful apathy. Although Brett didn't need to be at the Ski Bowl until twelve, he got up fairly early and took Roscoe, the family German Shepherd, for a gentle walk before breakfast. The weather wasn't bad: clear blue skies, crisp air, and about eight degrees. Fresh snow had fallen in the night and it clothed the neighborhood like linen.

He arrived back at the house and found his mother in the kitchen making pancakes. She amply filled her fuzzy pink terry-cloth pajamas with the picture of the raggedy bear on the front, and her red hair stuck out at wild angles. A smear of flour graced one freckled cheek.

Roscoe lumbered in happily, tracking sludge marks with his paws. He threw himself down in front of the fire with a contented groan.

"Brett? Did you tire that poor old dog out running laps?"

That joke had been going long enough to be an antique; Roscoe wouldn't have run after two pounds of steak being pulled on a string.

"No, Mom."

Brett wanted, for a moment, to go and kiss her on the cheek, flour and all. Too soon now, he knew he'd lose all of this. It had been slipping away since high school finished, and once he went to college, he knew he'd never be able to come back and find things exactly the same. This moment, right here, held the traces of every perfect morning he could remember. His childhood, his whole life—the comfort, the closeness, and even, best of all, the boring mundanity of it.

Weekdays, he wouldn't have minded losing, if you'd asked him. All those years of rushed breakfast cereal, lost homework, and his father getting frantic because the car wouldn't start. Perhaps any day after ten a.m., he'd have said the same, that leaving home would be the biggest, brightest, best adventure he could have right now. Only this moment, this time, Brett wanted to savor.

This meant home.

MONICA DERWENT looked up at her son standing strangely quiet in the doorway. She still had a tough time believing he could ever have grown so big. He towered over her in height now, though she made up for her short stature with the kind of ample hips and bust that used to get Rubens excited. She smiled.

"Well, go and take a shower. Breakfast in ten."

"Okay."

Monica watched him go, watched him linger a little on the way. Her boy. Her son. No two words in the English language so satisfying. She bit down on the impulse to frame her lips around them, as if she could keep him close like that. No. He'd be going. She had him for one more summer, and then....

Somehow, she couldn't quite accept it would work like that. She'd lose her boy to college, she knew, because he'd come back more or less his own man. But he *would* come back. He might go, but he'd always come back to her.

Her son.

AFTER breakfast, Brett checked his e-mail and bummed around the Internet for a little while. He thought about reviewing some of the forms for his application to Washington, and then decided to go to work early. There were only so many times he could reread the same pages.

The class dragged on for what seemed like years. Lisa gave the impression of being pretty pissed at him over yesterday, though not as pissed as he guessed she must be at herself, and the kids—a different, slightly older group—acted all restless and fidgety. It came as a relief when the class finished and Brett had time to take a few runs himself.

The new lenses worked great, equaling out the weird light conditions on the advanced trails, and he enjoyed taking some of the downhill bumps, feeling free and light and at one with the mountain until his knees and the bruises from yesterday started to complain. Fresh snow came down too, already falling thickly by the time Brett got back to the Bronco and prayed to the god of engines for this one to actually start without a fight.

With a little tender loving care to persuade it, the Bronco did what he wanted, and he'd driven halfway back into Havre before realizing how much he was looking forward to the chance of seeing Tommy. He'd said he wouldn't go back 'til Monday, but… well, he could change his mind, right?

Brett hoped his disappointment as he bounced into the ski shop and saw Mr. Klass—small, round, and white-haired, beaming happily at him from behind the register—wasn't too obvious.

"Hello, Brett!"

Mr. Klass had sold Brett his first pair of ski boots, his first helmet, and pretty much everything else in between, so he hated to appear anything less than cheerful.

"Hey, Mr. Klass," he said, trying to pass off his glances around the store as nonchalant. "Uh, I came by to pick up a pair of girl's skis. A student's. Your, uh… Tommy, he was going to fix the DIN?"

"Oh, sure. Yeah, he did. Girl's parents came in to collect 'em this morning and paid the bill. Said to thank you."

"Oh." Brett tried not to sound crestfallen. "Oh, okay. Uh…."

He floundered, trying to think of some other reason to see Tommy but coming up short. He didn't want to mention the free torque check in case Mr. Klass didn't approve, and there didn't seem like much else to say.

"Heard you took a tumble for little Jenny, huh? Quite the hero." Mr. Klass grinned. "That's what Tommy told me, anyway, and her parents seemed to agree."

Brett groaned. "Oh, no… really? I, uh, I might just have to have words with him about that."

"You can do." Mr. Klass jerked his head toward the storeroom as the door opened to admit a gaggle of high-school ski bunnies. "He's out back. Probably be glad of the company, even if the company does want to kick his ass. He don't know a lot of people in Havre. Go on through."

"Oh. Uh… okay. Thanks."

Brett beamed. Providence rocked!

Tommy stood in the narrow storeroom breaking up cartons, his hair falling over his face and the sleeves of a red plaid flannel shirt rolled up to his elbows. Paper dust spiraled in the air, and Brett tried, nominally, not to look at his beautiful brown arms or the way his hands worked on the cardboard. Another cotton crewneck bagged attractively against his neck, only today what looked like a deerhide thong rested against the skin there. Brett made out a couple of beads that appeared to be polished jasper before he dragged his attention away.

Okay, this has to stop. Right now.

Tommy looked up and smiled. "Brett. Hey."

"Hi."

Again, he just couldn't make Tommy's name leave his lips.

"Mr. Klass tell you the girl's parents came in? Had really nice things to say about you."

"Aw, hell."

"Yep. Figure it won't be long 'til we see you in the paper, savin' somebody's cat from drowning or gettin' a kid out of a tree or something."

He shot Brett an evil grin, and they both laughed.

"Yeah… somehow, I don't see myself as the Captain Hero type."

Tommy gave him a look that, just for a second, made Brett feel oddly vulnerable.

"I don't know. Maybe you've got a secret identity."

Brett's heart thumped so hard he hardly dared open his mouth. He tried to think of some smart movie line, some clever way of coming back to that, letting Tommy know exactly what secrets he did have. Well, perhaps some of them… but his mouth dried out at the thought.

"Uh, maybe."

Oh, classy. That's just beautiful. What the hell's the matter with you?

Brett swallowed heavily. "So, uh, you want a hand there?"

He couldn't think of anything smoother, but he would have taken any excuse not to have to leave. Although Tommy looked surprised, he happily accepted, and they shot the breeze while stomping down the cartons.

It turned out that Tommy had graduated high school eighteen months ago, making him a little under a year older than Brett. He'd worked a succession of jobs since then and he, like Brett, liked to ski, though his taste ran to backcountry rather than downhill. He'd never thought about being an instructor, he said, despite the fact that he had qualifications in equipment repairs and maintenance.

"Could take you anywhere, huh?" Brett said, suggesting the lure of Aspen or Crans.

Tommy shook his head.

"Nah, I don't think so. I'll stay here. I could never leave Montana," he added, with the air of one reciting a poem.

Brett caught the reference. "Ah…. 'When it's springtime in the Treasure State, and the gentle breezes blow—'"

"'About seventy miles an hour, and it's fifty-two below'."

"'You can tell you're in Montana, 'cause the snow's up to your butt, and when you take a breath of springtime air'—"

"'Your noseholes both freeze shut'!" Tommy added, in chorus. "'But the weather here is wonderful, so I guess I'll hang around. No, I could never leave Montana'—"

"'My feet are frozen to the ground'!"

They collapsed into laughter, not over the poem—everybody knew it, and only out-of-staters worried about getting ice in their nostrils while shoveling the driveway—but because of something shared, something communicated.

As they bullshitted and goofed their way through the rest of the job, Brett started to look at Tommy with new eyes; he wasn't just attractive, but fun to be around.

"Whew!" Tommy whistled and straightened up, glancing at his watch. "Look at that. Near enough to clocking-off time. And I'm starving. You wanna get something to eat?"

Brett brushed paper dust off his hands. "Sure."

"All right. You know Julie Red Dog's taco place?"

"Uh… yeah. Yeah, I do."

Brett nodded. He knew it, though he'd never been in. Even Indian tacos could be considered pretty adventurous in a town that didn't normally expand its gastronomic repertoire much beyond four seasonings: salt, pepper, ketchup, and ranch dressing. Besides, something about going in to Mrs. Red Dog's made him feel slightly uncomfortable.

"Okay. Give me a couple minutes to finish up, and I'll give you a ride over. It's only a couple blocks. The brown Chevy pick-up," he added, tossing Brett his keys.

"All right. Cool."

Brett tried not to grin. All right, so Tommy might just be being friendly, but it was good enough for him. He left by the back door to the employee parking spots, Tommy's keys in his hand.

Brett remembered hearing about some so-called psychics who claimed to be able to "read" people through their belongings. Psychometry. Kind of the same way that old movies showed voodoo priests using hair and nail clippings to make dolls of a person. The idea was that traces of someone's essence stayed in everything they touched or used often, like it became a part of them, or part of them became part of it… shaped it, changed it.

Whatever, but it definitely explained Tommy's truck. Brett weighed the keys in his hand as he walked across the lot, looking at all the odds and ends on there. A bottle opener, a small dreamcatcher woven of red thread with what looked like stone beads, numerous keys in at least three different sizes, and a slightly dented metal picture frame about two inches across. It held a picture of a baby wrapped in a pink blanket and clasped in unseen arms. Baby sister?

Or.... *No way. He doesn't have a kid. No way.*

Brett pushed the day's snow off the windshield, wiped down the hood, and dug the worst of the snow out from the vehicle's tire rims with his gloved hands. He unlocked the truck and climbed in.

The Chevy smelled of worn upholstery, dry air, and a hint of marijuana. A pair of sunglasses, a pack of gum, and a roll of duct tape sat on the dash, in among a jumble of what looked like pretty ancient country and rock cassette tapes. Another photograph, tacked to the column behind the gear stick, showed Tommy together with another guy—had to be a brother, they looked so much alike—two younger kids, and a Chinese woman holding a baby wrapped in that same pink blanket. *Sister. Whew.* His mother, Brett realized. He hadn't seen that in Tommy at first, but he saw the resemblance between them in the eyes and cheekbones. And the rest of the family... only no father. *Hmm. Maybe he took the photo?* Either way, this truck seemed pretty well lived in.

"Ready to go?"

He'd barely noticed Tommy crossing the lot, but he had, and now he hopped easily into the truck, settling himself into the clutter of his life like some Persian prince reclining into the scattered silk pillows of his divan.

Brett shook himself. Man, he had to stop thinking like that.

JULIE RED DOG hailed from Box Elder, a small town on Rocky Boy's reservation. Her taco restaurant had the distinction of not only being virtually one of the first Mexican places in Havre, but being an Indian-owned-and-run business, which had gotten both the tribal council and the local chamber of commerce pretty excited. Her face having been splashed all over the local papers, Mrs. Red Dog catered to a big crowd, though the place was still predominantly Indian. As they walked in, the sensation of being a minority made Brett slightly uneasy.

It didn't last long though, perhaps because he was with Tommy or perhaps, he told himself, because it was a stupid feeling to have anyway.

They sat at a table in the corner and talked as they ate huge, plate-sized pieces of fry bread piled high with ground chili beef, beans, lettuce, and cheese. It was nice: relaxed, casual.

Tommy told Brett, with a laughing grimace, about his late grandmother, a cheerful Assiniboine (or Nakoda, as he called it) woman who'd lived in the same rez house for forty years and wanted him to learn to ride for the rodeo because she really thought it would be a steady job. He told joke after joke, using his humor—self-deprecating but never whining—to avoid talking about his immediate family.

He explained blood quantum: how, though his father had half-Assiniboine and half-Canadian ancestry, and his mother half-Chinese (and half-Seattle, he joked), Tommy and his siblings still had the right to official recognition from the tribal council if they wanted to claim it. Brett understood the basic concept. It jogged memories of some dumb project about Native American life that he'd had to do in school… alongside better memories of going to the Fourth of July Pow Wow at Rocky Boy with his friends.

"So it's a quarter blood for enrollment, then?"

Tommy nodded and took a swallow of Coke. "Mm-hm. We're not, though. Dad never bothered to file the papers. Guess I could apply." He cast a brief look around the restaurant. "Don't know. Maybe. It is a big part of life. I mean, we have friends on the rez, from Gramma bein' there, but…."

He wrinkled his nose and said no more about it.

Tommy didn't evade questions so much as outright ignore them, Brett realized. After a while, he got the hint. Tommy had his reasons, he supposed, however much he wanted to know. He didn't push it. Sitting here just eating and talking… that could be enough for him.

Couldn't it?

CHAPTER FOUR

IT STARTED like that, just the simple beginning of a friendship. They would see each other in the sports store on weekends, maybe meet up at the end of Tommy's shift. After a while, they started driving up to Fresno reservoir, Beaver Creek, or Grassy Lake, parking a little way from one of the fishing or camping spots and drinking a few beers. Sometimes, Tommy smoked a joint.

Brett tried his best to stay casual about it all—the beer, the weed, and the proximity to Tommy. He hadn't really drunk much before, as a rule. Not because he disliked it or found it morally repugnant or anything, just that buying booze when ninety percent of the local stores knew your real age could pose a problem. However, he didn't want to look like a kid in front of Tommy. Okay, so barely a year stood between them, but he felt younger. Being with Tommy caught him like that, making him feel nervous and clumsy, but not in a totally unpleasant way.

Slowly, winter started to edge toward spring or, to give the season between still winter and almost winter its other name, construction. The snow began to thin, though the first hints of returning green beneath the ice were the only suggestions of slow change.

For Brett, plenty had changed.

Now, on a late March afternoon much like any other, the last of the ice crusted the edges of the reservoir. Brett was leaning on the hood of Tommy's Chevy, staring out across the water. Tommy snagged two bottles of Miller from the trunk and opened them with the bottle opener on his key ring.

"Here," he said, passing one to Brett.

"Thanks."

Brett took it, careful—like he was every time—not to let his fingers touch Tommy's and careful to avoid meeting his eye. Tommy had just informed him that at the end of the month he would be leaving the sports store. The end of the ski season loomed, and the company Tommy worked for in Burnham had offered him a full-time apprenticeship.

"That what you're gonna do? Long-term?"

Tommy shrugged. He came to join Brett, leaning on the Chevy's hood, making the most of the residual engine heat, he with a joint cupped in his hand, Brett rubbing at the neck of his Miller. Before them, the gray and gritty shore of Fresno reservoir, caught in the slanting afternoon light, looked like a different planet.

"It'd be good money," Tommy said. "People always need kitchens fitted. Stuff built. Could go down the carpentry route, too."

"What about if you could do anything?" Brett took a swig of his beer. "I mean, what's your dream?"

Tommy shot him a questioning look, his mouth curled into a cynical little smile. Brett shrugged, guessing he'd said something stupid. Pretty inevitable, he supposed, when he got so preoccupied just looking at Tommy. It didn't feel wrong, though. Tommy never made fun of him, never acted like he felt anything was weird. Brett was grateful to him for that, despite the fact it left him more confused than ever.

Sometimes, it felt like they were flirting, dancing around each other and knowing exactly what the game was called, but other times, they were just two guys, exchanging loose strands of friendship. He liked it, he supposed. It was the nicer kind of waiting.

Brett knew how this thing usually played out anyway. He'd had plenty of crushes on guys before. You either spent months drooling from a distance, secure in the knowledge that if the object of your affections were any straighter he could be patented as a draughtsman's drawing tool, or you agonized over every little detail, wondering if just maybe you weren't the only one and perhaps he might actually respond if you made a move.

Brett remembered that feeling all too well. He wanted to know how the hell you even recognized chemistry in the first place. Did you stay in a horrible agony of indecision and insecurity until you actually kissed him? And did that worry ever go away? Whichever way he looked at it, he knew he liked Tommy, which set him up with a problem. He felt comfortable with him but still so nervous—and somehow felt like Tommy felt the same.

God. Everything he does is beautiful.

Tommy took a pull on his joint.

"Bein' happy," he said at last, looking out over the water. "That's what I'd like. Don't think it matters that much what I do, long as I'm makin' enough money to live. Don't mind most things... I like working with my hands more than machines though. Not so good with cars'n stuff. Scott's the mechanic in our house."

"Your brother?" Brett said, surprised. Tommy really didn't talk much about his family.

Tommy took a mouthful of his beer and swallowed slowly. Brett tried not to watch the movement of his neck.

"Mm. We're twins. Not identical. He looks more like Mom than I do. Got a way with an engine, though. So," he added after a small pause, picking up the conversation and turning it right around, "you got less work on the Ski Bowl; season'll be done in a couple weeks. You gonna go full-time with the job at that place up on Highway 2?"

"Oh." Brett pulled a face. "Yeah. Guess so."

He'd applied for it on the off chance, just something to keep him going over the coming summer. Thurston's, at least until Target got market coverage any further north than Great Falls, aspired to fill in the gaps in the local discount department store market. How ready the people of Havre felt for color-coordinated throw pillows at knock-down prices remained to be seen.

Tommy chuckled. "Even with that girl still tryin' to pin you behind the boxes?"

"Not funny," Brett said grimly.

He'd discovered on his first day at Thurston's that Kirsty Muir, who'd nursed a thing for him all the way through high school, worked there too, and now she wouldn't leave him alone. Wishing he'd never told Tommy about her, Brett swigged his beer.

"I just never know what they want, you know?" he said carefully. "Women. You try and try, but you still end up in the doghouse."

Tommy grinned. "Aw, yeah. I hear *that*."

TOMMY laughed, trying not to notice the way the light caught Brett's hair, making just the odd strand shine bright gold. A few freckles littered his cheekbones and forehead too. Dark ones, like birthmarks, stood out against his skin like tiny, random flecks of paint. You could only see them close up, but once he'd noticed them, Tommy couldn't stop wondering if there were more on the rest of his body, speckled out like stars.

He reached up and tucked his hair behind his ear. "But, ah, you still try anyways, right?"

"You do," Brett said, his voice sounding hollow.

Brett looked out at the reservoir. Tommy hoped he wouldn't turn around; he knew he shouldn't let himself get caught staring, though it didn't really seem to matter. Nothing much seemed to matter—especially not logic or reason—when he looked at Brett.

Probably has a lot to do with not getting laid in more than eight months.

A cold wind rippled its way across the water, and a little snow fell from the trees. *What the hell. Worse things happen at sea, and worse than that is nothing happening at all.*

It was stupid anyway, letting it drag on like this. He had to be right about the guy. The time they'd spent together, the whole feel he got off of Brett.... Tommy had danced this dance before, so why did the steps seem so clumsy?

He took a breath and cleared his throat. "So, ah, when did you know?"

Brett glanced up from his beer. The wind lifted Tommy's hair from his shoulders, whipping strands across his face, dark bars across Brett's panicky, startled expression.

"Huh?"

"Y'know." Tommy squinted a little as the wind blew harder. "That you, uh, went… this way."

BRETT thought for a moment about playing dumb. He knew what Tommy meant, what he'd just asked, what—more than that—he was saying about himself, but…. No way. It didn't seem possible. It couldn't be true, could it?

He'd have thought not, but Tommy looked so sincere. Making it so easy. Brett felt foolish for not having followed his instincts better, earlier, but it didn't matter. Nothing but the relief and the euphoria mattered, and it seemed that chemistry didn't involve any chemicals at all, unless you counted the hormones.

"Uh. I, er… um. It… well, since a while back, I guess," he stammered. "Sayin' about trying, it always felt like I'd be tryin' too hard, y'know? Not like it would be if…."

Tommy nodded and took another swig from his bottle. "Uh-huh."

Brett shifted nervously. "Is it, y'know, I mean, do I come off like that?"

"No. No, I just thought, ah…." Tommy smiled sheepishly. "Kinda hoped, I guess. There's not much of a community around here."

"Right. Sure."

"Wasn't any better when we used to live in Chinook. Guess I had to learn to… um, see it."

Brett studied the Chevy's paintwork again, trying to stay cool, calm, and collected and not do anything stupid like punch the air and whoop. *He's gay.* He wanted to say the words out loud, put his mouth on them and make them feel real. Make sure he believed them. *And he likes me.* But… just because Tommy had come out and said what he'd said didn't mean he automatically wanted that. Did it? Only, if he did, then all their flirting had really *been* flirting, and now Brett would have to do something about it.

Oh, hell.

Despite the cold, sweat prickled at the small of his back.

Shit, why'd this have to be so difficult?

"It's good to have somebody to talk to, though," he hazarded. "I.... Well, I'd kinda shelved everything until college, I guess." Brett watched the bare trees bend and rattle against the sky. "I figured if you're gonna experiment, you need somewhere people don't know you. City or somethin'."

"Not always."

Tommy looked at him, his hair wind-whipped and his eyes narrow, and Brett grinned awkwardly, shifting position against the growing pinch in his jeans.

"I guess I never really, uh," he fumbled, taking another mouthful of beer. "Kinda thought it'd all come with college. I don't, um, I don't find it easy here."

"Easy? No." Tommy turned around and leaned his lower back against the Chevy, beer bottle dangling from his fingers. "Neither do I. But I get along."

"So...." Brett looked curiously at him, sidelong, not quite daring to ask the question. "Um. What, uh, what... what now?"

Tommy just smiled, his expression strangely serene. The corner of his mouth curled softly, and a pensive, distant look clouded his eyes. Nervous, Brett cleared his throat, not sure how to read it all.

"Nothing," Tommy said, still looking steadily at him. "Not if you don't want."

"Oh."

Brett leaned forward on his elbows, aware that he was blushing and hoping Tommy couldn't see. It embarrassed the hell out of him. He stared out at the reservoir and drained the last of his beer bottle. His stomach felt like one big panicky knot, his mouth was dry, and if his knees weren't shaking, there must have been some kind of earthquake going on.

"Listen," he said, not looking at Tommy but instead at the patch of peeling paint on the Chevy's hood, "I, um, I really... uh."

Tommy touched him then. Ever so gently, his knuckles brushed along the sleeve of Brett's coat.

Brett looked at him, his insides turning to water, and did nothing but watch as—apparently totally without his control—he turned, his own hand sliding out and brushing along the front of Tommy's parka, fingers slipping into the storm flap.

"I really like you," Brett murmured. "I have since—"

"I know."

Brett blinked, feeling foolish. *What the hell?*

He didn't give himself time to wonder what to do next. He leaned forward, his body inclining to Tommy's as their faces drew closer together. Time seemed not to stand still but to draw out into a huge, endless thing without boundaries. Brett's pulse hammered, and the tiny dark world inside his head collapsed into a stream of panic like he hadn't experienced since his very first kiss, and perhaps not even then.

What if he did it wrong? What if Tommy didn't want him? What if....

The moment seemed to stretch out for as long as human tolerance could stand and then just a little bit longer. All the while they drew closer, but not quite meeting. Just before the world ended, Tommy's lips brushed against his. Rough, not flavored or sticky with lip gloss like Lynsey. The suggestion of beard growth scratched a little against his chin. Cold from the air, but his breath so warm. Thoughts melted away.

Somehow, Brett hadn't expected it to be so different. So unlike the whole performance of kissing a girl, knowing he'd entered into a statement, a bargain, something she'd judge him on and maybe even compare notes with her friends over. No, kissing Tommy felt real. No act, no competition, just... natural, and only getting easier to do. Tommy's breath warmed his mouth, and he sighed as their tongues touched. Brett tasted the beer and the weed. And... everything else.

"Damn," he muttered appreciatively as they broke.

Tommy laughed and took another gulp of his beer, pulling back, giving him space. It could have been awkward, but despite the panic thrumming in his ears, Brett didn't feel uncomfortable.

He glanced over his shoulder, back toward the campsite and beyond it the road, but there wasn't really any danger of anybody coming by. Not with the ground still so hard, the air so cold. Brett leaned in to Tommy again, a silent question. The smile left Tommy's lips.

"Sure?" he asked softly.

Brett nodded. "C'mon."

"All right."

The second kiss—exploration again, mapping mouths and finding balances—lasted longer. Noses bumped and teeth clashed, but it didn't much matter. Brett left his beer bottle on the Chevy's hood and slipped one hand behind Tommy's neck, into the smooth warmth of his hair. He seemed to like it, and then Tommy's arm went around his shoulders, the joint still held between two outstretched fingers, his other hand resting on Brett's hip like it was the easiest thing in the world. Brett only came back to himself when he realized his fingers were tugging on Tommy's belt buckle.

He blushed and pretended not to notice when, as they parted, Tommy brushed his hand away.

"Think we oughta get in the truck, don't you?" Tommy said, his voice perfectly tuned to chafe across Brett's nerves.

"Uh-huh."

Inside the Chevy again, a sudden discomfort descended as both of them tried to work out the other's next move. Brett shifted uneasily. A painfully stretched moment of eternity ensued until Tommy's mouth found its way back to his and things somehow seemed right.

Brett had gotten hard enough for it to be difficult to ignore though, and he wriggled uncomfortably. It had been either about ten minutes or three hours since he'd first kissed Tommy—difficult to be sure which—so would it be okay to push the boundaries and move faster than he would normally? Did he even *want* to? He might not see Tommy every day, but there would still come a time he'd have to look him in the eye again.

Brett descended into another spiral of panic; he felt Tommy's hand on his shoulder, then a gentle pressure as Tommy pushed him away. When Brett's vision popped back into focus, Tommy was looking at him with a dark, guarded expression.

"Let's take it easy," he said quietly. "Huh? This is, uh, kinda fast."

"Yeah," Brett agreed, privately relieved.

He wanted release, but he didn't want to screw up whatever the hell they had happening.

They'd flirted—he'd known that, whatever he'd told himself. They'd tested the water and skirted around this often enough without saying a word. Only now, desperate but scared and feeling like he'd already half fallen in love, things had a totally different complexion.

Right now, Brett hadn't got the slightest idea what he did want, but he did know that Tommy hadn't completely let go of him. Tommy's thumb rubbed against the side of his neck, and Brett leaned into the contact.

TOMMY swallowed, trying to ignore the urge to kiss Brett again, unable to remember when he'd wanted someone so much. Brett's hesitancy might be adorable, but he still wondered how much it would take to give him back his confidence. Tommy had noticed that from the very first minute he walked into the sports store, wrapped up in all that ski gear. It was the thing he'd liked most, even as it started to crack and show all the nervousness beneath.

How can it be so tempting to touch someone?

Hell, he'd hoped for this, but Brett made it all too simple. Too easy. Something in Tommy's gut warned him that this wasn't a good idea. Actions had consequences and all that shit. He really ought to think about getting home. Only with Brett touching him, leaning up on him, and moving in to kiss him again, that thought lost a lot of its urgency.

He couldn't really say no, not when it was so easy to put himself somewhere else, leave his worries on the edge of life and lose everything in all that wonderful, beautiful warmth. Brett was still grinning when Tommy left him—back in town then, by the bookstore, so no long, lingering kiss goodbye—and it didn't seem real, as if perfect things had no place happening in the world.

Tommy drifted home on a cloud, full to bursting with it all, and he finally got back to the house after eight. It seemed quiet, but he'd expected that because on his father's gun club nights it always seemed quieter. It was as if the tension Martin generated behaved like a moving wall of silence, sucking everything into it and spitting back a dull, white noise.

"Where the fuck have you been?"

He glanced up, still unlacing his boots. Scott was leaning against the far wall, a lit cigarette in his fingers and a scowl on his face. Tommy toed off the boots and kicked the door shut behind him.

"Out."

"No, really? I wouldn't'a guessed."

"Piss off, Scott."

Tommy turned his back on his brother and raided the refrigerator for something that at least looked edible. He had serious munchies, and he didn't want this now. No sniping, no arguments. He just wanted to take everything that had been so right, so clean, from today, press it into memory and let everything else wash over him. Pretend it didn't matter. Pretend he could still feel Brett's mouth against his and all that desire pushing in on them both. Hell, he should have let it go on. *Always finish what you start.* As things stood, he'd had to stop on the drive home to take care of the diamond cutter in his pants, and even then it hadn't done much good.

Scott passed behind him and scraped a chair on the floor. Tommy knew without looking that he'd be sitting at the kitchen table, arms folded and face locked into a scowl of disapproval.

"You stink. Tokin' again?"

Tommy grunted, taking a chance on a leftover portion of mac and cheese. He put it in the microwave, leaned against the sink, and tapped his foot lightly on the linoleum.

"So, he went out," said Scott. "Gun club."

"Yeah. Where's Mom?"

"Headache."

"Huh."

Tommy didn't need to hear more than that. Mei took to her bed at least a couple of times a week with a migraine, spending a few hours with the door shut, the drapes pulled, and the lights off, alone with her pain. She had prescription pills, but they didn't seem to help.

Scott cleared his throat. "So. Um. Who you been with?"

The microwave bleeped. Tommy shot him a look, part disbelief and part pure, unadulterated *go to hell.*

Scott shrugged. "Okay, not my business. I know. I just.... You look kind of... I don't know. Pleased with yourself."

Tommy grabbed his makeshift dinner and sat down opposite his brother, eyes narrowed. He wasn't going to have this conversation.

Scott looked steadily back at him, watching him eat. They had their differences, Tommy knew that. Where he wore his hair long, Scott's always stayed cropped short, coarse and springy despite the gel. Where Tommy easily passed for Indian, Scott looked more yellow than red and—in a town pretty much split between mostly white, then First Nation, and lastly mixed—that stood out. It caught him some crap, too, but he didn't seem to care. He never did.

"You meet somebody?"

Tommy looked up sharply. "What?"

"You heard. Have ya?"

"Mmn."

Scott laughed softly. "Dog."

Tommy said nothing, but a smile tugged at the side of his mouth as he finished the macaroni. The fork clinked in the empty bowl, and he was getting ready to throw it in the sink and hit the shower when Scott spoke again, his voice a little strained.

"So, ah, I need to talk t'you."

Tommy paused. Unusual. When did Scott want to talk to him? He lowered himself back into the chair and searched Scott's face for a clue. His mouth clamped tight, and the thin scar beside his right eye moved like a sprig of cherry blossom as he winced.

I'm sorry, Daddy. I'm sorry. Please don't....

"Whassa matter?"

"I, um...." Scott fidgeted, fingers rubbing at the gold belcher chain on his wrist. "So, Karen, uh, she told me she's late."

"Late?" It took Tommy a moment to catch up. He frowned as he worked through the semantics. "Oh... *late*. Okay. Uh. How—how late?"

On the wall above the door, the clock that had belonged to their grandmother—black feathers for hands and a stylized sunburst painted in the center of its face—seemed to tick more loudly than usual.

Scott cleared his throat. "Several days. She thinks... I mean, we don't know. She wants me to get her one of those tests. They have 'em at the drugstore, right?"

Tommy shrugged. "Not really my area. Guess so, though. So, she...? Really?"

Scott nodded slowly and stared down at the table. "Mm-hm."

"Shit."

"Yeah."

Tommy rocked back in his chair. He found it pretty off-putting even thinking about Karen and Scott doing it, much less her being pregnant. Scott took a long final drag on his cigarette and crushed it out on the glass ashtray in the middle of the table. The smell of it itched in Tommy's nostrils. He couldn't remember the number of times he'd fought with Scott about his smoking—everything from the toxicity to the expense. He never listened, just called Tommy an interfering pothead hypocrite who had no business to try messing with his life. And now he'd be somebody's father in less than a year.

Shit.

"So, what are you gonna do?"

Scott shrugged. Karen came from a fairly strict family, Tommy remembered. That kind of vaguely evangelical reservation-mission Christianity. He'd only met her a handful of times, and, he realized with a sneaking sense of guilt, he'd never really liked her, though he barely knew a thing about her.

"I don't know." Scott wiped his thumb over his mouth. "Don't say anythin', Tommy. You won't, will ya? Not yet, at least."

"'Course not. Not 'til you know. Not—not 'til you're ready to, uh… you know."

"Decide."

"Yeah." Tommy sucked a low breath over his teeth. "Jeez, Scott… weren't you—"

"Careful? Yeah! I don't know how it…. Oh, don't you *dare*," he added sharply. "I know exactly how it *happened*, thank you! Hell, I got a better idea on that score than you'll ever have."

Tommy quirked an eyebrow. "Hey, I don't even wanna know. But, if you need anythin', if I can… help…." He shrugged. He had no idea what he could do, what people even needed for this kind of thing. "You only gotta say," he finished lamely.

"Yeah." Scott's face softened, and a smile crumpled his mouth. "Thanks, man."

Tommy guessed he would have said something more; instead he looked up, hearing the thud of small feet on the stairs. Lila appeared at the kitchen door in her nightshirt and striped tube socks, face screwed up with indignant tears. Seeing Tommy, she pelted across the kitchen, wailed, and threw herself at him, landing in his lap with a thump.

"Robbie's horrible! I hate him!"

"Hey, take a breath. What'd he do?"

Lila pulled back, sniffing and gulping as Tommy smoothed her hair.

"H-he… took my bracelet an' he won't give it back, an' he says he's gonna sell it to this guy at school an' it's *mine*. Gramma gave it to me. It's not fair! He's always taking my stuff and…." She sniffed again, then frowned. "You smell funny, Tommy."

Across the table, Scott stifled a laugh. Tommy glared at his brother.

"Is it perfume?" Lila wanted to know as he stood up, carrying her like he used to do when she was little. "It smells like… lemons. And somethin' spicy, like—"

"It's not perfume," he said hurriedly, as realization dawned. What she could smell wasn't just the weed, but Brett's aftershave, and he really didn't want to have to explain either. "Come on. Let's go see about this bracelet. And you can come too," Tommy added, shooting a look at Scott.

"Hey! What'd I do?"

Tommy winked at his brother. "Well, you oughta start getting the parenting practice in early, right?"

Scott scowled. "Asshole."

CHAPTER
FIVE

IT COULD have been easy to pretend that nothing had happened that day at Fresno. They hadn't really been seeing each other that often— just a casual friendship of snatched moments—and both Brett and Tommy had plenty to think about outside of it. Tommy had work, the kids to mind, Scott to keep from panicking, and his parents to stand buffer between. Brett had his own life, his job, plus the extra classes he'd enrolled in at the MSU campus as part of his preparations for college.

In among all those obligations and expectations, it would have been, perhaps, easy to let it slide, let it taper away into the distance. Leave the whole thing as a road untraveled.

Of course, the thing about easy options is that they never seem it at the time.

Tommy sat on the edge of his bed, tossing his cell phone in his hands. The early afternoon sunlight brightened the room. With his father out, Mei at the store, Robbie and Lila in school, Katie sleeping in her crib, and Scott at work at the auto shop in town, it seemed weird for a house usually so full of people to be so empty, but Tommy liked it. Scott had left a leaflet about obstetrics on his nightstand. Karen's home pregnancy test had been positive, so he'd said the next step would be an appointment at the clinic... not that he'd mentioned telling either set of parents.

Tommy worried about that, but what could you do? Right now, he had a rare afternoon off; he should have been working, but the plumber had overrun on his contract for the houses in Kremlin that the company would be outfitting, so the granite worktops wouldn't go in for another three days. It meant pushing payday back a bit, which Tommy wasn't so happy about, but there wasn't anything he could do about that either.

He caught the phone one last time and wondered how you could tell if it had landed on heads or tails. Tails meant calling Brett. Heads meant leaving it up to fate for another day or so. Brett hadn't called him yet; perhaps he wouldn't.

Nerves, or maybe regret.

It had been five days since Fresno. Tommy wanted, no, *needed* to know where he stood. If what had happened might lead anywhere or... not. It wouldn't be the first time he'd gotten the "I'm not gay, really" brush-off, even before he'd finished zipping up his pants, but... nah, Brett hadn't seemed like that type. Then again, it wasn't like you could tell, not first off.

Tommy flipped the phone open and stared at it. He could count the number of not-exactly-boyfriends he'd had on one hand, but he'd gotten sick and tired of counting on his hand.

No, he should just call.

Just as abruptly, he shut the phone, threw it onto his bed and, stretching, got up to go check on Katie. She was still sleeping peacefully. He hung back from tucking her in, scared to wake her.

Soft black hair wreathed her tiny ears and cheeks, her eyelashes dark and improbably long against rosy-gold skin. The shoulders of her pink babygro rose and fell steadily with the rhythm of her breaths, and she seemed so small, so warm... and too perfect to touch.

Tommy shook his head and backed out of the room—too much like his mother in there with all the pale walls, floral curtains, and bright rag rugs over the stains on the carpet where his father had thrown up. Martin slept on the couch more these days, while Mei hid behind the baby.

Mustn't wake Katie... Katie needs a night feed... Katie has to have the light on until she goes to sleep....

Privately, Tommy thought there was a hell of a lot of pressure on that kid. He leaned against the landing wall and rested his head against the cool plaster. Pressure. Funny thing. Brett probably wasn't going to call. He wouldn't want… nah, he wasn't interested. He wasn't even going to be around that much longer; he'd be going to medical school or whatever come fall, up in Washington. So probably… yeah, bad idea. Yep. He shouldn't call. Just forget about it.

TOMMY regretted telling the gods of chance to shove it a few days later, while driving back from the job at Kremlin. Cutting through the center of town, he passed the southern end of the college campus and spotted a familiar figure hiking along the road. He honked the horn, and Brett glanced over his shoulder, grinning as he turned around.

"Hey!" Tommy pulled over and wound the window all the way down. "Hey. You need a ride?"

Brett narrowed his eyes against the afternoon sun. He looked tired, and Tommy wondered if everything was okay. That his first thought should be such a sudden lurch of concern surprised him.

"Would ya?" Brett blew out a short, grateful breath. "Truck's at home. Dad was meant to pick me up, but apparently he's working late."

"'Course. C'mon."

Brett smiled and got in. Tommy became suddenly aware of the seriously old-school country rock coming from the stereo. Embarrassed, he made to shut it off, but Brett stopped him.

"It's all right."

"You don't mind? Really?"

"No." Brett grinned and picked up the ancient cassette case from the dash. "It's, uh, kinda cool. Um. The Nitty Gritty Dirt Band?"

"I listen to other stuff too."

"Yeah?"

"Sure." A smile curled the edges of Tommy's lips, and he spun the wheel. "Levon Helm'n The Band, John Fogerty, J.J. Cale…."

"Holy shit, you're a cowboy!"

Tommy laughed. "No! Kidding. I like Beck too. Good Charlotte—what? Oh, I see. Gonna educate me, are you?"

"I didn't say that." Brett placed the case back on the dash and held up his hands. "I mean, you might *need* it, but I didn't say that."

THEY turned off the main road, and the truck bumped a little. Brett chuckled as the only cover of Buddy Holly's song "Rave On" he had ever heard involving a harmonica crunched around the cab.

"I'm not a cowboy," Tommy insisted.

Brett raised an eyebrow. "You sure?"

"Ah-huh."

"Betcha are. Secretly." An image stole softly behind Brett's eyes. "Bet you're just dying for the opportunity to strut around in leather chaps and spurs."

He glanced over at Tommy, gauging his reaction to that, and was pleased to see that it made him laugh, hard, which was something well worth watching.

"Oh! Oh, no, my friend... I think that might be your problem, not mine. I don't play dress-up."

"Aw... not even for me?"

Tommy slipped him a sidelong glance. It amazed Brett how happy he looked: something in his eyes, in the way he grinned. It seemed as if a weight had lifted off him, though Brett couldn't work out how or when. He couldn't remember when flirting had been this much fun either.

"Gramma used to take me to the rodeo," Tommy said, the laughter dying down. "When we were kids. It's all right. I mean, I like horses and I can ride okay, but I can think of better ways to smash yourself up, y'know? Though if that whole Brokeback thing really floats your boat... well, I guess I could arrange somethin' for you."

Brett just smirked, too distracted for a moment to think of anything clever to say. Tommy grinned again and turned his attention back to the road.

"Damn," Tommy muttered, as if to himself. "Finally found a way to shut him up. So, how do I get to your place?"

Brett gave him directions, the tension seeping out of him, and for a while, they just drove while the music played on.

"It's good to see you," he said, out of nowhere.

Tommy's gaze shifted to him; the sunlight sliced over his face in flickering slabs of gold.

"You too."

"I, uh…." Brett began and lapsed into silence, not knowing what he meant to say—what he *wanted* to say.

Tommy laughed softly. Brett loved the way it sounded, like acceptance, not mockery. Like he understood. No clarification, no questions, no apologies needed. He wondered if falling in love felt like this. Kinda the same as walking along a narrow cliff ledge and wishing you had something more to hold onto. Except he didn't feel dizzy. He felt safe.

Oh, for crying out loud. I only kissed him once. Well, for kinda a long time, but… what the hell is happening to me?

Tommy changed a little bit as they got closer to home. The houses here—largely 1920s-style dwellings with pastel-colored siding, feature windows, and big, airy rooms—had picket fences and well-tended yards.

No, Tommy wasn't smiling so much, and he'd definitely turned quiet.

"You wanna come in?" Brett asked as casually as he dared.

Tommy shook his head. "Be nice, but I can't. I have to pick my sister up from school and get her to dance class."

"Oh."

Brett filed that one away in his head. He'd been piecing together how much Tommy did for his family from all those little dropped references. He wished he had the courage to call him on it, find out the whole story. In the meantime, he made an effort not to sound disappointed.

"Oh, well. It's, uh… thanks for the ride."

"Pleasure. Um. I did mean to call. I…."

Brett glanced out of the windshield at the empty road. Then he leaned over and kissed Tommy. Hard. The look on his face—surprise, wonder, and not a little lust—made Brett smile.

Priceless.

"Yeah. Me too. I guess next time one of us better do it. 'K?"

"All right," Tommy said weakly.

Brett got out of the truck and let himself in the front gate, dropping the latch behind him. His boots crunched on the white gravel. Tommy hadn't pulled away; Brett could hear the thumping beat and tight-strung guitars of his tacky music. He turned, thinking maybe it wouldn't be so bad to invite him in one more time.

Tommy was still watching him from the truck. He smiled, looking away quickly and turning the engine over. At that moment, Roscoe bounded arthritically out from the side of the house with a joyful bark. Brett fussed with the dog as he tried to jump up, tail wagging and tongue lolling, and didn't manage to call out to Tommy before he drove off.

Had he really wanted to get gone so quickly?

SLOWLY, March inched into April. With the end of the season, Brett's job at the Ski Bowl finished, as did Tommy's work at the sports store and all opportunities for illicit kisses between the packing crates. Fresno reservoir, already a trusted friend, assumed an even greater importance, and they spent as much time as they could spare up by the water while the ice melted and the land bloomed. Despite all the new growth, the temperature still lingered diffidently around the low thirties, and there never seemed to be quite enough room in the Chevy. The Bronco wasn't any better.

No, getting quality time together meant a constant struggle. Tommy realized that; he understood very clearly the concept of compartmentalizing life.

It gave him the idea of applying for the fishing license.

He had the thing in his pocket, burning a bigger hole than money ever could, when he walked into the kitchen that evening. He was whistling as he came through the side door, like he usually did when he got home from work, but all the joy died on his lips.

Mei must have been chopping vegetables, because she was still holding the knife, the handle gripped tightly, her hand close to her chest and the tip pointing out at Scott.

"I don't give a damn what you do!" she spat.

In her powder-blue highchair, Katie whined—the kind of high-pitched, keening cry that could explode into a full-blown wail at any second. Scott rolled his eyes and pulled a packet of Marlboros from the pocket of his jeans.

"Hey, don't you dare smoke in this house, Mister. Not around the kids. I don't know how many times I have to tell you."

"Thought you didn't give a damn, Ma?"

Mei glared at him. "You know perfectly well what I mean. I don't care what you're doing when you're out with... *her*, but I expect you to—"

"Her? She's got a name. Her name's Karen."

"I really don't care, Scott."

"No? I know. It's pretty fuckin' obvious."

"Don't you use that language to me! And not in front of your sister."

"Or what?"

"Scott!"

"Like I said, I'm goin' out. Good night."

Tommy stepped back as his brother shoved out of the door, the keys to the Pontiac in his hand. The cup that Mei threw smashed on the doorframe just behind him. Katie screamed, loud and long. Scott ran down the steps and climbed into the car in a cloud of aftershave, a gold chain glinting at his neck. He wouldn't be back tonight. He still hadn't told anyone about the baby either, and he'd left Tommy sworn to secrecy. Tommy sighed.

"Would you close the door?" Mei asked.

Tommy nodded, stepped into the kitchen, and shut the door behind him. Mei put the knife down and wiped her eyes. He wondered whether it would make any difference if she knew she'd be a grandma by this time next year. Katie was still yelling as he picked her up from the highchair and cuddled her.

"Hey, Starfish. Shh. Yeah, I know."

After a few moments, she quieted, her damp face pressed against his neck, trailing snot on his skin. Tommy patted her diaper and glanced over at his mother.

"She's wet. I got it."

"Thanks."

Mei looked pale. He knew she hated fighting with Scott. Everybody did because he never left any way to win. He just put his head down and pushed on through, and to hell with the consequences.

Tommy carried his sister toward the stairs, pausing to look into the living room. The TV was blaring, as usual. Martin sat asleep, his head dropped back on the top of the couch, as clean-shaven as any man might be by 8 p.m., still wearing the recently ironed flannel shirt and third-from-best jeans he'd worn to the doctor's that morning. The room had been tidied. Lila, curled up on the couch beside him, nestled under his arm as he slept. She looked up, seeing Tommy's shadow on the carpet, and smiled at him.

"Hey," he mouthed.

She had her hair braided. Her attention wandered back to the TV show—some angst-driven teen drama thing that Tommy wondered if she really ought to be watching—so he went upstairs to change Katie. Robbie, in the bedroom, at least appeared to be doing his homework. Tommy didn't disturb him, though Robbie looked up briefly and nodded.

BRETT lolled back against the door of his closet, more than slightly drunk. It had been a pretty late night, and one of his friend's brothers had brought the booze. There had been a lot of it. He clamped the phone to his ear, not because he couldn't hear Tommy, but because he couldn't believe it.

"You wanna what?"

It had been too long since Brett had seen him last. Things had been busy, and he missed being able to swing by the sports store and say hi. He missed the brief gropes in the storeroom and the long meaningful looks in public places. Both very melodramatic though also really, really frustrating when nothing else followed them up.

"I got a fishin' license. Gonna go up to Beaver Creek this weekend, just wondered... if you wanna come. Do ya?"

A slow, dirty grin spread across Brett's face. *That* was a good idea. Much better than snatched moments and perpetual rain checks, though he definitely hadn't expected it.

"The whole weekend?"

"I guess you've probably got plans."

"Yeah, I sure do. *Now*."

Tommy hesitated, then the line crackled as he laughed, realizing what Brett meant. Brett leaned his head against the wooden louver door.

"You are so smart."

"Yeah?"

"Mm." *And so fucking sexy....* His grin widened, the temptation to say it beer-heightened and almost irresistible. He licked his lips. "So, when and where?"

"How about around midday Saturday? Just look for the Chevy up by the campground."

"All right."

"Okay, then."

"Look forward to it. I'll see you there."

Brett broke the connection, smile still glued to his face. He fell into bed half-dressed, and the practicalities of this shiny new plan didn't start bothering him until the morning.

"YOU'RE going to what?"

Monica Derwent looked at her son with wide eyes. She'd probably have had her hands on her hips, only she was already holding the dog's flea-treatment packet. She curled her lip instead.

"Brett, you hardly ever go fishing. I thought you hated it."

He shrugged, elbows on the kitchen table and fingertips gingerly tracing the edges of a cup of coffee. She hadn't said a word about him coming home late and beered up last night, and he loved her for that. That and all her self-consciously liberal parenting.

Brett's parents had given him his first glass of wine at the age of fourteen, so that alcohol "wouldn't be a mystery." Now he frowned slightly, stifled a belch, and looked down into his coffee. He'd managed to get through this morning so far without throwing up, but he still wasn't convinced he'd escape the hangover completely unscathed.

"Not hate, not really."

"All right, but you used to say you found it boring."

"Yeah, but maybe I need some boring. Relaxation. Y'know?"

"Hmm." Monica peered at the leaflet that came with the flea treatment and counted out vials per ten pounds of Roscoe's weight. "And this is with Kevin?"

Brett sipped the coffee, taking time with his answer. It wasn't lying, not really. Just a little omission... perfectly acceptable when dealing with parents, or relatives of any kind.

"Uh, no. No. Tommy. This guy I met through the ski thing."

She looked at him, and he sensed all those questions bubbling on her tongue—questions he'd been prepared for because Brett knew exactly how his mother's mind worked. She'd want to know all about Tommy in excruciating detail: how old was he, was he from the same school, what were his plans for the future, who were his parents...? She'd want the whole CV, before she even suspected that he'd become anything more than a friend.

Brett guessed he could have lied. Said he planned to go with Kevin or some other guy from school. But she didn't really deserve it. Monica and Stephen Derwent had married young but conceived late, and Brett had grown used to the layers of cotton wool that wrapped an only and unexpected child.

Even so, no matter how liberal his parents considered themselves, he wasn't ready to set off the full chain reaction that would be caused by telling her exactly what he was planning to go to the creek for. They'd be supportive if he came out, he knew that—he hoped so anyway—and fear only rubbed a little bit of the edge off his certainty. But Brett somehow sensed that his sexuality as an abstract concept might be one thing for his mother to deal with, while the thought of him actually having a lover would be something totally different. It wasn't even really a gender thing; he certainly hadn't dared tell them he'd been sleeping with Lynsey Schaeder.

Then again, he wasn't about to pretend that Tommy didn't exist.

His father came downstairs, tie half-tied and one shoe laced, still searching for some misplaced piece of paper. He was saved from the inquisition—for the moment.

Stephen Derwent worked as an accountant and tended to struggle with the parts of life that didn't fit easily into columns. Monica rolled her eyes, re-knotted his tie, handed him a muffin with one hand and his briefcase with the other, and told him to do up his laces before he broke his neck.

"Your son's going on a fishing trip this weekend," she added pointedly.

"Oh?" Stephen, one foot up on the chair as he tied his lace, mouth full of muffin, looked at Brett. "Really? With Kevin?"

Brett mumbled a noncommittal response, really not ready to go through the whole thing again. He loved his parents, but sometimes he wished he saw less of them.

CHAPTER
SIX

ALL the rest of the week, Brett convinced himself that Saturday couldn't come quickly enough. Then, when it finally arrived, it seemed like it had swallowed the whole world up with it.

He got to the entertainingly named Beaver Creek at around twelve thirty. Shutting off the Bronco's engine, he cursed himself for his stupid, ridiculous nerves. Sure enough, Tommy's Chevy was parked at the edge of the campsite, but where was Tommy?

God, am I sweating?

Telling himself to pull it together, Brett got out of the truck and started to walk over.

This time of the year, it was hard to believe that the land had ever been such a frozen tundra. It was a comparatively warm day, with little signs of life sprung up all over the place: spring flowers, grass, birds. There might even be bears around somewhere, just starting to think about waking up.

The thing that leapt out of the bushes wasn't a bear, despite the low growl. Brett yelped as he pitched toward the ground, caught in a fierce hug around his back. He pivoted on his left foot and swung around to right himself, hanging onto Tommy's sleeves and ending up neatly in his arms. Tommy's growl morphed into laugher, soon smothered.

"Hey," he said as Brett pulled back from the kiss.

Brett grinned. "You normally hang around in the bushes waiting to jump out on unsuspecting passersby? 'Cause there's a name for that."

"Nah. S'only you. Actually, I'd just been gettin' lunch, and then I saw you comin', so I thought I'd, uh, say hi."

"Well, hi, then. Did you say lunch?"

Tommy smiled. *Ouch... that's still a killer.*

"Sure. C'mon. Hope you don't mind, but I already picked a spot," he said, leading Brett through the trees, down toward the water.

A weathered tent stood pitched between the pines and the creek, a small campfire already burning, a pot and kettle hanging over it. A large trout, cleaned and gutted, sat on a skillet waiting to be cooked. Brett stared.

"Wow. So, you really did mean fishing, huh?"

Tommy laughed and, to Brett's surprise, bussed the back of his neck.

"C'mon. Come have a beer."

They sat on an old red plaid blanket, and Brett drank his beer while Tommy cooked the fish. He was clearly the more experienced outdoorsman, and Brett didn't mind leaving him to it, though he felt a little ashamed of how new and unused most of his own gear seemed in comparison. They ate, watching the sunlight skim on the water like golden pebbles, and talked about pretty much nothing.

After the second beer, Brett started to mellow. The worries that had plagued him over the past couple of days—how did he go about moving things on with Tommy, and did wanting it make him ready for it?—seemed both less immediate and less disturbing.

Tommy leaned across him to toss his beer bottle into the trash and stayed there, passive and hopeful, waiting for Brett to close the gap between them. He found it easy to do, easy to fall into a slow, seductive rhythm of kisses. The blanket rucked beneath them, the occasional sharp stone making itself known.

Breathless, they parted, and Brett went to fetch his sleeping bag and ground mat from the Bronco. There had never been any question of needing a second tent, even though Tommy kept being so careful with him. Briefly, the feeling of being treated like a virgin bride annoyed Brett.

It passed quickly, though, especially when Tommy broke out marshmallows. Brett expected him to smoke some weed, too, but he didn't appear to have brought any. He wondered why, but between the beer and the marshmallows and the making out, he forgot to ask. It just felt good to see Tommy so happy. So… light.

BY RIGHTS, the sunset should have been spectacular, some beautiful symphony of reds and golds. Instead, the dusk snuck in guiltily, the light gradually failing and the sun sinking into a faint purple corona of cloud.

Brett, full of the last of the fish, more marshmallows, and the potatoes Tommy had cooked in the depths of the fire, lay back on the blanket and watched the bugs bat against the sky. Tommy swatted a mosquito.

"Shoulda brought a shotgun for these damn things," Tommy muttered, getting up from his spot by the fire to go to the pit.

Brett watched him go, his… what? Boyfriend? It seemed strange to think of Tommy like that, though they had, he supposed, been seeing each other for almost a month now.

Hardly a conventional courtship, though. They didn't go out, not in public. He guessed Tommy might, if he asked, but getting time together had proved hard enough already. With Brett working full-time at Thurston's now—and according to Glen, his supervisor, on track for a managerial promotion by the end of the summer if he kept up the pace—he didn't have much spare time. The extra foundation classes he'd taken up at MSU dealt with most of it. Plus, with Tommy always dashing somewhere too, doing something for somebody, spending what time they did have sitting in a burger joint making eyes at each other across the table would be a stupid waste when they could be alone somewhere like Fresno, or here at the creek where they could….

Brett stalled on that thought.

Funny thing, but they really hadn't *done* that much. They'd even stayed pretty much above the equator, afraid of starting something they couldn't finish or, perhaps, afraid of making that next big leap. Weird, he thought.

It wasn't at all like Brett had imagined it would be. He'd pictured meeting somebody at college, sure, but nothing too serious. Just a…

well, maybe not a fuckbuddy, but a guy he'd feel comfortable with, someone to help him explore that side of his nature, those needs. Not someone he'd find himself falling for.

Shit. Guess that does make him a boyfriend.

An odd word, kind of a secret passcode. He'd grown used to thinking of himself as Lynsey's boyfriend, but that meant something completely different. Something safe and comfortable that protected him from whispers, rumors, and from having to make any decisions or choices for himself. *Damn.* He hadn't intended to think of her. Lynsey. She wasn't much of an outdoors girl. She skied, rode, biked, windsurfed a little in the summer, but she'd hated hiking, camping— all those things that could get you out into the woods together. Alone.

Brett thought of how easily he'd thrown himself into that rut with her. How they'd both given each other confidence, ticked off all those necessary high school boxes. How he'd been so mad at himself for using her, hiding behind her like that, even while he kept doing it. How, despite everything, it had been good to go out with her on his arm, so to speak, and feel like he'd triumphed in some small, stupid way. That he could be—not normal, exactly… but maybe untouchable.

He couldn't see that happening with Tommy.

No, what he had with Tommy still meant something you didn't publicize, didn't flaunt. *Don't flaunt it.* God, Brett hated that word. As if the right to touch your lover in public could somehow be akin to running through town naked except for a red feather boa.

He sighed. Lover. That felt like a good word, though rolling it around his head worried Brett. He'd tucked condoms and a small bottle of lube into his pack, but would they actually need them? And what if they did? How exactly did you…? He swallowed, excitement and anxiety thick on his tongue.

Aw, hell….

The dusk deepened out into soft darkness, the air getting colder and the ground dampening. Tommy came back through the trees, and Brett's stomach tightened in anticipation. He sat up, watching him. Tommy stopped, one hand raised over his head, hanging his weight from the low branch of a ponderosa pine. He smiled, and Brett stared—because he could. He wanted every detail clear and perfect, from the way Tommy's faded jeans hung on his hips to the dark strands of hair escaping from his ponytail and brushing the collar of his fleece.

"You okay?" Tommy asked.

Brett nodded, too quickly. Tommy pushed away from the tree and crossed casually in front of the fire, pulled the fleece over his head, and tossed it down on the blanket. Then he followed it, dropping lightly to his knees in front of Brett, just waiting. His fingers trailed over Brett's outstretched leg, barely skimming his worn jeans. Brett leaned forward, his breathing shallow as he closed the space between them.

Tommy held him tight. Kisses tumbled into each other, pulling the breath right out of him. As they parted, the trees seemed to spin, and something that sounded very like a whimper escaped Tommy's lips, fluttering against Brett's cheek.

"Wanna take this indoors?" he murmured, jerking his head toward the tent.

"Mm-hm." Brett nodded, pulling him back for another quick kiss; his way of asserting, however briefly, a little control. Buying himself some time. They crawled into the tent, padded with the softness of sleeping bags and the red plaid blanket. Brett felt light-headed, convinced that every drop of blood in his brain had gone south for the winter. Tommy rubbed hypnotic circles on his thigh through the denim. Brett fidgeted under his hand and almost quivered under his words.

"Can I touch you?" Tommy whispered, his mouth grazing the rim of Brett's ear. "Properly?"

Brett wanted to tell him that he didn't have to ask, not ever, but he knew the question only represented a formality, like his whispered "fuck, yes," and the kiss of possession that passed between them.

It proved hard to breathe for a while, and it seemed to take forever for Tommy's hand to work into Brett's fly, creeping beneath the fabric of his boxers. *Damn the Northwest climate. Damn the mud and the cold and all these goddamn layers!* But then Tommy touched skin that had never known... okay, skin that had known his own hand,

and Lynsey's, and actually a lot more of Lynsey than just her hand, but none of it had ever felt like this.

God. Tommy… just *touching* him. Brett gasped. Tommy laughed a little, the whisper of breath warm on the side of his neck, and damn if that wasn't incredible as well.

"Is that okay?" Tommy asked, his voice little more than a low hum under Brett's ear.

He struggled to nod. Yes. God, yes, definitely very okay. Why hadn't they managed to do this before?

"Uh-huh."

"Good. I'm helping you out, right? You like me helping you out, Brett? That's all right, isn't it?"

His questions seemed sane, rational, and his tone didn't change. Tommy just leaned up against him, his forehead resting on Brett's jaw.

"I—" Brett choked out, embarrassed to find it appeared to be even tougher to speak with Tommy pressed up against him like that. "I wanna… touch…."

Tommy smiled. Brett shuddered. Then Tommy moved, the sleeping bags rustling under them, and he took his hand away. Brett growled softly with frustration and want, rolling over to meet Tommy again, pulling his fly open, cursing the thick denim and stiff buttons. He didn't understand how it could be so easy to touch him. Tommy felt like silk. Warm silk, crisp hair, and supple heat. The hardness of his chest pressed against Brett's through all those damn clothes and then—*oh, God*—Tommy leaned closer and filled Brett's world with the smell of his skin and his sweat and the damp earth. And then Tommy kissed him, and their bodies crushed awkwardly together, shoving and rubbing, the ballet of hands forgotten, fingers only there to grip hips, and Brett could never have thought anything would be so good.

He gave a loud, ragged grunt as he came, felt his teeth clash with Tommy's, felt Tommy still humping against him, still hard, where Brett had already grown slick and started to soften, and that amazing elation withered so fast. In its place, a cold void of panic opened up inside Brett, the edges steep and sharp and tinged with the shame of failure. He started to move away, but Tommy grabbed his arm, skin feeling hot enough to burn, leaving just enough space between them in the dimness for Brett to make out his face. He looked... beautiful. Powerful. Like a warrior.

"Don't," Tommy whispered, his eyes half-shut.

His head lolled forward as, unbidden, Brett reached down and stroked him, coaxing out those last moments, marveling at Tommy's lack of inhibition. He seemed to find it easy to be watched, touched, as he groaned, murmuring a stream of shapeless, desperate words. He cried out as he finished, locking them together with the mess they'd made.

Brett wiped his hand on his stained, sticky jeans, so turned on he could barely breathe. Tommy lay back, a dark flush spilling over his face and neck.

"Whew," he breathed, eyes narrowed as he looked up at Brett. "Y'all right?"

"Yeah." Brett smiled sheepishly. "My pants are so wrecked."

Tommy laughed softly. He hauled himself up on one elbow and peered at the damage. Brett squirmed, feeling vulnerable and over-exposed. He watched the intent concentration on Tommy's face, the... hunger. Uncomfortable, but also arousing, the thought that he could do that to somebody. That he could be so desired. He sucked the air over his teeth as Tommy touched him, so gently, peeling his jeans and shorts down, stripping him.

Brett hardened again, responding to the attention, and he reached out, tugging at the buttons of Tommy's shirt. He found it weird that the clothes couldn't come off slowly enough. He'd thought they'd just be an inconvenience, an irritation, but now they felt kinda like protection. Safe excuses. His throat tightened. Tommy pulled off the shirt he was wearing, and then the cotton tee beneath it. Brett couldn't believe he hadn't seen his chest fully before.

He ran his hand down Tommy's pecs, thumb brushing one tight, brown nipple. Fit, just like Brett had guessed the first time they'd met, but not really ripped. There didn't seem to be an ounce of fat on him, just fluid lines of flesh and planes of firm muscle. Brett decided that something in his brain had obviously been hard-wired to go weak at the sight of broad shoulders and solid biceps. If he convinced himself of that, he wouldn't feel so stupid about the way he'd started to tremble.

"You sure you want this?" Tommy murmured, tracing his fingers over Brett's stomach, tracking patterns on his hip.

"Been waitin'," Brett assured him, his voice shaking. "You know it."

Tommy just smiled and bent his head.

Brett closed his eyes. A thousand tiny, ticklish kisses brushed across his skin, across parts of him Lynsey had never even thought about touching—not because of any taboo, just because there'd never seemed to be a reason to. His knees, his ribs, the insides of his arms. Slowly, Brett realized he knew very little about his own erogenous zones.

"Ow! What the hell are you doing?"

He didn't need to ask, not really, but it made conversation. Tommy had Brett's nipple between his teeth, and he bit down gently while flicking at the captive flesh with his tongue. Brett groaned as Tommy released his hostage.

"Hey! I didn't say stop."

"Tough." Tommy blew across his wet skin, drawing another bone-deep shudder from Brett, and sat up. "I'm not your bitch," he teased. "Just 'cause I have long hair…."

He stopped when Brett reached up, running his fingers through the hair in question, and his face softened. Brett wondered what he might be thinking.

"C'mere. Please?"

He slipped his arms around Tommy's neck and pulled him close. As kisses went, it might still be a little awkward, full of negotiation and compromise, but that didn't matter. Sure, learning each other and losing that fear of letting go might take a while, but so what? It would be worth it.

"Mmnn," Brett murmured, somewhere between a yes and a no, as Tommy rubbed the back of his thigh. His leg rose of its own accord, like a puppy getting scratched. Tommy's hair tickled his bare chest. "Hold on."

He didn't want to stop, but—the ground being hard and the night being cold—there wasn't enough room in the tent to get too crazy. Besides, he wasn't a hundred percent sure what Tommy wanted to do and, although at this point Brett didn't want to refuse him anything, the sudden reality of losing his second virginity scared the hell out of him.

"All right," Tommy whispered, his mouth on Brett's ear, lean fingers caressing, *oh God*, caressing the curve of his ass and sending untold thrills shooting up Brett's spine.

And then he stopped.

"Oh… okay, no. No, don't stop," Brett pleaded.

Tommy sniggered and Brett wriggled against him, now not only incredibly horny, but annoyed at being laughed at. Tommy shook his head, his smile even sexier on top of the dark flush in his face.

"You just told me to hold on. You want or don't want?"

Brett bit back a little growl of frustration. "I do. I-I want everything. Just… here?"

"Out in the *wiiiild*," Tommy purred, leaning in to nip at Brett's neck.

"Oh, God. Seriously? In a tent?"

Tommy slipped down, lavishing his attention on Brett's chest.

"Yep. Mine are an ancient and proud people, full of deep mystic shit," he said, somewhat muffled. "We can do it anywhere."

Brett leaned back, putting his weight on his hands. *Wow.* Who knew male nipples had been made for that?

"Ah. I kinda thought," he said, trying to keep a clear head, "that it'd be nice to take the time to do it right. In a real bed. I… think I'd like to go slow, the first time. I know it-it might hurt, and…."

Tommy raised his head, and Brett's chest tightened at the sight of that face: the mussed up hair hanging over one eye, the frown of confusion on his brow, his mouth half open, and his eyes deep as a starless night.

"Brett, I was only gonna blow ya."

"Oh."

The blush burned on Brett's cheeks for a moment, and he waited to see if the ground would really swallow him up, but then Tommy

smiled at him, and there was such a look in his face that the
embarrassment paled a little.

"'Course, if you want to do that, we will."

"Yeah, maybe. Sometime. In a bed."

Tommy laughed. "Old-fashioned romantic, huh?"

"Nah." Brett's breath whistled through his teeth as Tommy
stroked him. "Just passionate about good lumbar support."

"Oh. Right. You want a pillow while I suck you off, then?"

"No. Just fucking do it before I explode."

"Yessir."

"Oh!"

It knocked the air right out of him. Brett threw his head back, his
weight falling on his elbows as Tommy sank between his legs and did
what it had taken him forever to convince Lynsey Schaeder to even
try. Tommy demonstrated far more talent, not to mention enthusiasm.
His hands roved everywhere, coaxing and stirring, and his *mouth*....
Brett found it hard to believe that anything could be so good.

He reached out, blindly, his hand resting on Tommy's shoulder,
kneading his warm, dark gold skin. So beautiful. Brett felt him
breathing hard through his nose, short bursts of air tickling against his
groin like laughter, amazed that the whole thing could be so natural.
Like he'd been waiting for this without even knowing it. Just another
door, unlocked.

Brett squeezed Tommy's shoulder. Tommy looked up, and damn
if he wasn't the most wonderful thing on the planet. Watching himself
slide in and out of Tommy's mouth drove the feeling even higher, but
Brett wanted more. He wanted to be part of the moment, part of how it
felt to do that... part of Tommy. He stroked his fingertips down
Tommy's cheek, holding the side of his head.

Tommy's gaze stayed fixed on him, but something like a
question seemed to pass over his face. He looked, for a moment, not
embarrassed but.... Brett wasn't sure. Hurt? How could it hurt him?
How could anything this perfect, this intimate, bring anything but joy?
He arched his back a little, his mouth too dry to give Tommy the
warning he wanted to, but Tommy knew. Right now, Tommy knew
everything.

Tommy *was* everything.

Brett closed his eyes, though he'd have liked to watch. Liked to see Tommy swallow, watch the way he moaned his approval, his voice humming through the core of all existence and finally, reluctantly, letting Brett slip out of his mouth. But, even if he'd opened his eyes, Brett wasn't sure he'd have been able to see. He whimpered at the cold air and felt Tommy draw up the blankets.

He couldn't believe Tommy had just done that. And, yet, it had seemed like the easiest thing in the world. Would it be so easy to do it to him? How many times had Tommy done it before? Unexpected jealousy assailed him. That thought, that sneaking jealous thought that came out of nowhere, led to an even worse one, a thought that left him cold to the pit of his stomach.

Is there anyone else?

Tommy settled beside him, not too close. Giving him space.

"Pretty intense, right?" he asked gently.

Brett blinked and forced a smile. He nodded. "The good kind."

"And you're all right?"

"'Course. I'm not a vir—" He stopped, blushing again though he hated himself for it. "You know what I mean."

Tommy chuckled. He looped his hands behind his head, just staring up at the tattered canvas.

Brett cleared his throat. "Uh, Tommy?"

"Mm?"

"What happens now?"

"Well, you could jerk me off."

"Oh." Brett's words stumbled on their way out of his mouth. "I-I didn't mean…. Of course I wanna, but—"

"You mean are we dating yet?"

Brett squirmed. "No! Yeah. Shit, man…! You can't ask me questions when you've just done that. I don't have my brain on right."

Tommy rolled over, half on top of him, laughing, his hair tickling Brett's face and neck. Brett craned up to kiss him, his hands cupping Tommy's ass. Tommy sighed contentedly, pushing back against him. That surprised Brett, almost as much as his lack of concern at kissing Tommy and tasting himself. If he hadn't been so satiated, he might have been embarrassed.

He reached down for Tommy, enjoying the needy little noises he made in the back of his throat, and massaging his butt as he stroked him.

"That good?"

"Hell, yeah. Yeah… want you, Brett."

Despite Tommy's encouragement, it felt kind of strange, and he wasn't quite sure what he was allowed to touch. Sex with Lynsey had been strictly traditional, and though he'd touched her ass—held it, squeezed it, kissed it—touching Tommy there held a whole different set of connotations. He wanted to, though. Brett realized it with something approaching surprise, and he wanted… hell, he wanted everything.

IN A perfect world—the world with reliably spectacular sunsets and mosquitoes that weren't armor-plated and three feet long—they would have made love all night, naked under the red plaid blanket. Unfortunately, nothing's perfect.

Tommy sat up, bleary-eyed in the dark and shivering.

"Jesus, I'm freezin'," he muttered, more to himself than anything.

Brett, still half-asleep and sticky-eyed, looked out from under the piled-up sleeping bags.

"Whzzt?"

He reached out, fingertips barely skimming Tommy's back.

Tommy, arms raised above his head as he pulled on his fleece, flinched, breath catching in his throat. "Sorry," he mumbled, glancing at Brett's frown of confusion over his shoulder.

"S'only me."

"Yeah, well. Y'know," Tommy said airily, burrowing back under the covers. "I kinda expected Hugh Jackman."

Brett snorted. "Tough. He can't have you."

"Oh?" Tommy raised an eyebrow, pretending that the possessive note in Brett's voice hadn't given him a perverse little thrill.

"Nope." Brett yawned sleepily. "Don't care if he is a big-shot movie star. There's no more room in the tent. C'mere."

Tommy scooted closer, feeling Brett's sleep-warm hands slip under his fleece. He wouldn't have had to put it on if Brett wasn't such a cover-hog, but he didn't care. Not much. So much pent-up need and want, all taken care of…. Who could complain?

"What's that?" Brett asked. His fingers halted in their travel, tracing a dip in Tommy's skin.

"Nothin'. Broke a rib, that's all. Years ago."

Brett pushed the fleece aside and peered at the spot. Tommy wriggled, not really wanting him to see. He knew what it looked like: an uneven patch on his left side, about the size of a tennis ball. It had healed just fine. Not worth anybody's attention.

"Does it hurt?"

"No. You can touch it."

Brett did so, gently. "How'd you do it?"

"Fell," Tommy said, too simply, twisting a short lock of Brett's red-brown hair around his finger. "It's nothing. Really."

"Nn-nn, musta hurt. When'd you say you did it?"

"I was thirteen. Now, d'you want my entire medical history, or have you got something more up-to-date to focus on?"

Brett pulled back a little to look at him, and Tommy captured his mouth in a deep, wet kiss, holding on to both sides of his head. *That oughta distract him.* Brett moaned softly as Tommy rocked his hips against him. Tommy smiled. It had been easy to forget how good it felt to be wanted. And, though he hated to admit it, Tommy kinda enjoyed making Brett lose it like this. Making him nervous.

Brett's arms slid around him. *Yes.* This place, this moment… completely theirs. Nothing else but this. Nothing else mattered. Brett held him tighter and moved with him. After a little while, Tommy pulled his mouth away and looked at him, stupidly surprised.

"Oh," he said quietly, his body tensing.

It had been enough for Brett, too. Tommy lay back, leaving him to pull up the blankets and settle down. Brett sighed contentedly and leaned his head on Tommy's shoulder. Tommy bit his lip, watching the dim wash of moonlight shape the darkness around him. As Brett started to snore, the blankets stealthily slipped over to his side of the tent.

Tommy smiled into the darkness.

BREAKFAST comprised slightly charred fry bread and flat Dr Pepper. Tommy woke, already in a good mood even before receiving the nicest, if clumsiest, blowjob of his life, and decided to mix up the batter in a can and cook it on the skillet. It tasted a little bit of fish, and the edges had caught because he'd been kissing Brett instead of watching the pan, but it still turned out edible.

They ate, looking out at the creek and the birds. At around a quarter to nine, an SUV pulled into the car park, and a family with two shrieking kids and a picnic hamper disappeared to the other side of the pull-in.

"Coulda seen some innarestin' sights if you'd come by a half hour earlier, folks," Brett observed, their noise dying away into the distance.

Tommy gazed at him consideringly over the last of the fry bread. "That bother you?"

"Hm? What?"

"Getting found out." He sucked his thumb and forefinger clean. "Caught. With me."

Brett blinked. "No. Why? Should it?"

Tommy shrugged, not prepared to admit that he didn't believe him. "You dated that girl for, like, forever. You're not exactly out."

"Are you?"

Another shrug. "Not the point. I just…. Guess I wanna know if you'll still say hi if I pass you in the street kinda thing. That's all." Tommy studied his feet, scuffing the edge of one boot in the grass. "'Cause, y'know, I've found, sometimes, people…."

He trailed off, embarrassed by the horrified look on Brett's face. He should never have started this conversation.

"What? Of course I— I mean, I would never.... Shit! No... you and me, I-I don't wanna screw it up."

Tommy looked up at him. He hadn't expected Brett's assurances to sound so genuine, so... desperate.

There's a "you and me?" Oh, baby.

"Thanks," he said quietly.

That subdued things, at least for a while. They took down the tent, packed up all the traces of that stolen time, and walked along by the creek a little, trying out the hand-holding thing.

"When, uh, when can I see you again?" Brett asked.

The cliché made Tommy smile. He'd abandoned Brett's hand in favor of gently nipping and kissing the back of his neck. He stood behind Brett, arms wrapped loosely around him.

"Soon," he murmured. "Depends when I can get away. Things are kinda busy at home right now."

Brett said nothing, but Tommy felt him tense. He cursed inwardly.

"I got a job in Kremlin on Tuesday, though. Maybe when I finish, I could swing by your place'n pick you up for dinner. You fancy a little dinner date?" Tommy rocked slowly against him and rubbed his hands over Brett's arms, chin pressed to the hollow of his neck. "Fine wine, fine dining... or burger, fries 'n' a coke in the Chevy. Park up at Fresno, put the radio on, fog up the windows. What d'ya think, huh?"

He planted a kiss just below Brett's ear, popping his lips against his skin, seeking out one of those sensitive spots he'd found last night. Anything to make him smile, hear him laugh.

"Quit that," Brett muttered, not terribly seriously. "Tickles."

"Will you, though?" Tommy persisted. "Tuesday?"

"All right. It's a date."

"Good."

CHAPTER
SEVEN

THEY didn't go out Tuesday. Tommy got a call at work from his mother, asking him to pick Robbie up from his after-school swim club.

"Well, where are you?" he wanted to know, clamping the phone between his shoulder and his ear as he threw his kit into the Chevy.

"I had to go out, that's all. I don't think I'll be back in time and I don't want him to be left there worrying. Please, would you do it, Tommy?"

He sighed tersely and slammed the truck's passenger door. He'd been about to complain that he had plans, but then he heard something in the background noise of her call. It sounded like a doctor being paged.

Oh, not again.

"Sure, Mom," he said, resigned. "I'll do it. You okay?"

"Of course. I have to go. Bye, honey."

She rang off as he was still framing his farewell. Tommy swore under his breath.

He left work at 4:55 on the button and gunned the Chevy back along Highway 2, glaring at the little white crosses that littered the side of the road. There were a lot of them; those, and the flowers bound to fences and posts, mummified memorials turned papery by the wind.

Robbie stayed silent on the drive home. Slumped beside his brother, all wet hair and sullen eyes, he kicked at Tommy's toolkit like it was the back of an economy airline seat, his arms folded. Tommy tried a few "how's school" and "did you have a good time at swimming" questions, but Robbie either shrugged them off or replied in monosyllables, so he gave up. He wanted to call Brett, but he could hardly do that with Robbie there.

They picked up takeout on the way home. Tommy sent Robbie into the house ahead of him, the greasy, spicy smell of the fried chicken tantalizingly fringing the air. He hung back in the Chevy, the engine still running, and found Brett's number on his cell.

"Hey, it's me."

"Tommy? Where are you?"

He glanced at his watch. Shit, it was already seven thirty. Even if he'd been planning to go over there, he'd have been late.

"I'm sorry, I can't make it. I'd've called before, but—"

"Right."

He winced. Brett sounded pissed, and who could blame him?

"I'm sorry. It's urgent, I couldn't…."

"Doesn't matter," Brett said after a long moment.

It didn't sound like forgiveness.

"I'll make it up. I'll—"

"It's okay, Tommy. You don't have to. We'll… whatever, okay? I'll see you around."

"Sure."

After he switched off the engine, Tommy sat there for a while, wondering how badly he'd screwed up. Eventually, the lure of the chicken got too strong, and he sloped indoors.

Mei had arrived home, and everyone was eating at the table. It took a moment for the agreeable little scene to sink in. Tommy had witnessed several like it before, but even then they'd never quite seemed real. As a small boy, he'd lived for evenings like this. Back then, they'd represented closeness and stability, but since he'd gotten old enough to see all the undercurrents, somehow they didn't seem so perfect.

Robbie and Lila were bickering over who had the biggest chicken leg. Martin sat at the end of the table, smiling at them, his face a little sweaty and a little red. To his right, Scott prodded at some coleslaw with a fork and an expression that suggested he thought it might fight back. Katie sat on Mei's lap pulling a French fry apart with intense scientific interest.

Hospital strapping and bandaging covered his mother's left wrist, but Tommy wasn't about to say anything. She glanced up, her gaze flitting almost imperceptibly between him and his father before Martin turned that crooked, slightly breathless smile on him.

"Tommy! All right, kid?"

He nodded. "Yeah. Hey, everybody."

"Come eat something, honey," Mei said, patting the empty chair between her and Robbie. "You didn't have to get all this."

He shrugged. Martin resolved the whose-chicken-leg-is-bigger dispute by seizing both from the kids' plates, taking a bite of each and then putting them back, to a chorus of appalled yelps.

"Daddy!" Lila scolded.

He stuck out his tongue, and she squealed at the mashed-up mass of chicken. Mei looked away, turning her attention to wiping Katie's mouth.

Basically a normal meal. Strange that it should feel like such a strain, really.

Tommy ate his chicken while looking mostly at the tabletop, glancing up when a sharp blow stung his ankle. Scott raised his eyebrows in a silent question. Tommy shook his head. No, there wasn't anything he needed to know about.

After dinner, Martin took the kids upstairs to look at their homework and supervise bath time. For all the fuss he made of it, he could have been some ancient emperor sweeping out of the Coliseum.

"Don't say anythin'," Scott murmured, passing behind his brother with Katie in his arms.

Tommy snorted.

In the kitchen, Mei was struggling with the washing up. She turned her head when Tommy came up behind her, wordlessly removing both the cloth and the plate from her hands and commandeering the job.

"It's only a fracture," she said quietly.

"He's in a good mood."

"It was an accident."

Tommy stacked the plates carefully on the dish rack. "Yeah. Same as last time."

He looked at his mother; she was trembling slightly. She turned away on the pretext of fetching a towel. He took it from her, dried and put away the plates, and pretended he couldn't hear her sniffling. From upstairs, the sound of running water reached them.

LATER that night, Tommy woke in the dark. He'd heard a noise, he thought, and he blinked in the gloom, trying to see if Scott had woken. He must have, because he wasn't there. His bed had been folded down, his clothes not in evidence in any of the usual places he let them fall… and there was the sound of footsteps creaking on the stairs. Tommy supposed Karen must be worth it and wished he hadn't thought that, because it made him think of who *he'd* rather be with right now.

Not that Brett would probably be too pleased if he turned up unannounced at—what? Tommy squinted at the imperfectly fluorescent clock on his nightstand—two a.m. and started throwing gravel at the window.

Still, good for Scott.

He lay still for a while, just listening, wanting to hear his brother get out of the front door undetected. Only they weren't, he realized, Scott's footsteps on the stairs. The door of his—*ha!*—parents' room opened and closed. After that, some low, dark rustling sounds. Then Mei's voice, muffled through the wall.

"No…! Martin, I said… I said—"

His father's response, an incoherent grunt, then a few muted scuffles and his mother's sharp, truncated cry. A little while later, the erratic, sonorous thump of the bed against the wall. Tommy put the pillow over his head and pulled the covers tight around him. His own private, safe cocoon.

It seemed to go on for so long.

Eventually, on the landing, the bedroom door opened again. Under the blanket, Tommy stopped breathing. His father padded across to the bathroom, pissed loudly, made his way back to his unwelcoming bed. Tommy, blood thumping in his ears and bile burning in his throat, heard Mei crying softly, the sound sucked away into the dark.

Tommy squeezed his eyes shut tight, as if it might somehow make them blind. On the landing, his parents' door shut with a gentle *click*.

"REALLY? Like a date night?" Brett asked.

Monica shot her son an old-fashioned look. "Date night?" she repeated incredulously. "Where on earth did you—"

"Oh, I don't know. Thought that's supposed to be good for marriages," Brett said glibly.

In truth, he hadn't been thinking of his parents at all. The moment Monica had mentioned they'd be going to dinner with one of Stephen's clients in Rudyard, only one thought had been on his mind.

"Well, it's nice you're thinking of us, honey. But it's hardly a date. Though I think it is gonna be too far to drive back again the same night. And I can't see your father staying off the vino, so I did think we might stay over. So, I want you to promise me: no wild parties, okay?"

Brett shrugged. "Sure."

"I don't mind you having a few friends over, but if you do, you know the rules. Nondrivers are welcome to the beer in the fridge, but you stay off the hard liquor. No drugs, and no wrecking the place. I want to be absolutely clear on that point. Okay? Promise?"

"Promise. But, Mom, have I ever—"

"No, but that doesn't mean there's a reason to start now. You can save all of that for college."

Brett grimaced, really more for show than anything.

Later that evening, he met Tommy up by the reservoir. He meant to bring the subject up, ask the big question. Brett had a hard time remembering what to concentrate on, though, because it had been a last-minute thing and the urgency of it had caught him by surprise.

I need to see you.

Tommy's words, his phone call from the road barely more than one rushed, sparse sentence. Brett had never heard anyone sound like they meant it so much, and he flung himself into the Bronco, no thought in his head but getting there as fast as possible. Their place. Their time.

Fresh back from a job in Box Elder—his jeans stained with paint and mastic—Tommy was tired and a little sweaty but unquenchable. Brett tilted his head, giving Tommy all of his neck, cursing the gearstick and the lack of space in the Chevy, as well as all of these damn clothes. They edged and wriggled, trying to find the best use of the little available room, and Brett found himself pinned under Tommy, one knee drawn up on the seat as they cleaved together. The hard bulge in Tommy's jeans rubbed against his thigh, mirroring his own arousal. He shivered, suddenly feeling very vulnerable. Tommy nipped at the point of his jaw, his fingers working under the hem of Brett's T-shirt, stroking the soft ridges of his stomach.

"Brett? You okay?"

Tommy pulled back a little, his face darkly questioning against the pale glow from the dash. Brett tightened his grip on Tommy's shirt, needing the heat of the connection between them no matter how much it scared him. Something had changed tonight; he sensed it. Tommy seemed different, and not from being weighed down with all the grime and dust of work. Brett felt it in his touch, in his mouth....

Brett nodded. "Fine. Are... are you all right? I... kinda have the feeling something's happened. Is that stupid?"

Tommy looked at him a little too long, his eyes shrouded in the dimness. The Chevy's heater rattled away to itself, the radio still churning out some ancient '80s power ballad. The days regularly hit the low forties now, but the nights could still get bitter.

"No," he said, fingers still working over Brett's body beneath the cotton tee. "It's not. I just... I have some stuff at home right now. It's nothin'. I.... You don't need to think about it."

"You can tell me."

"No."

The shortness of his reply stung, but Brett tried not to show how much. He knew he'd failed miserably by the way Tommy backtracked.

"I mean, it's all right," he said. "It's... it's nothing. You don't wanna know about it."

TOMMY cursed inwardly. He saw the hurt in Brett's face, and of all people, he didn't deserve to have this taken out on him.

"All right. Keep your secrets."

Brett sounded pissed off, but it didn't change the way he kissed. Tommy pressed harder against him, as if everything could be blotted out that way, as if he could erase himself, lose all the parts of him that he didn't need, exist nowhere except where Brett touched him. It didn't work. He didn't want to keep Brett in the dark, didn't want to lie.

Tommy pulled back again, lost and full and hurting, and Brett looked at him with such need, such want in his face. And it wasn't fucking *fair*. Tommy took a breath. He'd come too far, too fast. Thrown himself into this when he should have stayed out. This wasn't for him. It wasn't... meant.

Brett reached up, trailing just the tip of his thumb over Tommy's chin, and he nearly lost it. He felt the pressure, frustrated and twisted up inside him. Brett's mouth—so warm, his kiss so insistent—melded them together like the kind of slow, deep love Tommy knew they'd make, and he wanted that so much. Wanted everything. Only, all this poisonous melodrama had to stop first.

It wasn't good for either of them. He wanted Brett so much, but Brett wasn't his to take, not his to chain.... Even if he could do that, Tommy knew he'd never forgive himself. No. Brett's future lay elsewhere, somewhere bigger and brighter. And Tommy wanted to say that, to say something—anything—other than those three little words that trembled perilously close to the tip of his tongue.

Brett spoke first and saved him.

"Tommy?" He exhaled tightly, squirming against the seat.

Tommy, bleary-eyed, blinked at him. "Whassa matter?"

"Uh… I don't know which is worse: my hard-on or my cramp."

Tommy laughed breathlessly, the tension bursting out of him, and right then, he'd never loved anyone more. He lifted himself up so Brett could move. Eventually, after an awkward tangle of limbs and some banging of elbows, Brett rubbed the leg that had lately been pinned up on the seat, and Tommy sat back behind the wheel, looking at him with a smile on his face.

"Jalopy sex doesn't do it for you, does it, babe?"

Brett shot him a look. "You just need a bigger truck. Or less crap in the back," he added, jerking his head at the building supplies and who-knew-what mess piled on old sheets and blankets.

Tommy reached over and rubbed Brett's thigh. "Aw. Better?"

Brett gritted his teeth. "Actually, worse. Quit it."

Tommy's fingers worked further up Brett's leg, and he smiled innocently. "What, this? You don't like it?"

"Bastard," Brett growled. "You're going to leave me like this, aren't you?"

"Hmm. Wish I could."

Tommy's nimble fingers unzipped his fly and slipped inside. Brett gasped and leaned his head back against the seat. More clashing of limbs and bodies got them into a slightly more comfortable position, bearable for as long as it took. Tommy watched the flush darken Brett's cheeks, the small crinkle that cut across the bridge of his nose as he screwed up his face and made that cute, hot, gorgeous little noise in the back of his throat.

"I am in such a mess," Brett murmured, though he made no attempt to move.

"Tissues in the jockey box."

"In a minute."

Tommy adjusted his position, wondering how Brett did that, took everything in him that hurt or didn't work, bunched it up and made it right.

Did he even know he did it?

"Oh, baby," he muttered as Brett's fingers closed around him.

He seemed to be getting bolder every day, as if he'd never been nervous of this the way he had that night at Beaver Creek. So confident in the way he touched, so goddamn good at it…. Tommy let out a soft moan, knowing he wouldn't last long. It seemed as if each time brought them closer, made them more unbreakable. He couldn't end this. It wasn't his choice anymore.

"Tommy?"

"Hm?"

"Got the house to myself Wednesday night." Brett's breath grazed his cheek, all warmth and smug coyness. "You wanna come over?"

His timing was incredible.

"Oh… oh, shit, *yes*!"

Giving up, Tommy thought, had never been sweeter. He looked over at Brett as he mopped up and tucked himself back into his jeans.

"Hell, yeah. What time?"

CHAPTER EIGHT

TOMMY supposed, as he pulled away, that he ought to feel guilty. He ought to be ashamed, leaving the house, the family.... He had responsibilities, he knew that. Obligations.

Unfortunately, all that shamed him was just how much he was looking forward to getting away. *Maybe there's something spiteful in me. Something angry, malicious... ugly.* It had sparked up when Scott complained about him going out, when their mother got that pinched, martyred look she got every time he made his own plans. No. They owed him this, didn't they? One freaking night. He deserved it. He deserved just one chance... because that's what Brett gave him. One chance to feel right.

It had been nearly a week since Tommy had seen him last. It sucked, but they'd both been busy. He had to expect that. He kept telling himself it would only get more difficult. And it wouldn't last forever. Only until fall, when Brett went to Washington. Even so, his hands were shaking on the wheel by the time he pulled up at Brett's place.

God, when did this last happen?

"Hi, stranger." Brett grinned as he opened the door, and he looked so good in gray sweatpants and a well-worn cotton tee, washed-out red fabric hugging his arms.

Tommy licked his lips. "I brought beer."

"Great. C'mon. Roscoe, get in."

The German Shepherd, busily sniffing Tommy, wagged his tail and padded obediently after Brett. Tommy followed on behind.

Inside, the house seemed clean, yes, but unpolished. Pictures hung on the walls, family photographs with dust on the top edges of the frames and generic modern prints that filled up the blank spaces on cream walls. There were even a few bedraggled houseplants.

They sat on the comfortable, deep couch in front of the natural stone fireplace in the family room, Roscoe flaked out in front of the flames and Tommy feeling like he'd never been so far away from anyone. It made him nervous, all of this. This casual comfort. Brett opened two beers, and they split a frozen pizza that had already been in the oven when Tommy arrived. Brett had rented a movie: *X-Men*, with Hugh Jackman. It raised a smile that he'd remembered that throwaway line of Tommy's, and the whole thing felt so... nice. Unpretentious. And Tommy couldn't have been more grateful to him for that.

Gradually, as he sat curled up on the couch next to Brett, not really paying too much attention to the climax of the film—excepting the parts where Jackman had at least some of his clothes off—Tommy felt less numb. He didn't rationalize it, couldn't pretend to understand it; it was like coming back to himself after being knocked out for an operation. So much held inside, and all Brett did, if he even knew it, kept him grounded and sane. Anchored him. Tommy leaned closer, wanting very much to sink into him and never surface. He kissed Brett's neck.

"When do they come home?"

"Relax. Not 'til the morning. We got as long as we want."

"Long enough?"

"Maybe."

THE credits rolled, and Brett closed his eyes. Tommy's mouth nuzzled his neck, those lean hands slipped under his shirt, and it felt so good. He lifted his arms, making it easier for Tommy to strip him, winding his fingers in Tommy's hair as kisses peppered his chest. It surprised Brett that it could seem both so new and so familiar. Just like the night at Beaver Creek, only with the comforts of soft upholstery and heating.

Nerves fluttered in his gut as he remembered what he'd said up at the campground about lumbar support.

Roscoe cocked an ear and whined softly but apparently couldn't be bothered to move from in front of the fire.

"I think your dog's offended," Tommy murmured, taking his hand out of Brett's pants.

Brett laughed, too out of breath to actually speak. He knew there'd be more room on his bed, though actually taking Tommy in there kind of scared him. It was nerve racking, with the feeling of ritual about it, like something irrevocable. Brett tried to shake it, tried to tell himself how stupid that sounded, but it didn't help. God, he wanted this, but it still felt so fast.

Brett shut the bedroom door behind them.

It shouldn't feel fast. It had taken a little over eight weeks to get here, week after week of waiting, and maybe that explained it. The waiting. He leaned back against the door. Tommy pulled his shirt over his head, and the sight of that body bypassed Brett's eyes and headed straight to every nerve ending he possessed.

The deerskin thong he'd seen before hung around Tommy's neck, two burnished jasper beads and a tiny silver disc nestling in the hollow between his collarbones. Brett thought himself ugly next to all that tawny, smooth skin, saw his own body as pallid and uneven, dappled with moles and the odd, incongruous freckle. Tommy seemed to like them, though, and he traced his fingers over every mark as if they formed some kind of three-dimensional map, some kind of blueprint he could memorize.

On the bed, Tommy uncovered him piece by piece, and he appeared to relish the opportunity to see Brett properly this time, to be with him somewhere warm, enclosed and—even if just for now—private. Brett wished they could last forever, those moments of gentle introduction, before the need and the desire pressed in, shortening both breath and time. He reached for Tommy, but he rolled away, and Brett let out a little cry of disappointment.

Tommy looked up at him coquettishly from the covers, lips curled into a dirty, impish grin. Brett's pulse beat in his throat, and he swallowed heavily as Tommy crawled up the bed, a whisper in the grass.

"You wanna fuck me?"

Brett groaned. The way Tommy said it killed him, the way he rolled the word around his mouth before finally spitting it out, slutty and disheveled.

"Hm." Tommy's hand inched up Brett's thigh, traced silent promises on his skin. "What d'you think, Brett? You think you wanna fuck me?"

Brett nodded—while he still could.

"Mm," he said, hoping he'd managed to achieve more of a lustful growl than a strangled whimper.

"Good. I'd like that." Tommy slid him another dirty grin and leaned across to whisper in Brett's ear as he sat up. "I want you to fuck me, Brett. Hard."

That *word*… the last hook on the "k" seemed to pulse right into the center of Brett's brain and turn the whole thing to jelly.

Shit. Do something, won't you?

He tried to jar himself into action, but as Tommy got off the bed, he just sat there. He sat and waited, the blood rushing in his ears. He remembered being nervous like this the first time he'd slept with Lynsey only… no, not like this. With her, he'd been scared he wouldn't be able to do it. He'd been a little bit drunk, too. Right now, he just seemed to be wound so tight he felt like he might blow up into a thousand pieces. Anticipation more than anything else. Excitement… his nerves so keen, senses so intensified. He barely noticed his waning erection.

Tommy came back, bearing a pump bottle of lube and a condom. Brett wasn't entirely sure where they'd appeared from—he must have come properly prepared, sneaky bastard that he was. Tommy kissed him, fluffed him, and spread himself out before Brett, legs wide and eyes trusting. The nerves made another attack, but Tommy guided him gently, without any hint of embarrassment, any sign of mocking. Gradually, Brett relaxed again, his touches growing more confident.

"How, uh, how much of this stuff should I be using?" he asked, pumping yet more from the bottle of lube into his hand.

"Twice as much as you think you need," Tommy muttered.

Brett complied, all quiet wonder at the way Tommy opened for him, so strong but so tender. Tommy's skin was flushed, and his voice a faint rasp in his throat as Brett's third finger slid in.

"A'right... you ready?" he asked, shifting position a little abruptly.

Even if he wasn't, Brett guessed, Tommy was getting desperate. He supposed he *was* ready. He wanted to, definitely. Never wanted anything more, every fiber aching to get himself in there, feel what it was like to fuck Tommy... to fuck another guy. Trouble was, his hands were shaking so bad he thought he might never get the condom on.

Shit....

Tommy knelt four-square on the covers and licked at his lips impatiently. "You ready yet?"

"Yeah." Brett nodded, intense relief as he managed to settle the sheath, every nerve still threatening to explode.

It was everything he'd imagined, everything he'd ever fantasized about, and a hell of a lot more. Different, too. So much, so many different things, all wrapped up in one.

He took it slow, worried about hurting Tommy, but that didn't seem to be what he wanted.

"More," Tommy rasped, part of a chain of orders, low-voiced and yearning, that would have made Brett's knees go weak if he hadn't been kneeling on them. "Gimme... like that."

Brett did his best, thrust after thrust with everything he had. He'd thought Tommy would want to take it gently, but that seemed to be far from the case. The wilder he got, the more Tommy liked it, bucking and arching against him, his breath harsh as he cried out. God, he could be so loud! Brett wanted to tell him to rein it in. They might not share any party walls, but the house still had neighbors, and for all Brett knew people could hear him all the way down the street. That thought thrilled and embarrassed him, and he tried not to think about curtains twitching to the sound of Tommy's sexual orchestra.

Instead, Brett covered every inch of him that he could, skin on skin, sweat-slicked together, his face in Tommy's hair, breathing in his scent, free hand running over the taut muscles in his arms, both their weight supported against him.

He used his whole body, aware of the bed banging against the wall, not caring now, no longer worrying about how long they had or even if anyone did hear. Time didn't exist anymore. Not when he felt like this.

"Pull my hair."

"Huh?" Brett grunted, not coherent enough to fully understand Tommy's tense whisper.

"Hair. Pull it. Least you can do if you're g'na ride my ass."

"Oh, God…!"

Brett obeyed, and Tommy growled, flinging his head back.

"Harder."

Brett wasn't sure if he meant the hair or the fucking, so he did what he could with both until he passed the white-hot point of actually being in control. He came, buried so far in Tommy, body and soul, that he wasn't sure he could ever get out again.

He tried to breathe slowly, bring his heart rate back out of the stratosphere, but he could barely manage to breathe at all. He leaned on Tommy's back, forehead on his shoulder, his fingers still tangled in that gorgeous, silk-heavy hair. After a while, he grew aware of his eyelids drooping. Tommy fidgeted beneath him.

"Move," Tommy muttered.

"Hm?"

"Move," Tommy repeated, elbowing him in the stomach. "Love ya, but I can't breathe like this."

"Oh. Sorry."

Brett obliged, carefully extricating himself and collapsing on the mattress with a theatrical groan. Tommy rolled over and sat up. He grinned down at Brett and reached out to pinch his nipple.

"Don't think you're fucked out yet, boy. What time is it?"

Brett raised his head a little and peered at the clock, wincing as Tommy slicked the condom off him and tossed it.

"Nearly eleven."

"See? Early."

Tommy lay down beside him, chin propped on his arms, just looking at him. Brett reached out and tucked his hair behind his ear, mirroring that little mannerism of Tommy's, one of the first things he'd noticed about him. Tommy's eyes softened and a muscle clenched briefly in his jaw. Brett decided to believe that he knew what this moment meant. That he understood it, and that they didn't need to talk.

It might be bullshit, but he couldn't deal with anything else right now.

THE night wore on and gave way to the small hours of the morning. They'd showered, though the sheets remained sweaty and sticky. They hung heavily on Brett's hip as he lay on the bed, his head propped on one hand, the other tracing idly up and down Tommy's bicep.

Tommy wished he wouldn't do that; it felt like Brett's fingers were dragging his soul after them, nothing but iron filings behind a magnet. He didn't want to let out one of those paperback romance novel sighs, either, but he exhaled slowly, wishing he had the energy for one more round.

He'd been right that night in the Chevy, when he'd thought that it'd be slow. Oh, Brett could fuck like a jackhammer when he wanted, and that really was good, but that second time, on his back with Brett between his legs, surging like a tide and looking at him like…. Tommy didn't dare take that thought any further.

"You're beautiful," Brett said, quietly but very matter of fact.

Tommy turned his head away and swallowed heavily. *What the fuck is this?* He hadn't cried in years, but now his eyelids felt leaden and the bridge of his nose stung.

You're pregnant and hormonal, you stupid bitch, said a tiny voice at the back of his mind, somewhere out of the mists of memory. He smiled bitterly. He was still smiling when Brett kissed his cheek and laid his head on the pillow, one arm draped across Tommy's chest, heat pooling at the point their bodies touched. Tommy stared at the ceiling for a moment, his cheek burning and his throat tight.

"What time is it?" he said after a while, his mouth dry. He'd wanted to say "I love you," but the silence scared him; too big and too deep.

Brett rolled over to check the clock. "Almost one," he said, snuggling back down beneath the covers. "Better get some sleep; the alarm's set for five-thirty."

"Yuck."

"I know, but it was your idea. They won't be back 'til after nine. You could stay later."

"Nah, better I'm back early. Gotta get the kids ready for school and get up to Burnham by eight thirty."

Brett mumbled something unintelligible. Tommy didn't care what it had been; he was warm, comfortable, satiated, and more than that, he was... safe.

CHAPTER NINE

THEY took what they could get over the rest of the spring. With skill, luck, and a tight eye on the time, an hour or so could sometimes be snatched before either of Brett's parents got home from work, and they would, as Tommy joked, always have Fresno.

Brett found it frustrating, but he made a point of not complaining. Not because he thought he had a reason to bear it, but because he saw that Tommy had something on his mind.

He started to notice the bruises too. They came and went, but their regularity worried him. Oh, the more he'd got to know Tommy's body, the more scars Brett had seen. Always little ones, but each one a secret. He wouldn't talk about it, and at the same time, the mentions of his family all but stopped, as if he just disappeared into the mist every time he left.

It pissed Brett off, but he knew he couldn't push it. They only went around in circles... the closest they'd come to a real fight, so far. He'd wanted to know what happened when Tommy showed up at the reservoir with a swollen purple bruise on his forehead fading to a thin, shiny bloom around his left eye. Tommy had shrugged, said he did it at work, looking at his feet as he lied. It had been the last week of May, the lazy sunshine blissfully warm after so many cold months. They should have been making out by the water, resting against each other in the grass.

Instead, Brett had called him out on it and immediately wished he hadn't.

Bullshit. Who hit you?

Nobody. I told you—

Crap, Tommy. You gettin' trouble? Who's—

Nobody.

Tommy....

Look, he's a drinker, all right? He always has been. Got worse a couple years back when he lost his job. He swings when he's drunk, or when the painkillers don't cut it or don't mix. I shoulda learned to stay out of it before now. Keep my mouth shut. That's all. Just drop it, will ya?

Brett knew he wasn't going to forget hearing that. He wouldn't forget trying to pull more out of Tommy, trying to ask sensitive, prompting questions, as if he'd just tumble, quivering, into Brett's arms and share all his burdens. Instead, he'd gotten mad, driven away, and taken three days to simmer down.

Brett didn't want to risk that again. Their time meant a lot, and as things stood, it seemed like everything else was conspiring to remind him that soon there would be even less of it. He had his college acceptance letters; he'd gotten into Washington as well as his second choice, Strayer.

"Virginia?!"

Tommy's eyes widened, his beer paused halfway to his mouth. Brett couldn't help but laugh at him.

They sat overlooking Beaver Creek, clothed but a little tangled in each other, sun-warmed and tranquil, as if they'd never been at odds. The middle of June loomed on the horizon.

"Yeah, but I'm not going to Strayer. And Washington's less than eight hundred miles away."

The corner of Tommy's mouth twitched into an almost-smile, and he swigged his beer. Brett scuffed at the dusty grass with one foot. If you looked east, you could see the part of Bear Paw Mountain that, in winter, held the Ski Bowl. He felt, right now, so connected to this place that even he had trouble imagining going away.

"I'll come back on holidays. And weekends when I can."

Tommy gave a noncommittal grunt. Brett said nothing. That either meant Tommy didn't believe him, or didn't believe there'd be anything for him to come back to, and that thought made Brett angry. Sure, they hadn't talked about where this thing could lead, and maybe nothing lasted forever, but he loved Tommy.

That realization had been sneaking up on him for a while now. He didn't like to say anything because nineteen might be considered pretty damn young to say you'd found the person you wanted to spend your whole life with. But maybe not all love meant that. Maybe love was wanting to spend as long as you could with them. As long as you lived, or as long as you were the person you were at that time.

He'd change. He knew that. College would change him, life would change him. Tommy, too. Maybe they'd still love each other— if Tommy even felt that way, because Brett wasn't sure how to tell, and the thought of asking made him queasily nervous—and maybe not. Maybe all this would be gone. It scared the crap out of Brett, but he knew it could be true. And he hated it.

He glanced at Tommy, just stared at the hard line of his jaw, his high cheekbones, the set of his face against the sky. The bruises, mottled and ugly. Brett nudged Tommy's knee with his own.

"You sure you're okay?"

"Mm."

You're sure your father didn't give you a concussion?

It hurt to admit it, but Brett knew he didn't have a shot at pushing that subject.

"Are you coming by tomorrow?" he asked. "It's my day off."

"Sure." Tommy nodded. "About three thirty, right? I should be able to get off work by then."

"Cool."

BRETT stared up at the ceiling of his bedroom, the faded blue curtains closed tight against the daylight as if they could pretend the shelter of the night had already settled outside. It didn't stop yellow shafts of sun picking at the lint and the dust and the clothes discarded on the floor. Tommy was crashed out beside him, radiantly disheveled. Brett would never have thought, as little as four months ago, it could be so tender with someone like him.

Then again, he'd recently had a lot of preconceptions about sex rearranged. He shifted slightly on the mattress at the memory. A little over a week ago, Tommy had fucked him for the first time. They'd tried it before, and he'd wanted it so badly, but he'd been nervous and found it too hard to relax. This time, Tommy had tickled him mercilessly... and it should have been ridiculous.

It should have just been bizarre, but they'd been so close that day, like nothing else in the world mattered. Tommy had really made him believe that. Nothing existed except how he felt. He'd been ready, all tangled up in feeling so damn good that he'd lost all that tension, all that anxiety. It had been incredible.

Brett stretched against the sheet, wishing there could be more hours in the day, or at least a little longer before anyone might come home. They'd managed to squeeze in a heavy session this afternoon, Tommy bent double on the bed, begging him—actually begging—to be fucked. Brett had obliged, working them both up to the most intense orgasm. He'd sucked Tommy afterwards, and it had been like trailing his fingers through the water of a lake, touching something that ran deeper than he could see.

If only there could be just another hour or two... enough time to work up to taking him again properly, to feeling so full and complete, so close to him. Connected, but more than physically. Brett squirmed at the thought and rolled over to glance at the clock.

"Shit! Tommy?"

"Hnnn."

"It's almost five o'clock."

"Ugh... screw it. I'm too comfortable."

Laboriously, Brett sat up and swung his legs out of the bed. He limped a little as he stood, still feeling the burn in the backs of his thighs.

"Ouch.... Seriously, babe. My parents can't find you here. Not like this. I mean, they're pretty open-minded, but.... Gotta at least get dressed, all right?"

Reluctantly, Tommy pushed back into a cat-stretch and sat up.

"All right, all right. Shit…. Pass my pants?"

Brett let his gaze trail over Tommy's chest. The hard angles, gentle swells and ripples of his muscles, and the solid lines of collarbones all fitting together in a beautiful collage. Small brown nipples, the delicate shading of a treasure trail down his belly, his neat, dark navel… the broken rib that he'd refused to talk about.

He reached out, because there had to be time. Just once more.

"Ah-ah." Tommy slapped his hand away. "I wouldn't want to give your mother a heart attack."

"Changed my mind," Brett muttered. "There's time. If we're quick."

Tommy swung his legs out of the tangled bed. "Nope."

"But I can be quick…. I can be so quick, baby. I promise."

Tommy laughed, snagged his underpants from the floor, and tugged them on.

"No," he repeated, pausing to give Brett a quick kiss. "And you might wanna open a window. It's a little funky in here."

Brett started to pull on his own clothes. "Uh. You could stay. Meet 'em," he suggested, off the cuff. No idea why he'd said it. "Or not," he added, looking down, fastening his zipper.

Tommy had already dressed. He scoffed and flipped his hair out of his collar. "Yeah. 'Hey, Mom. This is Tommy, he's just'—"

"My boyfriend," Brett cut in. He looked at Tommy, part question, part challenge. "Y'know, they actually wouldn't freak out."

Well, probably not.

He tried to judge Tommy's expression, tried to gauge whether he'd said the wrong thing. Did they really have to keep on playing this game?

"You've told them?"

"No, but they're… they're good people. They're not, like, Bible-bashing Neanderthals or anything. They'd like you, I know it. And… well, you'd always be welcome here," he added awkwardly.

Tommy made a small, sarcastic noise in the back of his throat, though his expression didn't change.

"Yeah," he said dryly. "Well, that's nice, Brett. I'll think about it on my way back to the gutter."

"Oh, come on," Brett started and moved for the door, trying to pretend that hadn't hurt like a sucker punch. "I didn't mean...."

He trailed off lamely, looking at the fading bruise on Tommy's forehead. He'd gotten a couple of new ones, too. Brett had tried not to show his revulsion when Tommy had stripped down, revealing the twin welts on the back of his waist, the raw bruise on his upper arm... the fresh cigarette burn. Tommy had just shrugged, said it had been a tough week, and then he wouldn't answer another damn thing.

Brett sighed tersely. "You shouldn't take that from him. I know—"

"You know what?" Tommy snapped, the viciousness of it sudden and violent. "You know shit, Brett. Nothing! Nothing, okay? Not about me, or my family. Just... not everybody has this perky little *happy* existence, all right? Sometimes... sometimes people fuck up. They... they think they can do things they can't."

His voice dropped again quickly, as if he felt ashamed of shouting like that, and he looked at Brett with sad, hard eyes.

"Kinda like this."

Fear rose in Brett like bile, but anger—hurt, reflexive anger—spilled out instead. "What the fuck is that supposed to mean?"

"You know damn well. I can't... I can't keep doing this."

"What?"

Tommy shrugged dismissively at the rumpled room. "This," he said dismally. "Sneaking around in the back end of the afternoon, pretendin'.... Ah, forget it."

"Pretending what?" Brett demanded. "'Cause I don't know what you mean. Pretending what your father does to you is okay? Or is it us? Pretendin' we've got something worth being honest about? I mean, we only sneak 'cause—"

Tommy winced. "Brett, I really don't wanna get into this."

Brett saw him trying to back down but—though he didn't understand it—he didn't want to let go of the fight.

"Get into what? Why we never go out together?"

"It's not about that and you know it!" Tommy snapped. "That has nothin' to do with it. I just… I have other commitments, okay?"

"Commitments?" Brett saw red, barely listening to Tommy as he tried to climb out of the mess he'd made.

"You know I-I got a lot of stuff at home, Brett. It's hard to balance that with anythin' else, and I—"

"Yeah? Well if you don't want this, if it's too hard…. If you're saying you want out, you know where the damn door is!"

Tommy stared at him for a second, his eyes narrowed but his expression inscrutable. Then, with a small shrug, he turned. "Fine."

With that, he left. Just left. Brett stared. It seemed impossible. He thought of their first kiss, how it had taken star-crushingly long seconds to feel Tommy's lips touch his. So how could his leaving be over so fast? He stood there like an idiot, his feet bare and his world in tatters, and then he heard the sounds of the Chevy's door slam and the engine rev….

No.

No, no, this wasn't allowed to happen. Brett ran out of the house and he couldn't understand how Tommy had made it out there so fast. The Chevy gunned down the road, and Brett couldn't keep up, especially with no shoes. He swore and yelled and hopped up and down, clutching at his scuffed toes, and slowly, he realized that Mrs. Evans at Number 165 was peering out of her window at him. He waved guiltily and limped back inside, muttering a litany of curses under his breath as he turned the room upside down, looking for his cell phone.

CHAPTER
TEN

"SO YOU'RE really just going to go? Now?"

Scott sighed. He tossed a sweater into the open suitcase that lay on his bed.

"Yes."

Tommy said nothing. Scott glanced at him, a mixture of pity and pride on his face that left Tommy sorely tempted to smack him. That he could do this, barely with a word…. *Bastard.* And Scott had actually had the nerve to ask *him* what was wrong. He shook his head.

"I don't believe you."

"Look, Tommy… I know it's gonna be hard, but it's gotta be now, don't you see? Karen's father offered us a loan. I talked to her parents. I said we're gonna do the right thing… she wants to, too. We're gonna get hitched, and they're gonna help out with the apartment."

Tommy folded his arms. "So, bam, that's it. You up and go? Now? You haven't even told Mom and Dad about the baby."

Scott pulled a couple of books off his nightstand. Thrillers, with the authors' names in raised gold print above the titles. He threw them into the case.

Tommy widened his eyes, the sting of realization burning behind them. "Wait, you're gonna…? Tonight? You're just going to dump this on them and fuck off? Wh—"

"They're not going to understand," Scott snapped. "'Specially not Mom. You know that. This is my future, Tommy. Mine, Karen's, the baby...."

"You selfish bastard!"

"Hey! I have a kid on the way here. You really think I ain't gonna take every chance there is to give it the best start I can?"

Tommy pushed off from the wall and stalked into the room. "And what about us? Mom? Lila? Robbie? Katie?"

Scott turned, facing him straight down. "I can't keep doing this! I can't keep being there, Tommy. Somethin' has to give sometime, man. This time it's me. I'm choosing."

Tommy stared at his brother. *How can you? How the fuck can you even say that?* Scott didn't blink. His jaw clenched, his mouth tightened, but he said nothing. Tommy felt the anger, thick and bitter, rising in his throat, as if it could split his skin in two and burst out like a wolf. He took a deep breath.

"Fine."

"You can come to us. Soon as we're in the new place. If you need to. And the kids.... I told Mom the same thing. It might actually be better like that."

"Sure." He turned away, not even wanting to look at Scott.

"I'm sorry. I-I just can't keep doin' this. I told you that, Tommy."

I can't keep doing this....

Tommy spun around, blind and hurting. "For Christ's sake, Scott! Did you even think? You ever do that? Think we need you? You got responsibilities here!"

"Yeah? I got others too."

"Because you couldn't keep it in your pants! You're weak, that's what it is. You're a selfish, weak little bastard, Scott!"

Scott met him, word for word, not giving an inch. "Maybe, but I'm not the one turning into Dad!"

That landed on Tommy like a weighted glove. He didn't remember throwing the first punch, barely realized he'd done it until

Scott's fist connected with his stomach on the rebound. He caught Tommy's shoulder as he doubled over, whispering fiercely in his ear:

"You don't touch me. Not ever. You hear that? You ain't him and you don't fuckin' forget it!"

Tommy wheezed, fighting for breath. His eyes watered. "I'm sorry. I'm so sorry…. Scott?"

AS PREDICTED, Scott's parents didn't take the news well. The ugly scene lasted well into the night. At ten thirty, as if by some pre-arranged signal, Karen arrived in her father's sedan, a T-shirt that said "Rez Diva" on the front stretched too tight over her baby bump.

Tommy had been convinced it would come to blows. It didn't, at least not then. That got saved for later.

For days after Scott left, a dull kind of dread hung in the house like cobwebs. Mei sported a deep cut on her lip and a hunted look in her eyes. Katie, fidgety with teething pangs, had caught a cold that made her temper worse, while Tommy kept his head down and tried to keep the peace. It felt like trying to tread water in an ocean of molasses. Even the kids sensed it. Robbie disappeared one evening, sending everybody into a panic. They found him out back at the bottom of the yard, sitting behind the shrubs, just drawing patterns in the dirt with a stick.

It had been a little less than two weeks since Tommy had walked out on Brett. He felt bad enough about it, but Brett had called more than once since then, trying to apologize, of all things. Tommy had taken to leaving his phone switched off in the evenings and deleting the messages unheard and unread.

He couldn't trust himself, he knew that. Better just to hide. Brett would get the hint. He'd be hurt, but it would be better for them both this way. Wouldn't it?

He didn't expect, when he answered his cell at work, to hear Brett's voice. He'd been halfway through his lunch break, taking a drink of water and joining in the other guys' general banter.

"Tommy? Don't hang up."

The smile died on his face. "Okay."

"Can you talk?"

Slowly, Tommy got up, leaving the laughter behind him. The house the crew had been assigned to refit—a new, high-end ranch-style property—had a number of outbuildings and grassy paddocks. Water bottle dangling from his fingers, he walked down toward where he'd parked the Chevy next to the brand new barn.

"I'm at work."

"Then let me see you. Tonight, or—"

"I-I don't know."

"I just wanna know what happened. Please. I know you want to shut me out, but just this one time. That's all. Please?"

Tommy sighed, knowing he would crumble even as he cursed himself for a traitor. "It's complicated," he said wretchedly.

It sounded so pathetic, just like he knew his behavior had been. And yet, Brett still wanted to see him. Torn between being humbled by that and just getting pissed at him again, he knew he'd relent.

"Tommy, please. I'm beggin' here. Please. Just once. Just to know."

Tommy hated him then. Hated the way those words broke him, how simple Brett could make things, the way it made him feel trapped and beholden. Hated how easily he gave in.

"All right," he said. "I'm in Gildford. I can see you up at Fresno, about four thirty, maybe?"

"I'll be there."

"'K."

He swore as he turned off the damn phone and threw the water bottle at the side of the barn. It bounced, twice, emptying the last of its contents onto the ground, dark patches spreading out on the dirt.

TOMMY leaned against the Chevy's hood. He watched the Bronco pull up, watched Brett get out, white-faced and looking ill. Tommy folded his arms. It took a long time, waiting for him to cross the gritty, coarse dirt. The late sun, low in the sky, warmed his skin.

"Hey," Brett said, his voice small and thin.

Tommy nodded in response. God, this hurt like hell; his chest grew tight, his pulse raced. He wasn't sure he dared speak or move.

He really does look awful.

"You okay?"

Tommy nodded again. "Yeah," he said quietly. "You?"

Brett shrugged. He'd left a lot of distance between them, Tommy noticed, and he was just standing there, rigid and uncomfortable. Brett's left hand moved as if to rest on the Chevy's headlight but then flexed and dropped to his side.

"What happened, Tommy?"

Tommy looked at his feet. He wasn't sure which smarted more: Brett asking those questions, or hearing the truth dragged out of his own mouth like a rotten tooth.

"I-I can't do it. That's all. It's not.... I shoulda talked to you, I know, not just— I'm sorry for the way I acted."

Brett nodded, but it didn't look as if he took any pleasure in hearing that.

"Did... I mean, if it's the sneaking around thing, I'd stand up with you. You gotta know that. I've wanted to. I've wanted everybody to know. I mean, I—"

"It's not that." Tommy shook his head quickly. "It's never been that. It-it wasn't about us. It's everything else, y'know? I can't... I can't do everything," he finished dejectedly, staring at his work boots.

The sunlight picked at the grit, mica flashing in the dirt.

"Can I help, then?" Brett asked, hesitant but so sincere.

Tommy glanced up at him, looking for... what? Something, any sign of mockery, of condescension. No. He really meant it, damn him. He shook his head again.

"No. It.... Look, I just can't do this now. Scott's left. Y'know I told you he got his girlfriend pregnant? Well, they moved in together. Things haven't been good since he left. Dad...." Tommy swallowed, trying to find the courage to say it. "Scott's always been his favorite and he…. This has hurt him. Dad don't react well to that. He's like a kid, y'know? He gets… spiteful."

"Shit."

"Yeah."

"Well, can I—"

"Brett, don't."

Overhead, birds swooped in by ones and twos, coming to rest in the dusk. Branches shook with their landings.

"What?"

"Don't. You… you'll be off to Washington in, what, eight weeks? So—"

"So what?"

He glared at Tommy, and Tommy smelled his unevenly worn off aftershave, saw the endless colors in his eyes.

"Don't make it any harder for me to lose you," he said softly. "Okay? Let's just say, yeah, we had a good time, and—"

"I love you."

Tommy frowned, glancing down quickly at the ground again.

The breath stung as it left his lungs. *Oh… you bastard.* That wasn't fair. Not fair at all.

"Brett, don't," he said again, his voice thick.

"Well, I do. Does it make a difference?"

"Y-You're gonna leave. You're going to Washington. You—"

"Then come with me."

"What?"

The last fingers of light stained the sky, the bugs clouding out over the water. Tommy felt heavy, leaden, useless. Brett looked at him in the gloom, so luminous and hopeful, all that idealism and faith wrapped up in hazel eyes and a face like Michelangelo's wet dream. Tommy just wanted to hit him, slap some sense into that faultless head.

No one person should be so innocent; it makes everybody else feel dirty.

"Seriously. I mean it. You could. *We* could. We could get an apartment. We could—"

"Stop it! Brett, stop. Please. I can't do that. You know I—"

"No, you could. You could end it, Tommy. I know this isn't about us; it's about your father. About you tryin' to protect everybody; don't think I haven't seen that. You put yourself in the way, you try to keep everybody happy. That's not the answer. Not forever."

Tommy stared at the ground, the dirt inexplicably blurring.

"It's not all the time," he muttered. "The doctor put him on anti-depressants. They help, when he takes 'em. And he don't.... He never touches the kids. He just...." Tommy hung his head, hair falling over his eyes, and loosed a faint, mirthless laugh. "Shit... you hear that? I sound like my fucking mother."

Wordlessly, Brett stepped closer and pulled him into a hug, a simple embrace, without demands, without duress. Tommy knew he should go. Knew he should shout, scream, kick against it. He should never have come here. Instead, he buried his face in Brett's neck and hung on.

You're gonna be the end of me. You're gonna rip me up, and then you're gonna go. And I'm not gonna make it when you do.

"You can't protect people like that," Brett murmured. "You know that, right? You can't make excuses, put yourself in the way all the time. I-I know it's not my business; I know I should never have.... You never wanted to tell me, and that's fine. That's your right. But I can't see you hurtin' like this."

Tommy's jaw clenched, but he said nothing.

I wasn't hurting... 'til you.

The water lapped on the shore, the brush alive with birdcalls.

Slowly, they parted.

"Please. Even if you still want to end things with us, don't—"

"I never wanted to, Brett. I-I just can't do it. I'm sorry. And I do... love you, I mean. Love you so much."

Fuck. He hadn't meant to say it. He'd never meant to say it, never meant to admit that to Brett's face. Tommy rocked back against the Chevy, his hands flat on the truck's paintwork because, God help him, if he touched Brett again now, he'd never let him go.

It wasn't fair. They'd spent so much time keeping things light, easy. Tommy had put so much effort into that, into not staining Brett with something that didn't concern him... and now he couldn't stop this—this thing—from splashing out onto the dirt between them. Brett moved in, but Tommy turned away from his kiss.

"Tommy...?"

"Don't."

"But—"

"Don't try to make me choose. Please."

"Tommy, I'm not. I'm trying to help. I'm tryin' to—"

"You wanna help? Don't give me all of this, just to take it away."

Brett inhaled sharply. Tommy knew he'd wounded him, even before he pulled back, and he guessed he'd meant to hurt, only he couldn't feel it anymore. He couldn't feel anything. He looked away.

"You'd better go," he said, silently praying for Brett to get mad, to refuse, to yell at him... to do anything but leave. "I'm sorry."

Brett took a step back, a frown settling on his brow. Tommy guessed he'd come here for a reconciliation, not a face-off. He wished he'd been able to give it to him.

"I just wanted to help," Brett repeated.

Tommy nodded slowly. "Yeah. Then don't ask me to do things I can't."

I'm so sorry. Don't go. Please....

Brett stuffed his hands deep in his pockets.

"You know what? I won't ask you to do anything."

Tommy closed his eyes, not daring to speak. He opened them again to see Brett pacing backward awkwardly, his face white in the gloom.

"Bye, Tommy. Be careful, yeah? And... well, I'll see you. I—"

He stopped abruptly, turned, and headed back to the Bronco. Numbly, Tommy watched him get in. Time seemed to inch by; it seemed to take hours—and more willpower than Tommy thought he had—simply watching Brett go.

Eventually, the Bronco faded out along the road, nothing but tire marks left in the dust. Tommy exhaled shakily and slid down the door of the Chevy until he hit the ground, his head cradled in his arms. Tears didn't matter so long as nobody saw them.

After a while, he wiped his face on his shirtsleeve, pulled himself up, and climbed into the truck. Yeah, it would be better this way. In the long run. If he kept telling himself that, he'd believe it, sooner or later.

Tommy swiped at his eyes with the back of his hand and started up the engine. He didn't get back to the house until almost eight. Bone tired, cold, and still gritty with masonry and timber dust, he sensed something wasn't right as soon as his key turned in the lock.

The answering machine bleeped, its light an angry red, and he hit the playback with clumsy fingers. First, three messages from the school. Robbie and Lila, left uncollected. Then the hospital, what sounded like a middle-aged woman asking for his father, waiting for him to pick up, promising to call back. Last, Scott's voice, pulling Tommy from his sinking panic.

"Tommy, if you get home before I can get a hold of you, we're all at the hospital. Mom had an accident. You need to come up right away. I'm sorry… I've been trying your cell all day, but I couldn't get you. It's, ah, it's six thirty now. I'll call home again later if you don't show. Just… just come, okay?"

CHAPTER
ELEVEN

WHEN Tommy arrived, Scott was pacing by the door that led to the corridor outside the small and drab relatives' room, obviously desperate for a cigarette but disinclined to go outside. Robbie and Lila sat on the lumpy gray couch beside the water cooler, and Martin slumped in an armchair by the window, Katie dozing on his lap.

"Tommy!" Scott pulled his brother into a raw hug.

As they broke, Tommy tucked his hair behind his ear. "What happened?"

"We don't know. She went out to the store before picking the kids up. Left Katie home 'cause she had a fever, thank God, or I don't know what would have…. Car hit a utility pole, they said. Doctors say there's a head injury and some neck trauma, but they don't know how bad, some internal bleeding, coupla broken bones, and a ruptured spleen. She's still in surgery, last they said. I kept tryin' to call you."

Tommy winced. He'd been with Brett. Had his phone turned off because he'd been so busy with his stupid fucking melodrama, busy giving up the only thing that… no. That didn't matter, not now.

"Been at that Gildford job," he lied. "No service."

"Dad panicked when he got the call. Doctors've given him some tranqs."

"Shit."

Scott rubbed his arm. "Hey. It'll be all right. It'll be— Hey, baby girl!" He turned from his brother as Karen came around the corner of the corridor. "Aw, now *that* is why I love you. C'mere."

She held two Styrofoam cups of coffee and an armful of vending machine candy, her hair braided back and a chunky long-line cardigan buttoned over her bump. She passed Scott one cup of the coffee and took up what Tommy thought of as her normal position: about six inches to the right and two inches behind Scott, as if ready to spring into action at the snap of his fingers.

Tommy knew he wasn't being fair. As Scott reached out an arm and Karen slotted under it as neatly and naturally as a dovetail joint, her small, dark face tilted slightly toward him, Tommy knew it wasn't his place to judge. He saw the love there.

Even if dumpy little Karen, with her soft-spoken voice, slightly shuffling walk, and total lack of any apparent conviction about anything didn't sit that well with Tommy, he at least saw that everything Scott did—the way he held her, spoke to her, looked at her—said "this is mine." He'd made his choice, and they suited each other.

Tommy realized that Karen had seen him eyeing the chocolate ravenously, and that not all his sick dizziness could be attributed to shock or the sudden, violent ache of loneliness.

"Can I have one of those? I haven't eaten since lunch."

"Sure." Karen handed him a fistful of candy. "For the kids too, ah?"

"Thanks. That's… nice of you, Karen. And how are you? How are, uh, things?"

"Good," she said in her customary clipped syllables, one hand coming to rest, already proprietary, at the top of her stomach. "The apartment's beautiful."

"Good," Tommy echoed, feeling oddly empty. "Um. That's… great. And the baby? Is everything…?"

"It's good."

"Cool. I'm gonna, uh, go give these to, uh… yeah."

He slipped back into the relatives' room, suddenly desperate to be as far from both her and Scott as possible.

Tommy glanced at his father. If Martin was sleeping, it wasn't heavy slumber—more like the waking stupor of booze, painkillers, and Valium. Still, he didn't stir, and Katie stayed quiet. Robbie and Lila looked exhausted. Tommy sat down on the couch between them, passing each a candy bar and tearing the wrapper off his own.

"Karen got you candy," he said, needlessly but somehow feeling like he ought to put in a good word for her.

Robbie scowled. "I don't like her. She's a stranger."

Tommy considered this as he ate the chocolate, Lila pressing up beside him. He draped his arm around her and wondered how long it would take for Karen to win the kids over. They had a point; she'd never spent time at the house. Why the hell would Scott have brought her back there? She wasn't family, so she'd have been an outsider. *Them and us.*

Tommy wasn't sure whether it was that which made him feel hollow, or the knowledge that his mother was probably still lying in the operating room. Perhaps both. Everything seemed to run together, like wet paint in a rainstorm. One big mess of emptiness.

Robbie might have decided he didn't like Karen, but he ate the candy anyway. Lila didn't touch hers. At length, a doctor came by and told Scott that Mei had been taken to the recovery suite. They'd removed the torn spleen and dealt with the fractures in her arm and leg, but they would be keeping her out for a while longer to assess the severity of the head and neck trauma.

He took Scott aside, and Tommy guessed their hushed discussion referred to the bill and perhaps the prior injuries. Katie woke up and began to cry as he strained to work out what the doctor was saying, so he picked her off Martin's lap and carried her for a while.

She quieted and didn't feel hot to the touch anymore, but the kids had all had a long day. The doctor eyed them briefly before, with the business-like flicker of a weak smile, departing again.

"I'll take 'em home," Tommy said, though he hated to leave.

"No point in hanging around," Scott agreed and gave Karen a squeeze around the shoulders. "We oughta get going, too."

Tommy nodded. He'd hoped, however foolishly, that maybe Scott would come back to the house with them. Just for now. He didn't say anything, turning instead to Martin.

"Dad? You wanna come?"

Martin shook his head, standing up slowly, one hand on the wall. "I'll be at Deacon's."

Tommy tilted his head and tried to evade Katie's probing fingers. She'd woken up crabby and kept trying to pull his lips off.

"You sure you oughta drink, with the pills? Or drive?" He caught the look Scott shot him and lifted one shoulder in a well-what-am-I-supposed-to-say shrug. "You can always come back, get the Pontiac in the morning."

"Day I'm not good to drive after a beer's the day you can put me in the fuckin' ground," Martin mumbled. He grabbed his coat and stalked off down the corridor.

Tommy watched him go. Karen cleared her throat and looked at Scott.

He shifted awkwardly from foot to foot. "Well. Uh. We'll, um… I'll see you, Tommy. Okay?"

"Okay," Tommy said wearily. "Sure. See ya. Bye, Karen."

She nodded to him, and they left.

Great.

THE first few days proved hard. Tommy dropped by to visit his mother after work, and it wasn't the knowledge of how much worse it could have been, or the injuries she might have had, but the halo—the hard, menacing brace holding her head still—that scared him most. The metal almost seemed alive, wrapping around her like interlaced fingers.

He sat, held her hand, being careful not to dislodge the monitors clipped to her or the IV drip. He rubbed her knuckles with his thumb and talked to her in a low voice, just on the off-chance that she could actually hear.

Tommy left the ward, ready to head back out into the dusk, pick up some dinner, and collect the kids from the after-school activities that kept them quiet and kept them safe. The nurse called out after him, and he turned. Her footsteps echoed sharply on the polished floor.

"Mr. Hawks? Could you just confirm this number for me, please?"

"Huh?"

The nurse ran a hand over her hair, sweeping back a loose blonde strand. She held out a crumpled piece of paper.

"This number. Your, uh, your father gave this as a contact, but nobody seems to be able to get through. Could you...?"

Tommy glanced at the paper. "Yeah." He nodded. "That oughta be a seven, not a four. He probably got... uh. How come you needed...?"

The nurse smiled awkwardly. "There's, um, a social worker trying to make an appointment. Nothing to worry about, I'm sure. Just, with your mom's injuries and your father being listed as having a disability... y'know," she said, tipping her head to the side a little. "The system's there to help."

Tommy stared at her, caught like a deer in headlights. "Sure," he said, tucking his hair behind his ear. "I, ah, I have to go. But I'll make sure this gets.... I'll deal with it. Thank you."

She started to say something else but stopped and just nodded. Tommy stuffed his hands in his pockets and left the hospital as fast as he could. Why couldn't people leave things alone? Throughout his childhood, no one had listened if he or Scott said Daddy had got mad. Stuff like that just happened, and no one thought anything of kids with bruises. You'd been clumsy or stupid, or you'd just been roughhousing. That's what kids did.

It had surprised Tommy to find that his family differed from other people's, but he'd thought little of it. Then, after Robbie's birth—when Mei had talked about leaving for the first time—it had started to get worse, with Martin getting jealous of the new baby. Ironic, really, that he'd got his wife pregnant for the third and fourth times just to keep her.

Tommy slammed the Chevy's door and sat there, hands on the wheel.

Nobody had any call judging. And he didn't touch the little ones. Not now. It wasn't anything that couldn't be dealt with, and Tommy would deal with it.

His knuckles whitened as he tried to get Brett's face out of his mind.

It's not the answer, trying to protect people like you do....

Tommy gripped the wheel harder. No. Better that stayed buried, because however much he could have done with a friend right now, it wasn't going to be *him*. Better it remained a clean break.

Better that than his pity.

ONLY, for a clean break, it festered. It lay beneath the surface, even during those first few days when Tommy felt too tired, scraped too raw to do anything but go through the motions. After that, he had work, the kids to mind, the house to look after, and Martin, dead-eyed and lost, sloping around the place in the time he wasn't either at the bar or the hospital. He'd accepted a prescription of tranquilizers from the doctor, and that made him easier to deal with, though unpredictable.

"Ain't you gonna shut that fuckin' kid up?"

"Which one?" Tommy snapped rhetorically. Then, into the phone he held clutched to his ear: "Yeah, Scott, I know. But I could really do with—"

The television blared. Katie, sitting on the floor by her hammer and peg toy, was screaming violently, while Robbie and Lila appeared to have released a hellgate in the hallway and looked to be headed toward a full-blown fistfight.

"Tommy! Get off the fuckin' phone! Jesus Christ.... Hey!"

Tommy rolled his eyes. "You know what, Scott? Forget it."

He blipped the phone off and tossed it on the couch, stepping over the discarded pizza box on the floor to pick Katie up, lifting her into his arms just in time for her colicky scream to cease and for her to throw up all over his chest. A loud crash came from the hall, and something that sounded like a vase smashed to the ground as Lila began to cry. Martin turned the TV up.

"Oh, Chr— Katie!" Tommy held his baby sister out at arm's length, turning to yell over his shoulder. "Robbie! Leave your sister the hell alone, will ya? And Lila, for fuck's sake, will you quit whinin'?"

He looked at the doorway. She stood there, her mouth quivering, sagging on her feet like a rag doll.

Oh, shit….

"Just… just go to bed, Lila! You too, Robbie."

"No," Robbie shouted, appearing behind his sister and shoving her hard between the shoulder blades.

Lila spun around, a wordless howl on her lips. She swung, landing a club-handed blow to Robbie's face. He yelled, clutched his bloodied nose, and flew back at her. Tommy, a squealing, kicking Katie tucked under one arm, crossed the room and hauled Robbie up by the back of his T-shirt.

Canned game show laughter blasted out of the TV, the bright colors reflecting back on Martin's loose, expressionless face as he stared at the screen. Laugh on screeching laugh piled up behind Tommy, and he gave his brother a rough shake.

"Stop it! Fuckin' stop it, right now, both of you! What the hell is the matter with you? Huh? Just…." Tommy let go of Robbie abruptly, his own words echoing in his head. "Just stop. Please…? C'mon."

He started to usher them upstairs. Martin came out into the hall, keys in hand. He glanced at the kids, then Tommy, a sneer on his lips.

"You ladies have fun now. I'm goin' out."

IT TOOK Tommy more than an hour to get them settled. He let Lila sleep in Mei's bed, his apologies and I love yous running off her like rain. Robbie cried for the first time that Tommy had seen in months as he cleaned his face, and he wanted to be held. It didn't last long. Afterwards he retreated back inside his shell, refusing eye contact, conversation, and even chocolate.

He found Katie easier; she only required a cuddle, a few spoonfuls of gripe water, and a verse or two of "Rock-a-bye Baby" before she settled to sleep. Tommy had already stripped off his shirt. He threw it in the washer-dryer and sat down at the kitchen table with

the baby monitor, a bottle of cheap whisky, and his hash tin set out
before him on the scarred surface. Martin had fed Katie chili beef. Of
all things. Tommy poured himself another shot.

He rolled a fat joint and smoked until the air turned to velvet on
his skin. It seemed like the house hadn't been this quiet for days, and
he almost wished it wasn't, that he had something there to keep his
thoughts at bay.

Tommy drank the shot and poured another, glancing up at the
clock. The black feather hands read ten thirty. He remembered it
hanging in his grandmother's house and, as a small boy, asking
Grandpa Tim about the feathers. Raven, he'd said. Bird of the north,
the Secret Keeper.

Grandpa Tim, with his big red face and stubbly beard, had gone
into the story of how, as a younger man, he used to drive the winter
road, hauling loads up around Yellowknife and Diavik, where only the
sound of ice cracking beneath your wheels stood between you, your
truck, and a cold, watery grave.

One time, a raven had flown alongside the truck, riding the
updraft, flying beside him for damn near three hundred miles, all told.
By the end of the run, Grandpa Tim said he had it eating out of his
hand. Tommy remembered how his Gramma had smiled at that, saying
Raven had come to him as his journey guide. Tim had smiled back at
her and told how that winter he'd made enough money for them to get
married.

Tommy drank the second shot and wondered where the fuck the
spirits had been the year Grandpa Tim drove home drunk from Harlem
and wrapped his pickup around a tree. He took a pull on his joint,
wondering which was blurring his vision more, the whisky or the
weed. He wanted to cry, but there weren't any tears. Nothing inside
any more.

Why should there be?

Outside, he heard the Pontiac draw up, the clatter of garbage cans
as Martin half-fell out of the car, then the heavy footsteps and the
scratching of his key in the door. Tommy downed a third shot, closed
his eyes, and waited.

"T'my? Wha' the hell're you doin' sittin' half naked in the dark?"

"Shirt's inna wash."

Martin stumbled into the kitchen, cigarette dangling from his lips. He lurched to the fridge, got himself a beer, and leaned heavily against the sink as he tried to open the bottle. He breathed through his mouth, the tar wheeze loud in his lungs and the thick haze of booze rolling off him.

Tommy took another pull on his joint, eyes closed, quietly sinking into hatred of him. Not just him. Everything he did: the look of him, the smell, the noise of his breathing, the ugly, corroded voice that scraped like broken glass on Tommy's nerves. The utter oppressiveness of him, always fucking *there*, even when he wasn't in the house.

"Whassa matter with you?" Martin demanded, finally cracking open the beer.

Tommy glanced down; his left hand was shaking, beating out a staccato rhythm of its own on the table. He stared at it impassively.

"Whassa matter, cocksucker? That your jerkin' hand?"

"Fuck off," Tommy muttered, his self-censor somehow dimmed.

Instantly, the aura of Martin's body seemed to change, the air in the room adjusting itself around him differently. Tommy tensed up, waiting.

"What'd you say?"

"Nothin'."

"Fuckin' did, you little faggot."

"Don't call me that."

Tommy's eyes flicked open, as if staring at the words as they left his mouth. *What the hell?*

Martin laughed shortly.

"Don't? S'whatcha fuckin' are. Don't think I don't know that. Ain't entirely stupid. Y'got no balls, Tommy. At leas' your brother managed to get his bitch knocked up. What you got, huh? Y'got nothin'. Ain't got nothin', you worthless little shit."

"Shut up!"

Tommy was moving before he even realized it, turning in the chair with the shot glass in his hand, aiming his throw right for his father's head. He missed, hopelessly, the glass smashing on the counter, and Martin's retribution came fast.

The rabbit punch hit Tommy in the back of the neck, shooting his head forward and cracking it against the table. The second blow caught him on the recoil and sent him sprawling sideways to the floor, though he didn't stay down.

All blind fury and panic, Tommy barreled up and caught Martin around the middle, pushing him into the counter and knocking the wind from him. Unfortunately, it didn't knock the beer bottle from his fingers, and he brought that down onto Tommy's bare back. It didn't break, but it stunned him for a moment, enough for Martin to bring his knee up into his son's groin, his fist driving hard into Tommy's ribs.

Tommy curled up as he dropped to the ground, arms over his head, retreating inside himself until Martin finished. It didn't take long; tired, he bored quickly.

"Next time you touch me," he growled, pulling Tommy up by the hair, "I'll kill you. You unnerstan' me? I will put a gun in your fuckin' mouth, let you suck on that. You wan' that? You know what that'd do?"

Tommy nodded as best he could with Martin's fist in his hair, tight to the back of his skull.

"Yeah."

"Yes, *sir*."

"Sir," he spluttered.

Martin forced his head further back and pressed his index finger gently to the soft skin under Tommy's chin, staring into his eyes with an expression of awful, serene calm on his face.

"Pow," he whispered, almost tenderly. Then, abruptly, he released Tommy's hair. "I'm goin' to bed."

"Lila's in Mom's room," Tommy called and struggled to his feet, sore and queasy. "She… she had a nightmare."

Martin curled his lip. "Fuckin' bitches."

He staggered into the living room and slammed the door. Tommy didn't hear him say anything else for a while.

CHAPTER
TWELVE

THAT morning dawned very much like a lot of other weekend mornings. Usually, Brett would have thought it precious, given how soon he'd be leaving for Washington, but he hadn't been sleeping well over the past few weeks, and, tired and irritable, he found it tough to be enthusiastic about anything.

He trudged through the shower, pulled on some clothes, and sloped downstairs, aware that his father had already taken Roscoe out. Monica occupied the kitchen, and Brett smelled bacon and coffee. His stomach rumbled traitorously.

"Mornin', sleepy!" she called, far too cheerful to be bearable in Brett's current mood. "Guess what? You're missing the excitement. There's been a shooting! Last night. You want juice?"

He nodded, took the glass she passed him, and slid onto a stool by the breakfast bar. "A what?"

"A shooting. Heard about it half an hour ago when I went out to get the paper. Mr. Cox says it was some Indian guy, over at that bar… y'know, just outside of town? Where the Ford dealership used to be?"

He knew of it.

Some Indian guy. The words caught on Brett's ear, just as fast as a bunch of others stood out, shining darkly from his memory.

He's a drinker, that's all…. He goes to this craphole, Deacon's, 'cause he used to hunt with the guy that runs it.

Brett swallowed hard. His mother hadn't stopped talking, but he couldn't catch all of it through the rushing in his ears.

"…came up that way and he said there's police all over, but there hasn't been anything on the news. Not yet. Awful, isn't it?"

"Yeah." Brett tried to marshal his thoughts, think clearly through the jumble inside his head. *No way. Coincidence. Isn't it?* "Uh, thanks, Mom. I have to, uh…. I'll have somethin' to eat later, okay?"

He got up and left the room, just as Monica set the plate of bacon and eggs down in front of him. She called out, but Brett didn't respond, already halfway to the front door as he pulled his cell phone from his pocket and sought out the number he hadn't had the heart to even think about deleting.

Come on. Pick up. Prove me wrong. Please….

It probably wasn't anything but a stupid, sentimental impulse, Brett told himself. He didn't even know why he'd thought it could be anything to do with—

"Hello?" A woman's voice.

His stomach lurched. "Who is this?"

"Uh, my name's Jacqui Austin. I'm with the Hill County Sheriff's Department. Who—"

Brett broke the connection quickly. *Fuck!* Why the hell would the sheriff's department have Tommy's phone? Unless— *Oh, God.*

He gunned the Bronco into life, driving without thinking despite the whirl of thoughts in his head. Brett turned off his phone when it rang; Monica, probably wanting to know why the hell he'd left like that. What could he tell her?

Brett drove through the Sunday morning traffic just on the legal side of too fast, taking a loop down by Deacon's Bar, passing close enough to see the scene of crime tape. He hauled the truck in and wound down the window to ask the woman from the florist across the road what had happened.

"Carl Delaney from the corner store found him," she said, sucking on a cigarette, squinting a little at this wild-eyed, crazy kid demanding answers. "Only a couple hours ago. Some Indi—"

"How old?"

"How old?" The woman frowned. "Why the hell w—"

"Please."

"Well… middle-aged, I guess Carl said."

"Thank you," Brett called. The Bronco's tires squealed.

Oh, God. Oh, Tommy… what did you do?

He hit the gas and just drove, not even aware he was heading for Fresno until he drew up alongside the campground. Brett stumbled out of the truck, sick to his stomach. Tommy wouldn't have, surely. He couldn't have. No… he could. *You can't keep protecting people like that. Not forever.* Brett's own words echoed back at him. He finally caught sight of the Chevy parked sloppily down by the trees that led to the water.

He's here.

Brett gasped for breath and glanced around him. No cars. No people. Good. He swore and pushed through the pines. Water dripped down the back of his neck. It had rained last night, that kind of summer drenching that leaves everything smelling like damp earth.

Tommy was sitting on the shore, huddled up in that worn old blue fleece, arms locked around his knees, facing out to the inky water. Brett ran across the gray, gritty dirt and he must have shouted, because Tommy turned around, stood up….

Tommy reeled backward, clutching his jaw, stumbling but not quite falling, until Brett shoved him hard in the chest.

"What the fuck did you do?" he yelled. "What did you do?"

If it surprised Tommy that Brett had hit him, it didn't last long. He scrambled up, fists swinging and feet kicking before Brett even fully realized that he'd thrown the first punch. Regretting it, Brett tried to catch his arms, calm him down, but Tommy fought him every inch of the way. Tommy's head connected with his nose, and he tasted blood. Brett spat and staggered back.

"Tommy! I'm sorry," he managed, his words muffled by the hand clasped to his face. He held out the other hand in a gesture of peace. "Calm down."

"I didn't do anything!" Tommy yelled, though the blows had stopped. "I… I didn't…."

His voice sounded cracked, hoarse, and his right eye was badly swollen. Blood, dried and black, caked his face, and he sported a cut lip and a bloody nose. Thick, finger-like bruises marked his neck. Brett wiped his nose on the back of his hand, blood streaking wet skin.

"I thought you…. Oh, shit, I thought…."

Tommy backed away a step. Panting, he pushed a hand through his hair, looked at Brett, and shook his head.

"You gotta go."

"What?"

"Go, Brett. You—whatcha doin' here, anyway?"

Brett stared. Could he really be so blind?

"What the fuck d'you think I'm doin'? I heard what—I had to find you. What happened?"

Tommy shook his head again, like he was trying to get rid of a bad dream. His face looked clammy, and his clothes were wet.

"Have you been out here all night?"

"You gotta go," he repeated, his voice dull and mechanical. "You can't… you have to go home."

"No. C'mere."

Brett grabbed Tommy's arm before he could pull away and pressed a palm to his forehead. He felt hot, damp, and his cheeks were flushed. The pulse fluttered in his wrist, and his breathing came too fast, too shallow. His eyes looked glassy and unfocused, and when he reached out with his free hand to straighten the collar of Brett's shirt, it was an incongruous, unconscious gesture, like he wasn't even connected to the world.

"I'm sorry. Forgive me?" Tommy murmured. "Brett? D'you forgive me?"

Brett gave up trying to count Tommy's pulse. "Of course I do. Tommy, you're sick. What happened?"

"I couldn't…."

Brett was still holding Tommy's wrist, and he squeezed tight for emphasis, trying to prompt him, wake him up. Tommy looked numbly at his clenched fingers, white skin on brown.

"He hit her," he said, his voice hollow. "And he wouldn't stop. All—"

"Your mom?"

Tommy blinked. "Nah. Lila. She only wet the bed. She didn't mean to... but I couldn't stop him. And he hurt her. He scared her so bad. Last night, I-I couldn't... I couldn't let him do it again. I just...." He looked up. "Help me?"

"Of course I'm gonna help you. Idiot. Come on." Brett tugged at his wrist. "Tommy. We can't stay here. C'mon."

Tommy stared blankly at him. Brett shook his shoulder.

"Come on. Don't zone out on me. Not now. We need to get moving."

Tommy seemed to snap out of it. He nodded. "Yeah... it... it's a school day, isn't it? I have to make lunches."

Oh, shit. He's completely lost it.

Brett laced his fingers through Tommy's and pulled him close, feeling for the first time how badly he was shaking beneath his damp fleece. Unhealthy heat radiated from his skin. Brett rubbed his nose alongside Tommy's.

"Come on, baby. Get in the truck, okay?"

Tommy did so, stumbling but obedient, and that worried Brett even more than his fever. They climbed into the Chevy, partly due to it being closer, partly because he wanted Tommy to feel safe and, somehow, because it just felt... right. The keys still dangled in the ignition. Brett glanced over at him as they buckled up.

Oh, Tommy. How the hell do we get you out of this?

Brett's first thought—to head south, to Great Falls and its international airport—collapsed even as the engine thrummed into life. No, they couldn't do that. They had no money, no passports, and the cops must be looking for the Chevy by now. They already had Tommy's phone, so.... He turned, ready to tell Tommy they should take the Bronco instead, but he'd either fallen asleep or passed out, his head slumped against the window, his breathing finally slowing.

It didn't matter. Nothing mattered except getting away. Somewhere. Anywhere, so long as it meant... what? That Tommy could be kept safe? Brett slammed the Chevy into gear, dismissing his own stupidity. If he really had shot his father, Tommy would never be safe again.

Brett cursed inwardly. He shouldn't even be here. He should…
he should never have let Tommy go. He knew that now, the
knowledge clear and burning, guilt brimming over in every nerve.
He'd seen the bruises, known what must be happening in that house.
He'd never thought, not for a moment, it would come to this, but… he
should have found a way. A way to help, to do something. Anything.

"Canada," he muttered, almost to himself.

Yeah, that would work. It would buy time. Only, what, fifty
miles to Govenlock? *We can make that.* They could get across the
border, with either speed or luck on their side, and then there'd be time
to think. Time to work something out. Just so long as he got Tommy
away.

Brett ramped the Chevy left, heading on up Wild Horse Trail.
Gotta stay off the main routes and the highway. He had to keep going,
hit the border, take the provincial route, find a motel or something. He
blinked, trying to shake the memory that suddenly reared up in his
head. Lying on the grass at Beaver Creek, between Tommy's legs,
leaning back on his chest, feeling the July sun on both of them, and
Tommy lazily rubbing his shoulders.

We could go to a motel. What d'you think?

Tommy had laughed. *Why? You want cheap coffee and porno
channels?*

*No! Just… somewhere that's not a pickup truck or a race against
time. I'm sick of just taking what we can get.*

I like what I got, he'd said, kissing the back of Brett's ear.

Brett took a sharp breath; tears stung behind his eyes. His hands,
slick and sweaty, slipped on the wheel. He glanced over at Tommy,
hearing him stir.

"Go to sleep," Brett said, aching with the desire to hold him, tell
him—even if it wasn't true—that he'd be all right.

"Hm?" Tommy blinked at him, then squinted at the road.
"Wh…? Brett, what's goin' on?"

"I said I'd help you," he said, staring straight ahead again.
"We're going to Govenlock. We can work it out from there. You have
any money?"

Tommy shook his head, his lip curling in confusion. "Govenlock?"

"It's only just over the border, but...." His pulse raced. Brett looked over at Tommy. "What happened?" An urgency filled his voice, one that hadn't been there before. "Tell me."

Tommy looked down at his hands and frowned.

"I... uh, Scott came over last night," he said hesitantly. "He wanted some of his tools, for doin' up the new apartment. We got 'em all laid out, on the kitchen table, an'... then Lila came down. She'd wet the bed. And she kept crying, and Dad just... he just lost it. I don't know why then, why that shoulda...."

Brett dragged his attention back to the road. He didn't know which felt worse: hearing it, or hearing the bewilderment in Tommy's voice. Why this thing, why that thing, should have made the unforgivable inevitable. Like wondering what made a faucet leak.

"He came in the kitchen and he picked up the steel ruler from the table and he hit her an' he wouldn't stop. Called her a dirty cu—" Tommy's voice caught in his throat. "He called her things you never call a child. Never! An' then he just kept... he just kept hitting her with the ruler. Like he couldn't even see her. I pulled him off."

His fingers moved to his neck, not quite touching the bruises.

"He didn't take that too kindly. He went out, to... to Deacon's. I... uh, I took care of Lila and the others and... and I asked Scott to stay with 'em. Then... I, uh, I took the Western from the gun cabinet, and—"

"Tommy," Brett warned. His chest tightened again, but this time in panic, not love. Maybe he shouldn't be hearing this after all.

"I drove down there," Tommy said again, as if unearthing some long-repressed memory, some shadowed recollection. "And I waited. And—"

A high-pitched wail cut through the air. Brett glanced at the rearview mirror and swore. Behind them, just cresting the unpaved road, flashed the flickering red light of a patrol car gaining speed.

Desperately, Brett looked for a way out. There wasn't one. Several miles still stood between them and the border, and if that car came from the sheriff's department, they probably already had border patrol on alert. He looked over at Tommy, his eyes wide and wet. Tommy just looked so tired. Fear etched his face, but fused with an odd, shrunken kind of acceptance.

"Let it go, Brett."

"But—"

"Please?"

Brett hauled the truck over to the side of the road, spraying up grit as he slammed on the brakes. A breath somewhere between a cry of anger and a sob broke out of him. He'd failed. He hadn't kept Tommy safe. He hadn't got them away. He'd screwed up, just like before. He looked over at Tommy and knew the only thing that mattered was sitting right there… and he'd let him down.

And, though he hated himself for it, Brett wished he'd hit him harder.

"I love you," he said wretchedly.

The patrol car's tires hissed on the road, the siren filling up the air. The look, just for a moment, of genuine disbelief on Tommy's face threatened to break his heart.

"Even now?"

Brett knew he couldn't answer that. Instead, he leaned over and kissed Tommy, just the gentle pressure of lips meeting, feeling his hot breath, the clamminess of his skin. Brett tasted blood. He smoothed a hand over Tommy's matted and greasy hair, aware that he was starting to shake again, and wished there could be a minute longer… that the whole year could play out from the beginning, and that this time he wouldn't fuck it up.

He heard the patrol car brake, the sounds of somebody—maybe two people—getting out, the shouting for them to come out of the Chevy, hands on their heads. Kinda like a movie, only knowing the bullets would be real put a different edge on it.

"I'm scared," Tommy whispered against his mouth, sounding like a kid.

"Self-defense," Brett said firmly, not wanting to let him go but not wanting to get either of them shot. "All right, baby? It's self-defense."

Tommy leaned his forehead against Brett's. His hand shook as he touched Brett's cheek. The shouting got closer.

"I—"

"Self-defense. Okay? And don't say a word until you get a lawyer. Not anything, you hear? Not 'til you got a lawyer."

"I'm so sorry, baby."

"Tommy! Promise me."

"I love you. I always—"

"Not 'til you got a lawyer," Brett said again, breaking away from him. "Promise?"

Tommy nodded wordlessly.

"Okay." Brett took a deep breath, hand on the door. "We're comin' out, and we're unarmed!"

Two patrol officers. Sheriff's department, as Brett had thought. Having a gun pointed at his head frightened him more than he'd imagined it would. He hit the Chevy's paintwork face first, grunted, felt the plastic wrist restraints go on. One of the officers yelled into his radio, confirming the Chevy's plates, Tommy's description.... *He sounds like he's panicking worse than we did, but then they probably don't get that many fugitives to chase around here.* The thought made him want to smile—hard to do with his face crushed against the Chevy's roof, the metal hot with the August sun.

He craned his neck, seeking Tommy but unable to see him. A hand landed on his back, between his shoulder blades.

"All right, cowboy, you just stay there."

Brett closed his eyes. "Yes, sir."

Tommy....

The patrol officer was conferring with his colleague, but Brett couldn't hear what they were saying. He guessed it wasn't a good opportunity to straighten up and make a run for it, though the thought tempted him. After a moment, the officer pulled him back off the truck.

"Okay, kid. This is gonna take a minute. You, uh, get in the truck. Passenger side."

He reached in, pulled the keys from the ignition. Tommy's keys. Then he walked Brett around the Chevy, sat him down and told him to wait. A tanned, blond guy of around thirty-five, blue-eyed, with a pleasant face. A wedding band on his left hand. He looked vaguely familiar, like one of the ski dads Brett had spent the winter dealing with. His nametag identified him as Officer Clairmont, but Brett didn't know the name.

He leaned his forehead against the frame of the window. The patrolman walked around the front of the truck, conferring again with his partner.

The wait in the Chevy seemed an eternity. If he stretched, Brett could just see Tommy, cuffed and bleeding in the back of the patrol car, staring straight ahead. Blank-faced, like he'd been at the reservoir. The restraints bit into Brett's wrists.

Look at me, he willed silently. *Fucking look at me, you bastard!*

But Tommy didn't. It took a few minutes before Brett glanced down at his leg and realized it was shaking. *He* was shaking. All that adrenaline, all the panic and the blind terror and the determined, desperate attempt to get away… and he'd failed. And now he'd been arrested. Hadn't he?

Shit, he'd be in so much trouble. But not as much as Tommy. Furious tears welled in Brett's eyes and dripped onto his jeans. He wished he could wipe his face, but the restraints held his arms tight behind his back. His shoulders started to ache. *Tommy, how could you have been so fucking stupid?*

Hot, guilty rage boiled in him, and he pressed his forehead back harder against the sun-warmed window frame, glaring across the trail. The two officers were talking animatedly by the patrol car. Tommy had bowed his head, his hair hanging over his face. Brett sniffed, and he could still taste the blood at the back of his throat. If he'd thought his feelings for Tommy had been addled after the fight they'd had at Fresno, he'd been wrong. That was nothing compared to this. But, if only Tommy would look up at him, Brett knew everything would be all right. Like it would be a sign or something.

He waited. Tears skidded down his face. Then, in one shining moment, Tommy lifted his head and looked straight at him across the dirt road.

The breath caught in Brett's throat. Tommy didn't say or mouth anything, and Brett couldn't read the expression in his eyes. He tried to look strong, until the ridiculousness of it occurred to him: sitting here, bruised and bloodied, dripping tears and snot, his chin shaking like a kid who'd just taken a fall off his first bike. Then it was over. Beside him, the driver's door of the Chevy opened, and Officer Clairmont got in. Brett hadn't even noticed his approach. He twisted his head, wiping his face on the shoulder of his shirt.

Clairmont said nothing, and he had Brett's gratitude for that. Brett glanced out of the window, watching the patrol car start up and drive away. Beside him, Clairmont grappled with the Chevy's keys. Tommy's keys, with the dreamcatcher his grandmother had made, and his photo of Katie....

Brett hated the thought of anyone else touching that. Touching the wheel. Being in the Chevy at all. It was their space, their private cocoon. Where they'd made out, where he'd learned so much about Tommy and, hell, even started to fall for him. Brett remembered the first time he'd got into this truck, and how much a part of Tommy it had seemed then. And now, this cop, clean-cut and whistling softly under his breath, would be driving it, while Brett sat here in wrist restraints. It was so wrong. Twisted.

He hung his head, took deep breaths, and fought the need to either throw up or pass out.

"Hell, kid," Clairmont said as the engine rattled and he pulled out cautiously, tailing the patrol car back down the byway, heading down toward town. "You got yourself mixed up in somethin' here, all right. What the heck you tryin' to do? Get across the border?"

Brett shook his head, determinedly silent. *Not until you get a lawyer. Promise me?* God, he hoped Tommy kept his mouth shut.

"Suit yourself."

They followed the patrol car at a steady sixty. Even so, it would take a while to get back to Havre. Keeping one eye on the road and one hand on the wheel, with all the insouciance of a college kid cruising on Spring Break, Clairmont fingered the photos tacked behind the gear stick.

"Quite the family album, eh?"

"Don't... don't touch those. Please," Brett added, his attention torn between the images and the road ahead.

Clairmont shot him an odd look but shrugged and left the photos alone. "All right. Probably evidence anyway, huh?"

Brett said nothing. If the cop wanted to make conversation, he couldn't stop him.

"Y'know, we haven't had a murder in a good couple years around here. Not since them two Indians dropped that guy in the river."

He stared at the officer in the driver's mirror, at that reflected band of his lined forehead and those clear blue eyes. *Great.* Suddenly, Brett saw it all stretched out before him. That's how it would go, wouldn't it? Tommy Hawks, murderer.

But... wasn't he?

Brett took a deep, shaky breath. He didn't know what to believe. He couldn't help but think of Tommy's first words, when he'd found him at Fresno. *I didn't do it... I didn't do anything.*

He couldn't split the two things in his head: Tommy being innocent and him not believing it, or Tommy lying to him, even in that crazy, unreal moment. He'd been in shock. Or something. Obviously. Brett gritted his teeth and fought down the returning nausea of panic.

I should never have let him go.

His mind slipped back to that awful day Tommy had tried so hard to end things.

Don't make me choose.

Oh, God. Did that explain why he'd done it? If it did, then Tommy could have planned this. All of it. Brett's head pounded. Tommy... innocent and guilty, sinner and saint. He'd never felt so angry, so scared, so hurt, all at the same time. Scraped raw and turned inside out.

He let his chin sink onto his chest and leaned as far back on his arms as he could comfortably. He didn't care anymore if the cop saw him cry, but the tears had stopped coming.

I'm so sorry, baby.

CHAPTER THIRTEEN

TOMMY found himself in an interview room that looked very little like he'd expected it to. The Hill County Sheriff's office, like Havre's city PD, dealt mainly with drug offenses, domestic disputes, assaults, and thefts, and the roll of employees wasn't exactly huge. Released from the wrist restraints, he sat at a plain gray table. There was a huge two-way mirror on one wall, just like on TV, only opposite it hung a mounted trophy buck. The chairs were upholstered in a weird, napped beige fabric—scratchy and kind of uncomfortable—and a faint smell, like cookies, was drifting in from somewhere.

Tommy wondered if he might be hallucinating and looked carefully at the buck in case it started doing anything vaguely David Lynch. He glanced up as Sheriff Laven came into the room and sat down in the chair opposite him with a long sigh.

He laced his thick, pink fingers together, blue eyes keen beneath bushy eyebrows. Tommy remembered seeing him on the news a few months back when some hiker had gone missing. He couldn't remember if they'd found the guy or not.

"All right, Tommy," Laven said, jerking him back to the present. "Why'd you do it?"

Tommy glanced at the mirror. "I... I don't... I think I need a lawyer. I'm supposed to have a lawyer, right? How do I—"

"Don't worry. He's on his way." Laven sat forward, his mouth a wheedling leer. "But, I'll tell you what... it's wastin' time, all this waiting. You'd do yourself a favor, laying out your side of the story now. Get it all straight, right? Could really help yourself."

Tommy looked into the man's open, clear face. "I...." He swallowed. *Self-defense, right, baby?* "I—"

"I, I, I? Come on, Tommy! You can do better than that. You really want to try for a needle? We have the gun. We have your cell phone. All we need to do is match your prints to the scene and that's only a matter of time. If you don't want to talk to me, I can always go ask your buddy. He's just down the hall."

"Brett didn't do anything."

"Oh, come on. You had him there, ready to help you ditch, right? Where'd you plan on going?"

Tommy shook his head. "No. No, we.... He didn't do anything. There wasn't any plan. We—"

"So, what? You two just out for a romantic drive?"

Tommy stared, struggling to find something to say. The sheriff's face slowly changed.

"No, we.... He just came to find me. I didn't call him, I didn't plan.... Wait, you're not charging him with anything, are you?"

"Well, right now, Tommy, he's an accessory to murder."

"No! No, that's not true. He didn't do anything. He... he didn't."

He shook his head again, bewildered and lost.

Don't say anything, Tommy. Not a word 'til you get a lawyer. Not a word!

He couldn't lose the image of Brett being parceled into the Chevy, then the memory of such... peace as he sat in the patrol car. Just silence as he looked through the windshield at the beautiful, open blue of the sky.

Funny, that.

"You do realize what you're looking at, right, Tommy?" Laven asked, leaning forward again but airing a different tactic. "I mean, if you took that gun, you went to the bar to find your dad... well, that's premeditation, son. You'll be looking at life without parole, easy. And—let's face it—prison's hardly going to be a cake walk for a kid like you, eh?"

Tommy looked up sharply. Laven winked at him and, for a moment, he thought the sheriff would speak, but then the door opened and a young woman came in. Introduced as a criminalist, she proceeded to test his hands and clothes for gunshot residue and took a cheek swab for DNA. Tommy sat passively and let her do it, watching numbly as she crouched in front of him, intense concentration on her face.

It made him think of his old school nurse, administering shots and cold compresses in a totally impersonal way, like she might as well have been wrapping salami on a deli counter.

"So," Laven wanted to know, "did he fire the gun?"

"Definite GSR," the criminalist said, scooping up all her little bits of kit and indicator paper. Her dark ponytail switched over her shoulder, and she shrugged. "He's either fired or handled a recently fired weapon in the past few hours, but I need to get the DNA to the lab to see if it matches what we found on the body. I'll need to take his clothes too."

Body.

Tommy frowned. They'd cut him up, wouldn't they? Like all that stuff on TV…. Somewhere, his father would be disassembled, deconstructed, weighed, evaluated, and notated. Only it wasn't him anymore. Nothing but meat.

Martin had gone.

No, he'd gone—he'd *gone* long ago—no. No, he'd stopped. That was it. He'd stopped the moment his eyes dimmed, the echo of the shot on the brickwork… the sharp smells of piss and vomit and beer.

The dull thud. That crumpling noise and that thud as he hit the asphalt. The sound of his breath, bubbling out, bloody and fading. His hands… God, his *hands*. Had they been reaching out? Or trying to push him away…?

Sheriff Laven glanced past the criminalist at his suspect.

"Aw, shit. What'd you do to him? Could he be allergic to any of that stuff? Hey… hey, kid, you okay?"

The criminalist glanced down at her kit and then at Tommy.

"I can't see that he would. Looks more like shock to me. Panic attack, maybe. He does look kinda sick. He's definitely running a fever."

"Oh, great." Laven leaned out of the door and called to one of the officers lingering in the hall. "Hey, can you get some hot coffee in here? Thanks, Gina."

Tommy balled his hands into fists, but that only made the shaking worse, so he folded them under his arms and huddled in the chair. It seemed so cold for August. He blinked and glanced up at the sheriff and the other two officers who'd entered the room. He recognized one of them—Clairmont. The other, a dark-haired woman, held a pot of coffee and a short stack of Styrofoam cups.

"Wh-who's lookin' after the kids? Is Scott still with them?"

"Now, Tommy...." Laven sat down again and poured out two cups of coffee. "You just calm down, all right? You don't have to worry about anything except telling us what happened. Here you are, you drink this."

Tommy looked at the cup in front of him. Getting it from table to mouth looked like it might be complicated. He wasn't entirely sure he wasn't going to throw up, either.

"Somebody needs to call my brother."

"We've spoken to him," Laven said.

Something in the casual tone of his voice worried Tommy.

The sheriff smiled disarmingly. "Soon as we found the ID on the body, we called your house. Your, uh, your brother'd got himself in a real state. His dad gone out, not come back, you not back either. What's everybody s'posed to think, huh?"

Tommy frowned. He wasn't used to this feeling of being at war with his own head. Like fighting through thick cobwebs just to think. He stared down at his fingers, watched them tense around the coffee cup, trying to understand why they didn't seem to be anything to do with him.

Laven rocked back in his chair, hands flat on the table.

"So... we know about your mom. That's sad, that is. But she'll be comin' home in a week or so, right?"

Tommy nodded. That's what the doctors said. She'd need rest, relaxation... time to recuperate. She wasn't going to get it. Maybe even less so now.

"Guess your pa didn't make life easy for her," Laven said, and Tommy wanted to know just how the hell he thought he had a right to judge, to make stupid understatements like that. "Or any of you. Hm? Your brother told us about him hittin' your sister. That why you shot him?"

"I—" Tommy stopped. *Don't say anything. Not a word.* "I think I oughta wait for the lawyer."

Laven shrugged. "Have it your way. Miss out on your chance. I'll go talk to your friend instead. Fair bet he'll roll on you nice and easy. It'd be the smart thing to do... could even save himself some jail time."

"Jail time?"

The words flew out of Tommy's mouth before he could stop them. His body tightened against the chair. As Laven looked at him, part smug and part questioning, waiting for him to stumble into the bear pit, Tommy knew he should have seen that one coming. He also knew he'd have walked into the trap willingly, even if it had been marked out with neon arrows and whistles.

"Wait."

Promise me.

Laven relaxed back into his chair, cocking his head a little bit to one side. "Yeah?"

"He wasn't there. Brett wasn't involved in... in anything. He just panicked, that's all. He wanted to, I don't know, get me away. He—" Tommy licked his lips nervously. "If you drop the accessory charge... can you do that? If you let him go, no charges, I'll give you a full statement. Confession... whatever. C-can you do that?"

Laven leaned forward, looking at him consideringly. "He's, uh... it's that important to you, huh?"

"Please. He's goin' to Washington next month. Med school. He don't need this... he doesn't deserve it. Not over just some stupid panic." Tommy wondered how soon they'd be finished here; his head spun with a sickening tiredness. "Please?"

"All right," Laven said eventually.

Tommy sagged with relief. "Thank you," he murmured, his eyes beginning to close. "So, what do I have to sign?"

"Not as easy as that, kid. C'mon. Hey, Gina... can we get some paper and a pen in here?"

IF BRETT had figured he'd landed himself in trouble already today, it paled in significance next to the feeling of dread as he walked out to the front desk to meet his parents.

Monica stood talking to Gina Anders. Brett knew her as Kurt's mom, one of the ski slope parents, though he wasn't sure if she recognized him. He guessed whether she did or not, this would be all over town by lunchtime, and that thought strangely lifted him. It was almost a relief, in a really, *really* weird way.

He didn't know why on earth he should think of it as a good thing right now, but he didn't have time to fixate, because his father, hand on Monica's shoulder, turned to look at him.

Stephen's dark brown chinos and gray sweater—his unofficial weekend uniform—seemed rumpled, and he had his glasses perched on his nose instead of the contacts he liked to wear at work. His face looked stiff, serious. Monica, so pale that each freckle stood out like buckshot on her cheeks, glanced from Gina to her husband, then to her son and back again.

Brett took a deep breath and walked slowly up to the desk.

"Mom. Dad. Uh...." He looked at Mrs. Anders. "I believe I have some forms to sign, ma'am?"

Brett took the papers and pushed the pen across them, his fingers fat and resisting. His name spilled out like it had nothing to do with him. They still hadn't said a word. Would it be like this, then? Cold silence?

Brett slid the forms back across the desk.

"Uh, Mrs. Anders? The lawyer... Tommy's lawyer. Is he—?"

"Collins. Yeah, he's in there now." She eyed his parents warily. "Um. Brett, you do know he's confessed?"

Brett stared, not understanding. "Wh... what?"

Gina smiled kindly at him. "Yeah. But you're okay. You go on home, hm? Go on."

"But—"

"Brett." Stephen's hand landed firmly on the back of his son's neck. "Come on."

Don't say a word. Promise me.

What the hell had Tommy done? Confession? Confessed to what? Brett's head thumped with horrendous possibilities. His father walked him out to the car, and Brett was aware of the people staring— white faces and big eyes, mouths framing whispers as he passed—but he barely saw them.

Monica unlocked the car. Stephen gave Brett a little push and sent him folding into the backseat. He slumped in the synthetic leather. His mother hit the gas, and the Ford pulled away, tires squealing. Brett closed his eyes. His wrists and shoulders still ached from the restraints, and his nose stung with every breath, but neither hurt as much as the knowledge that Tommy must have felt so desperate, so… alone. That things had got so bad—how had that happened? Brett shuddered, thinking of what Tommy had said about Lila, and thinking of his bruised, bloody face, his neck, his wrist. That broken rib that he'd first seen back in April.

I was thirteen.

How long had Martin been hitting them? Had it only been hitting? How— how did people live like that? On top of the questions came the anger. Boiling, bitter anger that Tommy had done this to him. *To us.* Selfish, maybe, but it burned. Brett couldn't stop seeing Tommy's face at Fresno, the broken capillary in his puffy eye, the blood still on his lip. He'd asked to be forgiven. Of course he'd said yes. But had it meant so little that Tommy really thought he'd leave for Washington and abandon him completely?

He'd thrown away his future—their future—without a word.

If only you'd talked to me… told me the fucking truth!

It made a mockery, a lie of every minute they'd had together, every touch, when Tommy could toss it aside so easily. Lie to him. Not tell him. Not… not want to involve him. Protecting him, maybe, but no one wanted to be protected like this. He could have helped, couldn't he?

Brett curled his hands into his sleeves. *Shit!* To be in such pain and still trying to protect him. He wanted Tommy. Just a minute, one more minute to hold him and promise that he understood. He didn't, but it didn't matter. He'd tell him it would be okay. And it would be. It had to be. He felt sick, but he swallowed the nausea down with all the bitterness and the anger. He had to stop acting like a kid. He didn't have time to do that. Not now.

Save Tommy first. Freak out later.

It occurred to Brett that neither of his parents had said a word, and the temperature in the car had dropped to that of the average January in Cut Bank. He saw both Monica and Stephen shoot looks at him in the mirror, but he had no idea what to say to them.

MONICA pulled up crooked on the driveway and got out of the car.

"Get him inside," she muttered, slamming the door.

Stephen exchanged glances with his son in the rear view. "Come on," he said hoarsely.

Within a couple of minutes, Brett was sitting at the kitchen table, not totally sure of how he'd got there but aware of how the next few hours were stretching out ahead of him, black and bottomless. His father sat down in his usual place, his back to the window, and Monica took the chair next to him, a damp tissue clasped in one of her hands.

"This isn't you, Brett," she said, her voice low but adamantine hard. "I can't believe you'd be involved in…. No, that you'd throw it away like this."

"What?" Brett stared at his mother, appalled.

Monica rubbed her fingertips across her forehead.

His father's gaze shifted guiltily to her, then back to him. "What your mother means—"

"Don't you tell him what I mean, Stephen! I know exactly what I mean and I just damn well said it. I am disappointed, Brett. And hurt. You didn't even think to *talk* to us?"

Brett looked down at his hands. What could he have said?

"I mean," she continued, eyes red-rimmed but blazing, "You've never even said you're... what? Bi? I mean, I'm assuming...."

Her voice faded out. Brett kept his head down. That way, he figured he could maybe get through it. Just like his interview at the sheriff's office all over again. He should have realized, when he knew they had Tommy's phone. The pictures on there—nothing hardcore, just mementoes that Tommy had wanted—gave away everything.

Well, then, smile for me.

Tommy, trying to take his picture as he lay in the long grass at Beaver Creek. Him, pulling Tommy down for another stolen kiss, snapped in the act of kissing him... never having realized that they looked so good like that, his fingers tilting Tommy's jaw, their lips locked. Like that's how they belonged, like nature had made them just for that, perfectly sculpted and balanced.

The officer had tossed it onto the table, as if Brett ought to be ashamed of the picture. *We know.* So what? It changed nothing. And everything.

"Um, no," Brett said, because it might as well be now that he started to clear up this mess. He took a deep breath. "Uh. Not bi, Mom. Gay. I... I'm gay. I didn't really think I'd be out 'til college. I-I didn't wanna... I don't know. But then I met Tommy back in January. He was workin' for Mr. Klass at the ski store, and we... we... uh. I, ah, I never told you 'cause, well—"

"Why tell your mother about your rough tricks, huh?" she sniped.

His mouth hung open, the breath knocked out of him. *Bitch!* Where the hell had she picked that up?

"Monica!"

His father's voice held a warning, directed not just at his wife but at him too. *Don't push her. She'll explode.* Brett didn't care. He'd never had a real stand-up shouting match with his mother. Yet. He wet his lips, preparing to defend himself, but his father got there first.

"You know we love you, Brett. But this is serious. If those charges hadn't been dropped...! What the hell has been going on with you that you'd be involved in something like this? What... what happened?"

Brett tried, but the words wouldn't come. He hadn't rehearsed this, hadn't imagined it would be this way.

You do realize you could get life without parole for what you did, son? The sheriff leaned over him, putting on his kind, concerned, fatherly face. *Accessory after the fact. And it's premeditated murder. Tommy took that gun and he went and waited for his father. And he shot him. You helped him, didn't you? Aided and abetted the escape of a felon, too. Why not make it easier on yourself, huh? Make a statement; we'll see what we can do.*

"It's my fault," he said quietly. "I knew what kinda thing had been goin' on in that house."

"Brett," Stephen leaned forward on his elbows, "what d'you mean?"

"Tommy's father. He hit them… the kids. His wife. I knew and I did nothing. Tommy didn't want…. He's proud. Stubborn, too. He didn't want people knowing, but—"

"Five kids, huh?" Monica steepled her fingers, tissue between them, breathing through her hands as if in prayer. "That's what Mrs. Anders said."

Brett glared at her. And who the hell had made it Mrs. Anders' business?

"The father lived on disability, mother had a part-time job at a drycleaners. Three kids under ten, and the… the other two are a mechanic with a pregnant teenage girlfriend and your… kitchen fitter."

The words left her lips with such disdain that Brett saw red.

"I met Tommy, not his family," he snapped. "And I didn't judge him."

"You clearly didn't use any damn judgment at all!"

"Okay, both of you. Just stop it." Stephen held up a hand. "Honey, you need to calm down. Brett, we're not…. Look, whether you've been… intimate with this person or not doesn't change how we feel about you at all. You know that," he added.

Too quickly, Brett thought. Of course it changed how they felt. They'd be angry, confused, upset that their son either hadn't felt that they needed to know, or hadn't wanted to talk to them. That he'd broken all the faith they'd had in him, in the person they'd thought him to be.

Brett understood that all too well now. He knew how much it hurt.

He knew Stephen would be thinking about all those talks they'd had, those excruciating man-to-man moments, like when he'd first started dating or when Lynsey dumped him. Brett had thought then about talking to him, explaining why he really wasn't as broken up as Stephen expected him to be. He'd wondered at the time whether his father knew. If he had, he hadn't wanted to talk about it.

"Brett?" Stephen's voice sounded firm, but not unkind.

Brett blinked, trying to hold on to the present. He couldn't have imagined for a moment, this morning, that today would have turned out to be quite as shitty as this.

"Just tell us how this happened, son. How you... *why* you didn't feel you could come to us. Wh—"

"Did you know what he was planning to do?" Monica cut across.

"No! I had no idea, Mom. If I'd known what was gonna happen, I'd have tried to stop him. I—"

"Oh, instead of trying to drive him across the border?" Her voice rose to shrill as she fought a losing battle to contain her anger.

"Honey...."

Stephen looked between his son and his wife, obviously not relishing the prospect of picking sides.

"Mom, it wasn't—" Brett broke off, and sighed wearily. "I love him. I couldn't hack knowing I let him down, that I... I let him push me away. You wouldn't... you don't understand, okay? Tommy tried to finish it. He didn't want me involved. And I tried to let that be okay, I really did." His gaze fell to the table, his eyes blurring. "I didn't try to make him fit in with what I wanted. I mean, not when I saw... I've been so lucky, and I never knew it. I didn't understand, when I wanted him to come to Washington with me, why he couldn't leave. I didn't—"

"You asked him to go to Washington?" Stephen frowned.

Brett swiped a hand over his face. "I wanted us to be out. I wanted... I wanted everything. I'm in for the long haul, all right? I-I still am."

He raised his head as he spoke, realizing the truth of what he'd said. Yeah, he might still be mad. Hurt. A thousand other things, too, but it didn't mean he could suddenly picture a future without Tommy in it. Whatever that would hold now. He couldn't walk away. Not again.

"I'm sorry." Brett looked guiltily at his father, seeing Monica wipe her eyes on the damp tissue. "I'm sorry I didn't talk to you. I just... I thought I could handle it, and then Tommy finished things, and I guess it woulda been the end of it all if... if this hadn't happened. But it did. And I-I'm not gonna give up on him now."

"Brett, he killed a man." Monica's voice softened, her temper under better control.

Tears dripped down Brett's cheeks, warm and full. He took a deep breath, trying to hold on. "Mom, if you knew what.... It was self-defense."

Self-defense, right, baby?

Tommy hadn't looked for a moment like he believed him. And then he'd confessed, they said. Of all the stupid, idiotic... beautiful things.

"He confessed so they'd drop the accessory charge. Don't you see?" Brett hung his head, the tears falling hot and uncontrolled now. "For me. God, I should never have...."

After a moment, Stephen's hand reached to stroke the back of his hair, pulling him into a seated, awkward hug, and Brett knew that, just maybe, there could be a chance he hadn't screwed everything up beyond repair.

CHAPTER FOURTEEN

BRETT had, in some small way, expected his parents to be supportive, even if he'd never foreseen the way he'd come out to them or the circumstances. He hadn't anticipated as much from the rest of Havre, because it just wasn't the kind of town that handed out blue ribbons for airing your business in public... and definitely not his kind of business.

Only four weeks ago, even though he'd been busy moping over Tommy, Brett could hardly have failed to miss the scandal of Lisa, the ski instructor he'd worked under last winter, receiving the full wrath of local society because Doug Petersen had finally left his wife and two daughters for her. Seemed like, suddenly, Lisa had a hard time getting served in the market, while the rumor mill had it that Doug's school ski-tuition contracts wouldn't be coming up for renewal.

And neither of them even shot anybody.

Kevin, whom he'd known since elementary school and had—up until Tommy—always been the person Brett had thought of as his nearest thing to a best friend, came to see him that evening.

Monica sent him straight up the stairs just like always, and when Brett opened his bedroom door he found Kevin standing outside it, cracking on a stick of wintergreen gum and looking nervous. Guilt welled up in Brett for all those years he'd never said anything, for all the times he'd been less of a friend than Kevin deserved. He was showing just how much he deserved too, standing here right now.

"Kevin?"

His friend shrugged, hands deep in his pockets.

"What are you doing here?"

Kevin looked at him with sad blue eyes, his ears burning red against his short-cropped blond hair.

"I heard some stuff. A lot of stuff that's goin' around. Figured I should come see if you had anything to say."

Brett slumped against the doorframe. Okay, it smarted, but he deserved that one.

"Fuck it.... I'm sorry, Kevin. What are they saying?"

As if he had to ask. Kevin shrugged again, but something new lingered in his eyes. A wary, guarded look that turned Brett's stomach.

"Y'know. That you're qu—that you're, uh, gay, I mean. And you got in with some Indian who's killed a guy. Or that you both did. And then there's all this shit on the news...."

Brett looked at his feet. Yeah, he'd seen that. So far, only scant details, because Tommy had yet to be formally arraigned and the whole messy, scrambling business of lawyers still had to be gone through, but a reporter from the local paper had already come by the house. He'd never been as proud of his father as when he went out there and got rid of her, all icy politeness and no comment, before coming in and sitting back down to dinner like nothing had happened.

"I mean... *murder*?" Kevin tilted his head, trying to catch Brett's eye. "I don't know what to think."

"Me neither. Not about that." Brett scuffed the side of one foot against the carpet. "I wasn't involved. The, uh, the other thing's true, though."

"Oh." Kevin frowned, and Brett wondered if he'd been expecting some kind of denial. Kevin nodded slowly, his mouth crunched into a weird curl of regret. "Right. You never said."

"No, guess not. I'm sorry. I should have, huh?"

Another shrug. Brett wondered if that meant Kevin didn't care, or if he thought it should have stayed unmentioned. An awkward silence fell between them and seemed to spill out into endless hours.

Kevin shifted uncomfortably on his heels. "So, uh, what? You did a *Natural Born Killers* with this guy, or what?"

Brett wanted to laugh. Trust Kevin to bring everything down to a movie. "No," he said. "I just... I can't really talk about it, Kevin. I did somethin' stupid, that's all. Tommy got himself in trouble, and I-I just wanted to help him. I shouldn't have, but—"

"Well, they always say you know who your real friends are when you need to move a body."

"Kevin! We didn't—" Brett stopped, catching the glint in his friend's eye. "You know what? That is not funny. Not even a little bit."

"Yeah, it is. So, what happens now?"

Brett sighed. "I-I don't know. I'm tryin' to find a lawyer."

"I thought they let you go?"

"Yeah, they dropped the accessory charges 'cause Tommy gave them a full confession. I told him not to say—" Brett stopped, feeling the anger swelling up again and not wanting to vent in front of Kevin. "He should have waited for the damn lawyer! Now he's got some public defender jerk who's never handled more than misdemeanor charges and... I'm scared that's not gonna be good enough."

Kevin frowned and dug his hands even further into the pockets of his jeans.

"So, you... you're sticking with this guy?"

Brett nodded. "Yeah."

"Oh."

Another frown. Kevin pulled one hand out of his pocket. "There's already a lot of this," he said, flapping his fingers against his thumb.

Brett shrugged. He hadn't expected anything less.

Kevin shook his head. "I just wish you'd said something, man. I mean—"

"I'm sorry, Kevin. I—"

"I'd've hit on Kirsty Muir before now, for a start.... Oh, you should probably know. She's the one doin' most of the, uh...." Kevin flapped his fingers again. "Woman scorned, I guess. Y'know. She's, uh... yeah, she's pretty mad. Guess she didn't know you were spoken for, huh?"

Brett winced. There had been a point at which he'd wanted to yell his relationship with Tommy from the top of the highest ski lift. Easy to say, then. Somehow, this seemed more excruciatingly embarrassing than he'd imagined it would.

"Uh. Yeah."

"Mm. So," Kevin said, tilting his head. "What happens now?"

Brett was taken aback. He hadn't imagined Kevin would ask.

"Well… Tommy needs a good lawyer." He shrugged. "I gotta fix that first, I guess."

Kevin stared. "Wh— You're gonna…? Brett, how the hell you think you can pay for a lawyer?"

"I got my college money. I'm gonna use that."

Brett stared at his feet. That didn't sound quite as logical as it had in his head. He wasn't totally surprised when Kevin started to laugh.

"You're what? Oh, shit, man! God, I…. Fuck, Brett. You're not serious?"

Brett looked up, unsmiling. Kevin leaned a hand against the doorframe, his laughter stopping abruptly.

"Shit. You can't—"

"Uh-huh. It's my money. Mom and Dad always said…. I mean, it's in my name. And I earned a lot of it. It's not like I'm stealin' it. I've spent half the afternoon lookin' up how to do this, and the college fund'll be enough for a retainer."

Disbelief edged into Kevin's eyes. Brett wasn't really looking at him anymore. He strafed a hand through his hair, talking out his plan.

"I spoke to this guy in Helena. He's handled domestic abuse cases and gotten acquittals, sentence reductions… he's really good. He'll give me a payment plan, and I can… y'know, if we can just get him on board, I can handle it from there. I just need Tommy to sign off on it. I-I need to find him."

Brett stopped, hearing the shake in his voice. He'd called the sheriff's department over and over, but they wouldn't give him a thing. No case number, no information. He wasn't family.

Kevin shook his head. "Dude, this is fucked up. I mean, are you completely insane? This... this is your life you're talkin' about. I know how much you wanna go to med school, how much you.... What if you never get another chance?"

Brett's jaw clenched. He wouldn't ever get another chance with Tommy. And if Tommy hadn't traded the confession against his accessory charge, he'd never have got the option to go to med school anyway. Not with a criminal arrest record. He said nothing.

"This is crazy," Kevin breathed. "I think you probably ought to stay low for a few days, all right? If... if there's anythin' you need, call me. Just... take some time. Chill out and think about what you're doing, yeah? I'll go by your work, tell 'em you're sick. Don't go in. All right?"

Brett stared at him, realizing that Kevin may as well not have listened to a word he'd said. Take some time? What time? Time enough for Tommy to get charged with murder one? He couldn't just sit on his ass and let that happen.

"Sure," he said, without much emphasis. "Thanks, Kevin. That... that's cool. Thank you."

"All right, then."

"Yeah."

Brett leaned against the door, these horrible last moments stretching out between them. With a useless wave of his hand, Kevin backed away. He looked back up the stairs just once as he left. Brett knew things there weren't ever going to be the same there, and that really sucked.

He glanced at his watch. Heading on to half past seven. Eight hours ago, they'd almost made it to Canada. Downstairs, the front door slammed. Brett gave the wall a halfhearted kick.

Only one thing he could do now.

FINDING the house wasn't that hard. He'd never been there before, but Tommy had—once or twice—mentioned the area and a couple of landmarks that gave Brett something to work with. He spent an hour or so knocking on doors, finally finding someone who gave him the right street and house number. Brett parked outside, taking a second to check himself in the mirror.

The sprawling neighborhood was mostly made up of houses built in the '80s; they were squat and dark, crouching on scrubby lots, but the dying sunlight turned the chain fences to gossamer and the glass in the windows to molten gold.

Brett screwed up his courage, stepped up onto the porch, and knocked on the door. After a moment, it cracked open, and the face of a guy who looked so much like Tommy that Brett's heart leaped peered out from behind the scratched wood.

"Yeah?"

"Uh, you're Scott, right?"

"Yeah, and if you're— Wait a minute. You're *him*, aren't you?" Scott Hawks opened the door fully, his tone hardening as he stood before Brett in worn jeans and an old Grizzlies sweatshirt, a gold chain glinting at his neck.

Different features, Brett realized now; the dark eyes less almond-shaped, more slanted, the chin narrower, the thick black hair cropped short.

Not so much alike at all.

"Yeah. It is you. Tommy's—"

Scott appeared to be casting around for a less than complimentary noun, so Brett got in first.

"Brett," he said, simply. "Brett Derwent."

"What d'you want?"

"I wanna help."

"Piss off."

The door started to close in Brett's face, so he stuck his foot in the gap. It hurt much more than he'd expected.

"Wait! Argh…! No, hold on. Please. I just… ouch! No one's telling me anything. Where he is, what's happening, if the lawyer's any good. I don't…."

Scott glared at him from the dimness, then opened the door and leaned against the frame. He dug a packet of Marlboros from his pocket and pulled one out, looking thoughtfully at Brett.

"The County Detention Center. He got arraigned this afternoon."

"Already?" Brett said, his voice rising in panic.

He couldn't be too late. Not again.

Scott nodded. "Yeah. Bail's set at a hundred fifty thou, so there ain't no way we can make that. Mom's saying she wouldn't want him back here anyway, but I think that's shock talking." He fiddled with the unlit cigarette, looking uncomfortable and avoiding Brett's eye. "She's not well."

"I didn't know about the accident. I'm… sorry."

Scott grunted. Brett didn't know what to say.

He took a breath. "How can I see him?"

"I dunno. Speak to the lawyer… the court-appointed one, I know that. I got a card somewhere."

He patted his pockets and frowned.

"Is he any good? The lawyer? 'Cause I—"

Scott shrugged. "How the fuck should I know? Here." He passed Brett a dog-eared business card. "I don't know. I think we have to find out about legal aid and shit, but…. Look. Brett, right? I have a mother still not outta hospital and already on the verge of another breakdown, two shit-scared kids and a baby to worry about, plus a very pregnant fiancée in an apartment I'm not going to be able to pay for because I have to sort out this fuckin' funeral. I'm really not down on my criminal law 101 right now, okay?"

He stared at Brett for a moment, his mouth tight and his eyes guarded. A soft breeze bowled down the road. Scott put the unlit cigarette between his lips.

"It's you that had Tommy acting the way he's been this summer, right?"

"What?"

Brett frowned. Did Scott somehow blame him for this?

Scott shook his head. "He's been… I don't know. Up, down, inside out. At first I thought he'd started tweakin' or something, but it wasn't that. Not even close. He looked... *alive*. Not just keepin' his head down and pushing through." He shifted uncomfortably from foot to foot. "I've known he's queer for years. So. Um. You guys, are you... I mean, is it, like, a thing, or are you just, y'know, parkin' it somewhere?"

Brett wanted to laugh. Desperately. But, somehow, that didn't seem like the most sensitive reaction. Scott winced, like this physically hurt him.

"I love him," Brett said as simply and as gently as he could.

Scott looked at him over the cigarette, his hands already half-cupped around the tip to light it. Relief flooded his face. And maybe even something a little bit like admiration.

"Tommy says he feels the same. I...."

Scott struck a flame from his lighter. "Uh-huh."

"I don't plan on going anywhere," Brett said determinedly. "I want to do what I can. Help. If there's a way for me to do it."

Scott took the cigarette from his lips; a plume of smoke slipped from the corner of his mouth.

"All right. Well, you can tell the lawyer I said you're as good as family. If you, uh, need anything, call me. Um. This number, not the house." He took back the lawyer's card and scrawled a number on the reverse of it with a stub of pencil pulled from his pocket. "You should go see him at County, if they'll let you. I... I have to go. But I'll see you around."

"Thank you."

Brett tucked the card into his pocket and stepped clumsily off the porch, unsure what else he'd been expecting. He started to make his way back to the Bronco.

"Hey, Brett!"

He turned. Scott leaned over the rail, cigarette in his fingers.

"Yeah?"

"Would you really have gone to Canada?"

"Sure." Brett smiled. "But only while I worked out how to get him somewhere with no extradition."

"Shit." Scott shook his head, a disbelieving grin on his face. "Y'know, he probably deserves you."

"I hope so," Brett called, watching him go back into the house.

The smile faded from his face as the door closed, echoing in the empty air. He couldn't keep from wondering what had happened inside that building over the years and, with that, there came a rational anger and a totally irrational guilt, as if he could have—*should* have—prevented it.

Brett's fingers closed on the card in his pocket. He might not have been able to do anything before, and he wasn't even close to forgiving Tommy for keeping him in the dark, but he sure as hell could do something now.

HILL COUNTY DETENTION CENTER fitted at least half the description Brett imagined when he thought of prison. The lawyer, Collins, had proved to be a complete jerk, but at least he'd told Brett how to apply for a visit.

The visiting cubicle had phones either side of a thick glass viewing window, set in a bench just wide enough to lean on. Chairs stood bolted to the floor either side of the glass, the privacy panels not as wide as they really needed to be. Brett sat down and waited, aware of how the guards seemed to stand oh so close. Sweat slicked his palms, and his pulse hummed. And then, finally, Tommy came in.

He looked awful, still bruised and battered, though at least cleaned up. He moved awkwardly, as if he was stiff and sore. Brett had hardly closed his eyes for worrying about him; it seemed Tommy hadn't slept either. Dark circles ringed his eyes, and the orange prison issue clothes made him look sallow and ill.

Tommy sat down. Brett fumbled for the phone, holding his breath until the other receiver rested against Tommy's ear. He didn't know what to say, and ended up speaking without thinking, the words tumbling out in an angry rush.

"What the hell happened?" he demanded. Tommy winced. "What in the hell happened to waiting for the fucking lawyer? Huh?"

Tommy smiled mirthlessly. "Hi."

Brett had the grace to be embarrassed. "Hi. I'm sorry." He sighed. "Oh, Tommy. I know why you... did what you did in there. I just—"

"You had nothin' to do with it. I couldn't let them treat you like you did."

"But what's gonna happen? How are ya? Is everything... I mean, can you—? What's going on? 'Cause they wouldn't tell me anything. No one would tell me anythin' at all and...."

Brett stopped. He heard himself, the words just pouring out with no control. Not what Tommy needed right now.

"I'm all right," Tommy said. He reached up and tucked his hair behind his ear. "I got, uh, arraigned on second degree. They set bail pretty high, though, so I'm here 'til the trial, I guess. Lawyer says so, anyway."

"Collins?" Brett snorted. "I spoke to him. Man's an ass. Kept talking about how you oughta be preparing yourself for a guilty plea, hope for leniency?"

Tommy opened his mouth as if to say something, but Brett plowed on. The thought that they'd been caught before Tommy had actually told him what happened that night passed across his mind only very briefly. He stomped on it, hard.

"No. You need to get a new defense. Woulda been better to have a new lawyer before the arraignment, but you can still do it. I got some numbers for you."

Tommy frowned. "Wh—"

"His name's Michael Ribideaux. Works out of Helena. He's really good. He says you could have a shot at voluntary manslaughter... maybe even an acquittal with a sympathetic jury, if they could prove sustained, uh, abuse."

Brett bit his lip. He knew Tommy wouldn't take kindly to that word; he never had. Brett remembered him flying off the handle when he'd used it once before. *He's not like that—it's never been like that!* Eyes wild, voice sharp... the strength of his denial had only scared Brett more.

Only, Tommy barely reacted at all. His frown just deepened.

"I don't know. Where'd you find him? I-I thought the legal-aid guy—"

"Internet," Brett explained shortly, praying Tommy wouldn't keep asking questions like that. "I did some research."

He'd spent hours reading up, searching directories and databases, learning a hundred and one things he'd never thought he'd need to know.

"But—" Tommy switched the phone to his other ear and cradled it against his shoulder.

"He has a great reputation. He's worked a lot of domestic ab— uh, a lot of cases he's gotten acquittals and lighter sentences on. He could really help. I've spoken to him on the phone. I got all the numbers. He says he'd be happy to take the case, and I really, really think you oughta—"

"Brett…."

"Please. I don't wanna see you go to trial with a legal-aid defender."

"Brett, I can't afford—"

"It's handled. Okay? Just call the guy. Sign off on it. That's all you need to do. Just say you'll do it, yeah?"

"I don't have the m—"

"Tommy, please!"

A short, hot silence flared between them. Slowly, horrified realization spread over Tommy's face.

"Oh, you don't mean…? You wanna pay? No, Brett. No. I can't—"

Brett hunched over the phone and leaned closer to the glass. "Baby, listen. You need a good lawyer. This guy's good. So just let me help."

"No! How are you gonna…?"

"I got a loan," Brett lied, meeting Tommy's eyes, willing him to just damn well accept it, whether he believed him or not. "I can pay. Let me help."

The air seemed to creak as they looked at each other through the cold glass.

"But it's your college money," Tommy said after a long moment. "Isn't it?"

In a way, it made Brett feel proud. Like it showed how well Tommy knew him, or what kind of kickass lovers' telepathy they had.

"Your ears go pink when you lie," Tommy explained. "I won't take it. I don't wanna…. I mean, you gotta go to Washington."

Brett deflated. He blushed, hating the heat that rushed to his cheeks.

"You can. I want you to."

"But…."

"Take it. Take the damn money, Tommy. Please."

"I—"

"Look." Brett sighed. *Stubborn bastard.* "It's not just for you, okay? It's for me, too. I can take a couple years out. Keep working, keep savin' up…. You're only gonna get one shot at your defense. You know what could happen. You did so much for me already. Let me do this?"

TOMMY hung his head. The raw wash of humiliation, the fear, the guilt, and the pain… everything riled up in him. It had become so hard to think right, so hard to make sense even of the simple things.

And Brett never made anything simple.

"Also, um, I called the lady at the tribal council in Fort Belknap…."

He glanced up, exhausted and bewildered. "What?"

Brett licked his lips nervously. Looking at him burned like it never had before: so much blind faith, hope, and yeah, even love in his face. Tommy knew just how badly he'd hurt him. He wouldn't have blamed Brett if he'd never wanted to see him again. But there he sat all the same, and he didn't look like he wanted to go anywhere.

"If they'll, uh…." Brett cleared his throat. "If they allow you to make an application—just so you got the tribal enrollment number, right?—there's all kinds of programs that could help. It's not just grants for college; there's special stuff for people in the penal system, so... y'know, it could take time, but it'd help."

"You're just a one-man defense team, aren't you?"

"Hey, I'm tryin' to help."

Tommy sighed. He knew that. But it wasn't the point, and he couldn't bear to look at that pissed-off, wounded face Brett had on now. He knew he was being an ass, but there wasn't much he could do about it; there's only so much charity a body can take. Tommy rubbed his face, then moved to touch the glass with his hand but somehow didn't quite get there. His fingers flexed on the bench.

He couldn't have seen this coming. Not for a minute.

Couldn't have ever thought he'd stay.

"I can't take the money. You're supposed to go to Washington," he said hoarsely. "We talked about it. I thought—"

"Shh. Washington can wait. Anyhow, I talked about you comin' too. And you never even thought about that, did ya?"

Tommy blinked. That sounded like recrimination, however calm Brett kept his tone.

"I...," he began, because it wasn't true.

He'd thought about Washington so much. But he'd known he couldn't leave. Known that it wasn't for him, that life. Accepted it, because they weren't his dreams. They shone too bright, bloomed too big for him. No. You had to accept your limits. Live with them. Within them.

Brett—in fact, the whole summer—had been the last gasp of his rebellion. One thing to call his own, to keep sacred. Tommy hadn't gone looking for it, and he hadn't expected it to last or to be so important. You couldn't put a river in a glass; all the dazzling water, the sound and the light and the whirling eddies... all parts of something else. He realized he'd fallen silent. His mouth grew dry, and Fresno filled his head.

"I thought you'd move on," he said quietly, looking away.

He couldn't see that in Brett's face. Not now, or he'd lose it. Bad enough having to do this here, in public, without embarrassing himself like that. He heard Brett swallow heavily, heard his stiff, controlled breath in. *Shit.* He didn't want to fight. Not after everything.

"Did you?" Brett asked, after a moment.

Tommy stared down at the bench. His hair masked his face. Brett couldn't possibly have thought college wouldn't come between them.

Even he can't be that naïve.

"Tommy?"

He couldn't stand the bitter ache in Brett's voice. That he was trying to hide it only made it worse, and Tommy couldn't bring himself to look up. The thickness of uncried tears ran under Brett's words.

"Is that really what you thought?"

Scared to speak, Tommy uttered a small mumble that started out as "don't know." Nobody had ever reduced him to this before. He shook his head wordlessly.

"You thought I'd leave you that easily?" Brett asked. "That I don't...."

Tommy lifted his head, and his fingers brushed up against the glass. Brett placed his palm opposite.

"It's no choice at all," he said softly. "I love you."

His voice—quiet, distorted slightly by the phone—hung on Tommy's ear like a caress. He pressed his lips tight together, and the tips of his fingers whitened on the glass.

"Thank you," he whispered. "I-I...."

A weak smile pulled at the corner of Brett's mouth. "I know. Promise you'll call the lawyer?"

"'Course."

"I'll be checking up."

Tommy laughed damply.

"Your mom's coming home next week, by the way. I, uh, went to the house. Saw Scott. He's gonna try to come up and see you soon. He said to say they're coping. Now, uh, what do you need? Ready cash? What about the phone account? I don't really know what...."

Tommy swiped at his eyes. "Underwear," he said, trying to concentrate on switching back to the practicalities.

How do you do that? Turn me around like this? It's not fair!

In truth, practicalities proved the least of the things Tommy had to adjust to now. He knew he'd have to reconcile all the things happening around him, all the chaos he'd caused. But every time he tried to recall them, those empty, black hours seemed less and less clear. Even Brett couldn't fix that.

"All right." Brett caught his eye. "Briefs, yeah?"

Tommy smiled, despite himself, despite everything, and nodded. "Please."

He tried to keep up with Brett as he cycled through all the sensible, mundane things he'd obviously thought of before he came here. He hadn't asked a single question about what had happened that night, Tommy realized. He wondered why, but he didn't know how to ask, and Brett wasn't giving an inch, focusing on the things they had to get fixed up, everything he'd taken it on himself to do, organizing lists, checking things off....

The visits had time limits, and Tommy hadn't a clue how long they'd been here. Time had never seemed to matter to him when he'd been with Brett—although, he realized, they'd always been counting minutes, one way or another.

Maybe now they always would be.

CHAPTER FIFTEEN

BRETT sat on the edge of the deck, his legs through the railing. The night wasn't that cold, though it wasn't exactly balmy. Montana didn't really do mid-eighties and sultry nights, even in August. He scratched Roscoe's ears; the dog groaned softly and snuggled up against him, stretched out on the deck, his tail thumping lazily once or twice against the wood.

Brett felt tired, empty, and drained. He felt like a fool, too, because he couldn't justify feeling sorry for himself when Tommy was moldering in the county lock-up with the meth heads, violent drunks, and... well, he didn't even like to think the word "rapist."

The past few days had been a blur of scrambling to try and do things, a desperate tornado of activity that didn't seem to go anywhere: submitting lists of phone numbers for approval so Tommy could call out—collect, of course, all recorded; bugging Scott to keep track of the lawyers, because nobody Brett called would tell him anything... obviously. He had, apparently, no right to ask questions. He wasn't family and, Brett thought bitterly, unless state law changed, he never could be. The detention center wouldn't even let him put money into Tommy's account because he wasn't a relative.

He kicked feebly at the shrubs below the deck. He couldn't just have a damn good bitch about it and feel better, either. Too much, too many conflicting things roiled in him for that. Oh, he'd expected the anger, the inability to understand what Tommy had done, but the sense of betrayal, of loss and abandonment and, God, yes, even hatred, of all things! That had taken him by surprise.

"Confused?"

He and Roscoe both looked up, and the dog wagged his tail again. A mug of hot chocolate hovered mysteriously at Brett's shoulder. He turned around to find it attached to his mother. She raised her own mug.

"I put a little something in it. Mind if I join you?"

He took the hot chocolate and shook his head. "Nn-nn."

Brett couldn't really deny her, he supposed, though he wasn't sure he wanted company.

Awkwardly, Monica got down onto the deck, blowing the soft red bangs out of her eyes as she adjusted her seat on the wood. Roscoe scrambled to his feet, joints clicking, and snuffed around to see if she had a biscuit.

"Y'know, Brett, it's all right to be mad at him. And it's all right to take a breather, think about yourself."

He winced, touched by her concern, but distinctly uncomfortable. Did they really need to talk about this? Now?

Monica sipped her hot chocolate. "Are you sleeping?"

"Not really," Brett admitted. "I just keep thinkin'... ah, I don't know. And you're right, I am. I'm mad as hell. That he'd do what they say he did. That he wouldn't let me in. I...."

He trailed off. Monica nodded, looking out into the yard, her hand absently stroking Roscoe's flank.

"I guess," Brett said slowly, "I guess I know what it's like when somebody lies, keeps you in the dark about something important."

Monica smiled, her profile softening against the dark. "Mm. I just keep thinking of that friend you used to have... Ben, I think? Campbell."

"Mom! That's going back to, like, fourth grade."

"I know. I just remember how well you got on. You two were practically bonded at the hip, then, after a year or so, we never saw him again."

Brett groaned. "I don't believe you remember that.... God, you don't think I had a crush on him, do you?"

Monica shot her son a curious glance. "Did you?"

"We were *ten*, Mom!"

"So? At seven, you said you wanted to marry the green Power Ranger."

Brett stared into the frothy depths of his chocolate. Monica had floated a marshmallow on the top of it. The endless capacities of mothers stared back at him, and he couldn't help but think how much he loved her.

"Yeah," he said eventually. "But he *was* really hot. And he had kick-ass ninja moves."

Monica chuckled. Brett smiled, relief washing through him. The nip of brandy in the hot chocolate warmed him, and he took another sip. A breeze prickled through the trees, and Roscoe padded off indoors, presumably in search of his bed.

"You'd like Tommy," Brett said after a while. "He's smart. Kind. Funny. I wanted him to meet you'n Dad. He got pissed with me. 'Cause of... of this. All this," he added, nodding at the hot chocolate, the deck, the yard. The beautiful, boring normality of it all. "I didn't realize that at the time, but I get it now. I don't think I ever understood how lucky I am, y'know? With you. Dad. Everything. Even with Tommy.... I mean, he's spent his whole life lookin' after other people. Tryin' to keep things together at home. He loves 'em so much. His mom, his brothers and sisters. Even his dad. After everything that guy did."

Brett shrugged and cradled his mug. He looked mournfully at his marshmallow as it melted into gooey nothingness.

"He's been so good to me. So... careful. And I threw it all back in his face. I saw the... the bruises. Burns. Scars. I didn't do anything. When he tried to keep me out of it, I let him. I just sat back and took the easy way with everything. I think I've been doing that my whole life."

"Brett, cut yourself a break, honey."

Monica rubbed his back with the broad, warm flat of her hand. She used to do it for him years ago, soothing away every childish ill from nausea to the pain of being picked last for softball. It worked even now. Almost.

"So," she said softly. "What did you think would happen when you went to Washington, hm?"

Brett closed his eyes. *Don't make me choose.*

"Don't know. I-I had this stupid fantasy like he'd come with me, we'd get an apartment or something, start living a real life, not just stealing time together. 'Cause it isn't, uh." Brett paused, running his tongue over lips that suddenly felt dry. How the hell did you say this to your mother? "It's not just... it's never just been about the sex. He loves me. He confessed for me," he added because he still didn't quite believe that himself. "I wish he damn well hadn't, but he's a stubborn bastard. Proud, too. But he's a good man, Mom. And I love him."

Monica's hand stopped moving. After a moment, she turned her head and peered cautiously at him. The shadows painted her face.

"I bet you do, honey."

That lit another flare of anger in Brett, though he tried to choke it down. He wasn't sure if it was because of his age or Tommy's gender that she didn't seem to believe him. Like it was some stupid teenage crush that would wear thin with time.

That wasn't true. He *knew* that wasn't true. It couldn't be.

"You and Dad got married right out of high school," he said, snappy and more than a little reproachful.

"All right, yes. But...." She sipped her hot chocolate, her tone irritatingly reasonable. "Well, it's hardly the same, is it?"

Why not?

He wanted to ask her, to spit out those words and demand an answer. He didn't, though, because then she made a point that ran too close to his own fears.

"I mean," Monica said, licking a blob of chocolate from her lower lip, "if it's because you feel guilty—"

"Mom!"

"I just think you really need to consider this. That's all, honey. I mean, think about what you're doing, and why. Is this what you really think you should do? Standing by someone who didn't trust you enough to confide in you?"

Brett looked away. He couldn't help but think of her vicious words as they sat at the kitchen table, hurtling into that inevitable, horrible argument. Did she still think so little of him, of Tommy?

Did she *really* not get it?

"He played martyr," he said. "I know that. But what I've realized—what hurts most—is that this has nothing to do with me. I couldn't have done anything. Not really. Even if I'd tried, I couldn't have saved him from any of it. He probably even did the right thing, tryin' to keep it from me. Doesn't stop me feeling guilty, but… it doesn't change how I feel."

Monica said nothing. After a little while, she took her hand away, and they finished the hot chocolate in silence. Brett was glad of that, in a way. He suspected she might blow her top when he finally dredged up the courage to tell her what he was planning to do with his college fund.

MICHAEL RIBIDEAUX, a tall man with broad shoulders and a high forehead, wore his hair close cropped, shaved down to a fade over his ears and the nape of his neck. Designer glasses with rectangular, red-rimmed frames sat high on his nose, and a sober, dark suit with a pale blue shirt and a deep gray tie gave him an air of devastatingly understated style. An antique gold wedding band glimmered against his dark skin.

"Good morning, Tommy. It's nice to meet you at last."

Tommy didn't know whether he should stand up or not. It seemed the polite thing to do, but they were sharing the interview room with a correctional officer, and those guys didn't like too much movement. He ended up doing some kind of half shuffle behind the gray table, rising warily to shake the hand that the lawyer offered.

"Uh. Hi."

Ribideaux sat down, popping the clasp on his briefcase and taking out a manila file. Tommy watched anxiously as the CO left, leaving Ribideaux to his client privilege. He wondered what the hell Brett had gotten him into. Talking to the guy on the phone had been one thing, but….

"So, where to start," Ribideaux said rhetorically, his voice deep and, Tommy had to admit, confidence-inspiring.

Easy to picture him commanding attention in court, with all the bailiffs and the jurors, the prosecutors... the judge. He gulped nervously, almost missing the enclosure of his cell.

"I read your statement," said Ribideaux, declining to call it a confession. "I've been going over the paperwork. I, um, I'd like you to meet with a lady called Melanie Kaczyk... she's a psychologist."

Tommy looked suspiciously at the lawyer. "I'm not crazy."

"Nobody's saying you are," Ribideaux replied smoothly. "But there are some, uh, discrepancies that I think we need to clear up before anything goes any further. Frankly, I'm amazed the sheriff's office didn't push it."

"What?"

Tommy frowned, the expression turning into a wince as it pulled on his black eye. He raised his fingers to it and pressed just below the swelling. The medical officer had given him an antibiotic shot and a couple of aspirin on his first night, and that had helped, but not a whole lot.

"I don't understand," he said, eyeing Ribideaux guardedly.

"You don't remember what happened, do you, Tommy?"

Tommy averted his gaze, staring down at the table. "I-I shot him. I took the Western Field rifle from the, uh, the cabinet. I drove out to Deacon's. I waited, then—"

"How long'd you wait? Half an hour? Two hours? Ten minutes?"

Goddamn lawyers, Tommy thought, as he fired the questions out like rubber bullets. What the hell was he trying to prove?

"Well, I... I don't know. Prob'ly not long, but—"

"And what did you do?" Ribideaux asked calmly. He leafed through his manila file and pulled out a page here and there with his long, broad fingers, laying them neatly on the dull, scuffed surface of the table. "Did you confront him? Did you argue? Fight?"

"N—well, yeah. I guess we did."

"Mm. Because your father had already gotten physical with you that evening, right? When you stopped him beating your sister. Your brother, uh… Scott, he said it got pretty nasty."

Tommy shrugged. Ribideaux adjusted the papers so they lined up, perfectly straight, perfectly symmetrical.

Next time you touch me, I'll kill you… I will put a gun in your fuckin' mouth. You know what that'd do?

He swallowed, his throat suddenly sore and tight, his hand tugging at the collar of the itchy, ill-fitting orange shirt.

"I shot him," Tommy muttered.

"Yes, but—" Ribideaux tapped one of the papers, taking it out of that perfect line up and spinning it round so that Tommy could see. His confession, all signed and dated. "How? It's not in the statement. Did they even ask you? How many times? In the head, the chest? Did you watch him die?"

Tommy rocked back in the chair, aghast. "What? I—"

The smell. That stuck with him. The alleyway behind the bar stank. Beer, piss, puke… the burn of the powder. Echo on the bricks. His eyes… the dull thud as he dropped to the wet, stinking ground. It had already started to rain.

"Once," Tommy said, "In… inna chest. No. Yes, in the chest."

Silence.

He looked up. Ribideaux pursed his lips.

"Oh. Okay," he said and pushed up his designer glasses. "Not, uh…. Oh, I don't know. Twice in the gut, once in the head?"

"Huh?"

The rain pelted against the Chevy's windshield. He watched so many cars pull away, so many people leave. Women in high heels squealing about the rain. Drunks who didn't even notice it. Only, he couldn't leave. Not now. Couldn't go back to that. Couldn't let him *go back.*

Not this way.

"Because that's what the ME's report says. Not touching on the, uh, defensive wounds on the body."

Tommy frowned, trying to clear his thoughts. "I…."

He got out of the truck. He tipped his head back, feeling the cold rain patter his skin. Somewhere, a cat yowled, a sudden screech in the night.

"Tommy?"

He saw the shape, a shadow backlit against the door. One for the road. Just ol' buddies.... He saw a broken, damaged man. He saw a monster.

And he froze.

"Tommy?" Ribideaux repeated, prompting him. "It's important that you're honest with me. Do you remember?"

"I... I don't know! All right? I don't know. I just... I know I went there and I took the gun, but I didn't— I just wanted to.... I don't remember," he finished miserably. Tommy scrubbed a hand over his face and coughed. What he wouldn't give for another handful of aspirins. "It's blurry. He—I think he laughed. Swung... he always swung when he got drunk, even if he thought you were funny. I musta taken the gun when I got out of the truck. I remember... his hands as he went down. I... I don't remember doin' it." He squinted up at Ribideaux. "I-I thought I would. Didn't expect to see anythin' else when I closed my eyes but...."

Tommy frowned. He must have reloaded the gun, if what the lawyer said was true, but he couldn't remember it. He closed his eyes, looking for those memories. Damp panic and hard, jagged breaths as he scrabbled for the ammo, hands shaking as he broke the gun and slipped the bullets in... *make sure the fucker stays down because, if he gets up now, you're a fucking dead man....*

Had it even been like that?

He didn't know. There was... nothing much. Just impressions, like pieces of glass that reflected only distorted snatches of images.

"Do you remember driving to Fresno reservoir?"

Tommy shook his head. The lights hurt when he opened his eyes, and he winced.

"Uh-uh. I remember bein' there. It was still rainin'. I didn't know what else to do, where to go. I knew what I'd... what I'd done. Like part of me had gone too. You know what I mean? Then Brett—"

He stopped. Ribideaux already knew, he must. Whole damn state knew by now, he supposed. *Pair of fags. Bobby and Clyde.* He'd overheard that one in the sheriff's office and more than a dozen like it since. Tommy hadn't meant for that to happen. It should have been Brett's choice. Didn't matter on his account; he'd never needed anyone's approval. But Brett....

"I don't know why the hell he showed up there," he croaked.

"Special place for you?" Ribideaux asked, shuffling through his papers again. "Perhaps that's why you went there."

"Safe," Tommy muttered, not really concentrating. "No. I-I don't know. Maybe. He should never have—"

"But he did," said Ribideaux.

Tommy glanced up at him, trying to read the meaning in his face. He frowned. The lawyer tucked his papers back into the manila folder.

"Well," Ribideaux said after a moment. "I think we can definitely use this. Very much so. But I would like you to consent to talk to Dr. Kaczyk. Will you?"

Tommy shrugged. "Sure."

After all, what difference did it make?

THE thing about jail was the time. It lost a lot of its meaning, but made up for it by tripling in importance. Ironic, really. Every second became a second stolen, a piece of freedom you'd never see again, yet you didn't think of them that way. Time ended up being hard to keep track of because it seemed to go by so slowly, the structure of the days never changing. The routine—the sheer weight of it, straddling the hours with huge, immutable demands—pulled everything that happened out of shape, distorted the importance of every little thing. And you couldn't get away from that.

Not being able to get away caused a lot of the fights. Tommy's unit spent most of Thursday on lockdown after an incident between two meth addicts waiting to be transferred into the treatment program. Come Friday, he relished the change of scenery, and though the interview room had become depressingly familiar, it still gave him a break. Tommy sat slumped with his elbows on the table, head down, fingers pushed deep into his hair. He glanced up as the door opened, admitting a woman he hadn't seen before.

"Tommy," she said, engaging him with a smile. "How are you doing?"

She looked about thirty-five, maybe, honey-blonde hair probably dyed, deep dimples at the corners of her mouth. Soft blue eyes, though.

"I'm Dr. Melanie Kaczyk. I've been asked to come have a talk with you. You feeling up to a chat?"

He shrugged. "Sure."

"All right, then." She started shuffling through her paperwork. "So, I've been looking over the notes your counsel sent me. You're one of five kids, huh? That's a lot to cope with… and I should know! I have four brothers, and my mom never lets me forget what we put her through."

She was using the kind of pleasant, sing-song voice usually applied to minors, the elderly, or the infirm. Tommy stared steadily at the tabletop, its once-glossy surface marred with scratches and the dulling of years.

He tucked his hair behind his ear and winced as his fingers brushed the scrape on the side of his face. It had begun to heal, the raw skin turning rough. Another day or so, he guessed, and it'd start to itch like hell. He'd had enough bumps and bruises to judge that.

Kaczyk wanted to talk about those, among other things. It didn't take Tommy long to decide that she asked too damn many uncomfortable questions.

"So," she said, "your father had his accident… almost three years ago, right?"

Tommy shrugged. "Fell off a scaffold at work. The company wouldn't pay compensation 'cause they said he'd been drinking." He glanced up at her impassively. "Prob'ly had."

"And why do you say that?"

He arched an eyebrow. "Because he always drank, okay? Even before he hurt his back. He'd swing drunk, he'd swing sober, and he'd swing when he tried to kick the booze. And he did used'ta try… it made it worse."

Kaczyk made a note on one of her bits of paper. "Uh-huh. And how did things seem between him and your mom?"

How the fuck do you think? Tommy said nothing, though he wanted to. She obviously sought her answers in how he responded to the questions, not in what he said. That made him uneasy. He wasn't used to being analyzed.

"Tommy?" Kaczyk prompted. "Did they fight? Argue? Did she give as good as she got, or—?"

"No!" he snapped, louder than he meant to. "No, she used to stand there and damn well take it, all right? And he'd make like it'd been a joke, or an accident, or… somethin'. And she'd let him. She let him get away with it. And we had to too. Not… not s'posed to make Daddy mad. Just… keep quiet and be good."

He looked down at the table, rubbing his fingers over the scratches. He couldn't believe he'd let her do that. Manipulate him that way. He glowered at her from under his lashes. Kaczyk returned his look with a blank sort of one-size-fits-all sympathy. She didn't understand. People didn't. People never did.

"You can do that when you're big enough to understand how," Tommy muttered. "Not when you're little."

Kaczyk waited a beat, then leaned forward, tilting her head. "Did he hurt the kids, Tommy?"

"No, he… he'd get jealous, 'cause they needed Mom's attention, and he used'ta take it out on her. Me 'n' Scott, too, when we got older. We were ten when Robbie was born. Bigger. He never touched the little ones."

Kaczyk tapped her pen against her files. "Ten's big enough for a beating, huh?"

Tommy shrugged, not looking up. "If you pissed him off. Embarrassed him. He… he used to have other women, up 'til the thing with his back. Used to leave us in the car while he'd… visit with 'em. Just… just look in my mother's medical file, okay? He gave her more'n sprains and fractures. Herpes, for one thing. He…." Tommy rubbed his knuckles over his forehead, wanting to push away the ache, not meeting the psychologist's gaze. "He never let her say no. You understand?"

"You're saying—"

"I'm saying I never grew up with a very balanced view of relationships."

Kaczyk pursed her lips. "You think that's why you find it difficult to connect with women?"

Tommy gave her a withering look. "What? No, I think that's because I don't wanna fu—Look. I don't find it hard to connect with women. And I don't think my father's to blame for me likin' guys. It just is, all right? It has nothin' to do with—"

"Did he know? Doesn't strike me he'd have been the most supportive parent."

You unnerstan' me? I will put a gun in your fuckin' mouth, let you suck on that... cocksucker. You want that? You know what that'd do?

Tommy blinked. "He'd never have won Father of the Year, even sober." He peered wearily up at her. "What do you want me to say? He kicked the crap out of me? Yeah... but he did that anyway. He used to call Scott a faggot and a cocksucker, too, and if *he* was any more red-blooded, he'd fall over."

Kaczyk smiled, the dimples by her mouth deepening.

"He looks more like Mom, too," Tommy went on. "Dad used to call him a chink. Say he looked like a poontang baby. That make it equal opportunities crap we had to take?"

The psychologist chuckled softly and made another note on her papers. Tommy watched her do it, mildly annoyed.

"I think you're starting to enjoy yourself here, Tommy," she said. "You're smart, aren't you?"

He shrugged, looking away.

"No, you are. You're smart and you're determined. You graduated high school. Your brother didn't."

"Doesn't make me any better. Brett's goin' to college." Tommy winced even as the words left his mouth. *Damn it.* He hadn't meant to mention Brett. "He's s'posed to, anyway," he mumbled, remembering the money... the money that had paid for the lawyer that had brought this damn woman here in the first place.

Tommy bit down on another burst of irritation. His fingers itched.

She kept smiling at him.

"Yes…. I wanted to ask you about your boyfriend."

"Brett's got nothin' to do with it."

Kaczyk ran a hand over her honey-blonde dye job, smoothing the immaculate strands. "Oh, Tommy, come on. The accessory charge got dropped. You don't need to protect him anymore."

He looked at her for a long moment, then sighed. She wanted to pick through his head, find out what made him tick? Fine.

"Look. When… when you get treated like trash, you act like it. Yeah? You lose pieces of yourself, and it's hard to get 'em back. Y'need someone to… remind you. I never made friends easy. Not good friends. 'Cause people, they see what things are like and they back off. 'Cause it's complicated. It's different. And different frightens people."

Kaczyk nodded, a small noise of encouragement on her lips.

Tommy dropped his gaze to the table and shifted uncomfortably in the chair. "I'd just got used to gettin' by. I didn't think I needed…. Brett never judged me. Not once, not even when—" He stopped abruptly. "He's special. That's why I wanted him to go to Washington and not be… trapped."

"Like you?"

Tommy grunted noncommittally. He remembered watching the Bronco drive off in the dust. The sound of the world breaking around him. The fact that it actually, physically hurt. He'd cried so hard he couldn't breathe.

Don't go…. Had he really thought Brett would have refused? Stayed and bullied him into coping? He wondered if it would have made any difference if he had.

"So, especially after your brother moved out and your mom had her accident, I mean, that left you in a very difficult position, didn't it, Tommy? That make you angry? Resentful?"

He shot her a scornful look, but Kaczyk had turned her attention back to her paperwork.

"And you… you broke up with Brett. He's given his account to Mr. Ribideaux," she added, by way of explanation. "Very eloquent young man. He should be a great defense witness. But tell me, Tommy. All that… totally selfless? Really? You loved him enough to let him go? Or did you want to protect him, maybe, from something you planned to do?"

He stared at her in disbelief. The soft blue eyes had turned hard, and her questions were like belt whips across the back of his head.

"Tell me what happened that night, Tommy."

He didn't… couldn't remember. Weird, because he'd thought— like he'd told the lawyer, even though he hadn't meant to say anything—that he'd see it every time he closed his eyes. Instead, only darkness filled his head, full of hidden things weaving and rustling in the shadows. Snatches of color, of impressions he didn't understand.

"I-I don't know," he said lamely.

Kaczyk leaned forward, her tone hushed and confidential. "You know, it's all right to be angry with the people we love. Especially when they treat us unfairly, or if sometimes they do things we know they shouldn't. If they hurt us. Or if they hurt the other people we're close to."

Something tinged her voice, something… ugly. Anger blistered in Tommy's throat.

"He never laid a finger on Lila before that night!"

Kaczyk's mouth twitched. "Did I ask if he did?"

Tommy blinked. It wasn't even anything in the way he touched her. The way he looked at her. *You're Daddy's girl, aren't you?* She'd started to grow up, they could all see that. And that thought—that black, slimy thought—had crossed Tommy's mind once or twice. When Martin wanted her to sit with him on the couch. When he told her she looked pretty.

"No, he never… he wasn't like that. I'm not like that."

"Tommy?" Kaczyk sounded concerned.

Maybe, but I'm not the one turning into Dad!

He remembered how hard Scott had hit him that night. Tommy pulled himself out of the memory and stared down at his hand. It had started shaking again.

Whassa matter? That your jerkin' hand?

"Look. I did what I did, okay? I... I musta done. There wasn't anybody else there. I don't remember doin' it. Just that he went down. And I panicked, I guess. That's all. I mean, do we have to keep talkin' about it? If I shot him, do the details really matter?"

The psychologist made a note on her paperwork, sleek black pen switching its way through words he couldn't read upside down.

CHAPTER SIXTEEN

MONICA did get mad when she found out about the money. She threw crockery, slammed doors. Brett had the first real argument—the first red-cheeked, testosterone-pumped, face-to-face yelling fight—he'd ever had with his father. The house stayed cold for days after, and he was glad he'd already sent the check to Ribideaux's office.

The days spun into a pale, edgeless mess. There didn't seem to be as many people he could go to as there once might have been. Kevin appeared to always be busy, or so he said. Brett tried going out. He sat in the coffee bar he'd sometimes gone to with friends, opposite the train station. Mainly, he remained invisible. A couple of people whose faces he knew looked at him, and for just a moment, Brett thought there might be someone coming up to say hi, but that didn't happen.

Nothing like that happened. On the plus side, he figured, he didn't actually get spat on in the street. Like he'd always said: Havre was as accepting as a place without real tolerance could be. You just didn't talk about it. Only, what he would have given for someone to talk to.... Brett couldn't get another visit scheduled at the detention center as fast as he wanted, and they told him it could take a couple of weeks for Tommy's phone list to be approved. Yet more thankless, lonely waiting. Brett worried that—if he did too much more of it—he might start hating Tommy again. Easy to do when everything you thought your life had been starts to unravel around you.

Then the first letter arrived.

Dear Brett, it read, and he realized he'd never really seen a great deal of Tommy's handwriting before. The words looked rounded and careful, as if he didn't do that much of it, and he seemed to have a hell of a time keeping the lines level on the page.

Please don't worry. I say that, but I bet you are. And I can't tell you what to do, I know that! But don't. I am all right. I miss you, but I was missing you before I got here, so that's that. There's not much for me to say....

Brett read on, savoring the scant details about the commissary and the conditions, the preliminaries Ribideaux had been organizing, the endless meetings and assessments. The psychologist.

They say it all comes down to premeditation. Mr. Ribideaux says taking the gun is reasonable defense, but the prosecution will say it showed intent. The shrink says I was in a dissassociative state (I think). This doesn't mean crazy, which I'm not. There is a lot of talking. Most of it I think is crap. I don't know what's going to happen, but I know I wish I'd never hurt you.

Those words cut into Brett, but not as much as the last paragraph. Tommy's writing—unaffected, free from flowery prose or high-flown words—struck him all the deeper for it. The way he asked, so simply, if his mother had been doing okay, and if she might come to see him.

I asked Scott when he came, but he said he didn't know. I think he lies as badly as you do. Please write back. I love you.

Brett leaned his head back against his bedroom wall and took a deep breath. Blame him? Yeah. Hate him? Sometimes. But it all paled into insignificance against the way he felt now. He sat cross-legged on the bed that they'd shared those precious few times—never for long enough—and read the letter over and over again until the words blurred.

BRETT shifted nervously on the doorstep. Funny. He'd never been to Tommy's house when he lived there, yet now it was getting familiar. He pulled himself up as the door opened, feeling faintly ridiculous, like he should have brought a bunch of flowers or something.

"Yes?"

Mei's height struck him first, or rather the lack of it. A small woman, with a sharp delicacy to her features and a slim, almost boyish build. It made the neck brace seem even bigger. She moved with difficulty, and he tried to work out how long it had been since her accident. Hell, he didn't know the extent of her injuries, either. Tommy had never even told him.

"Uh.... Brett. Brett Derwent. We spoke on the phone?"

Recognition flickered in her dark eyes. "Come in."

He did so, stepping into the dim hallway. A faint smell of damp permeated the air.

"You'll have to come through. I'm in the kitchen. It's Katie's lunch time."

Brett followed her, watching her stiff walk, the way she held one arm tenser than the other. Tan slacks hung shapelessly from her hips, teamed with a baggy, pale green sweater, her hair pinned into a loose, stubby ponytail at the nape of her neck. In the kitchen, the radio discharged a low babble into the background. A dining set that Brett generously thought of as shabby chic took up much of the small room, butting up against one cool blue wall.

Katie sat in her highchair, a toweling bib around her neck. She looked suspiciously at him as he came in, her mouth bowing into an incipient scream and her pen-stroke eyebrows pulling together. He smiled, partly in greeting to her and partly because, with that wary face, she reminded him of Tommy. Brett saw why Tommy adored his baby sister. She looked worth every one of the photographs pinned up in the Chevy.

Katie looked very solemnly at him, then puffed out her cheeks and made a raspberry noise. Brett grinned.

"Hi, Katie."

Mei glared at him as she crossed to the fridge to get a plastic-wrap-covered bowl with Katie's lunch in it. Brett choked back the smile.

"Um. Thanks for letting me come by. I...." He stopped. What did you say? Sorry for your loss? Kinda weird in the circumstances. "Uh. Thank you."

"I don't know what you want," she said stiffly, uncovering the bowl.

Slightly taken aback, Brett paused. Okay, it had been difficult, discussing it on the phone, but all the same....

Katie swung her pudgy legs, balled her hands into fists, and slammed them against the plastic tray of her chair. "Wanna down," she complained, scowling.

"In a minute, honey," Mei muttered. She placed the bowl in front of her and handed over a wide spork with a cartoon duck on the handle. "Eat up first. You gonna do it yourself?"

Mei turned to Brett, her gaze shifting, her forehead furrowed. He wondered, as she grabbed a towel from the counter and wiped her hands, if she looked older than her real age.

"I mean, I'm very grateful for what you're doing for Tommy. The money, the lawyer... I couldn't have done that. But you can't expect that...." She looked at the floor.

Katie pulled a piece of lettuce out of her bowl and sucked it loudly.

"Excuse me," Mei said, passing Brett and, with difficulty, pulling out a chair. "I can't stand for too long."

He moved, too late, to help her, watching uselessly as she lowered herself into the chair, wincing.

"Can I get you anything?"

She shook her head. Tommy said the doctors had put a pin in her thigh.

"No. Thank you. It... I just don't know what to think, what to feel," she said, after a while. "He's my son. I have always loved him.

Whether he's been good or bad... and he used to act up like anything, he really did. But—"

Tommy? Act up? Brett said nothing.

"I loved my husband," Mei whispered, sounding so close to breaking. "He wasn't perfect, but no one is, you know? And he needed... he needed help."

She avoided looking at Brett, but he saw the tension in her shoulders, the way she hunched in on herself. He'd seen it before. Katie addressed her bowl of chopped lettuce, tomato, and hardboiled egg, watching Brett and Mei with big, wide dark eyes. He wondered how many times she'd seen Mommy close to tears before.

"*We* needed help," Mei corrected herself, straightening up. She flashed him a quick look from under those dark lashes, her face pinched. "But not... I mean, I always found a way to love them both. But not now. Now, my husband's gone, my boy's gone, and... I don't know how to deal with it. With what he is, what he's done."

She held his gaze as if searching his face for some kind of answer. Brett didn't have one, but he didn't have the courage to look away, either. Of all people, how the fuck could she speak like that?

"So,..." Mei shrugged and rubbed her knuckles against the palm of her other hand. "No, right now, with your money and your lawyers and all your concern.... Right now, kid, you can have him."

What the hell?

Mei held up in her hands in a gesture of calm denial. "I'm sorry. I'm sure it sounds terrible, and I don't expect you to understand it. But there it is."

"But—" Brett began, knowing he should just shut the hell up and not say anything, even as his mouth opened. "But he's asking for you. You're not even gonna go see him?"

"No." Mei shook her head, bracing herself against the table as she stood carefully, going to help Katie with her salad.

Brett stared. How could she do that? *Say* that? Hell, he'd been an idiot to come here. As if, somehow, they'd all be one big happy family, and Mei would be grateful to him for helping, that he could see—just like she did—that Tommy's crime, if not excusable, could at least be understandable. Not right, but not evil. She could see that, couldn't she? That he'd made a mistake, not a decision.

Katie looked up at that moment, a piece of egg clutched in her stubby fingers. She looked at Brett, then at her mother, with serious eyes.

"Yucky egg," she said gravely, after a few seconds' apparent consideration, and then stuffed her hand into her mouth.

"Just eat it, honey," Mei muttered. She made another pass with the spork and wiped her daughter's mouth.

"Um." Brett cleared his throat. "Uh, would it be all right if I stayed in touch, though? I mean, if there's visiting orders and stuff, I wouldn't want to take any slots that you or—"

"I told you. I don't wanna see him."

"But—"

"I don't. Not yet. I have too much to deal with. The kids… they ask things I can't answer. He can call me here but, frankly, I don't want to hear him explain anything."

Brett rubbed his hand up and down his arm. He felt cold. Mei looked at him as she lifted Katie out of the highchair, the pain written on her face.

"You think that makes me a bad person? You're appalled by that?"

"No, I—"

"Well, that's tough." She wiped Katie's hands and face with the towel and tossed it down on the table. "You have all the fun you want, playing jailbird Romeo, but how long are you going to wait, huh? Ten, twenty years? More? Last killer in the news 'round here got the needle. You think about that yet?"

Brett said nothing. Of course he'd thought about it. He'd lain awake, sweat-petrified, convincing himself it wouldn't happen. She must have done the same, so how could she be so hostile? So venomous? How could she…?

"I'd probably better go," he mumbled. "I'm sorry I wasted your time."

He left as fast as he could and sat in the Bronco for a moment before pulling away, hands tight on the wheel.

"SHE just doesn't like admitting she failed."

Scott broke the edge off his taco and popped it into his mouth. Brett watched him, a slight frown on his face. They were sitting in Julie Red Dog's. Scott had brought him a holdall with some of Tommy's stuff in it; the things that Mei hadn't let him take and a few other mementoes besides. Some of his crewnecks, some underwear... a stack of photographs held together with a rubber band. Just in case, as Scott put it. Brett suspected that he'd just been being kind.

"What d'you mean?"

Scott sniffed, his attention wandering over the restaurant to where Karen was talking to a couple of guys at another table. One was middle-aged, a long gray ponytail hanging halfway down his back. The other was a younger, thinner version of him, a scrubby beard clinging to his chin and a T-shirt that read "Cuck Fuster" baggy over his skinny frame. They laughed. Scott smiled.

"Y'see that? She looks good on it, you know what I mean? She's starting to walk pregnant now, too." His gaze flicked back to Brett, and he shrugged. "Mom always thought she could cope with him. She'd never have left. She might have talked about it a coupla times, but it wouldn't'a ever come to anythin'. It'd be like saying she failed and she'd never have done that. With this... well, Tommy's said it for her. She'll hate him for that."

Karen patted the older guy on the shoulder and started coming back to their table. Scott had a point; she'd definitely started walking pregnant.

"She'll hate him for killin' the bastard too. She loved him. An'... yeah, I guess we all did." Scott shrugged dismissively. "Bein' a bastard don't stop him bein' a father. And you can't choose who... y'know. I mean, if that's the person you need to feel loves ya, then that's the person you need."

That remark stayed with Brett. They seemed very alike in that way, Scott and his brother. They should both have been philosophers.

Karen sat down, dangerously close to her fiancé. Scott's arm slipped around her, and Brett might as well not have been there. He ate his taco quietly, content in two things. First, that Scott had invited him here. Second—the thing he'd realized only after he started eating—that he was the only white person in the room, apart from one of the fry cooks. And it didn't feel weird anymore.

He finished his meal and tried not to let the cooing and the kissy faces across the table piss him off. Karen wasn't exactly a pretty girl. Engaging, but not pretty. Her small, dark eyes—always on the move—and her lively, animated manner when she really relaxed, like she did with Scott, reminded Brett of an excitable kid. And just as easily as a kid, she could also throw ferocious tempers and have dense black moods. Come visiting time, he tried to find a way of asking Tommy about it.

Tommy smiled, amused by his attempts at tact, and just for a moment, Brett's world glittered.

"Yeah, she has problems," Tommy explained, his voice a little distorted by the phone. "Attention Deficit, depression… a lot of stuff's pretty common with FA spectrum disorders."

Brett frowned. It had seemed like it had taken forever for this visit to come around, and he didn't want to waste it all talking about Karen, but he'd not really dared to ask anyone else.

"Huh?"

"Fetal Alcohol Effects. She doesn't have the full-blown Syndrome, but she still has a tough time with a lotta stuff. Scott manages her though. I think they're well suited."

"Does… I mean, is the baby gonna be all right?" Brett stopped, catching himself sounding like some clucky mother hen. It didn't even feel like his business. Not yet. Maybe not ever; it would always be Tommy's family, not his.

"Sure. It's from drinkin' in pregnancy, it's not congenital." Tommy smiled again. "Aren't you gonna be a doctor?"

That might, some other day, have struck a raw nerve.

Signing the check for the retainer had been one thing. Even as he put it in the mail, Brett had been worrying about the rest of the legal fees. He hadn't known how many there would be; it cost to get the lawyer to meet with the client, to go into court… even just to do some damn paperwork. Brett knew he'd really have to rack up the overtime at Thurston's, though he didn't mind. For one thing, it got him out of the house, out of range of his parents' cold, prickling fury. The job wasn't going so well, though. He'd been passed over for that promotion back in July because he'd been so down after splitting with Tommy. What had Glen said? *Customers need to see a smile, Brett. And team leaders can always smile for the team, whatever the weather.*

He remembered being hard pushed not to be extremely sarcastic.

He didn't want to tell Tommy, but since the day of the arrest, Brett hadn't exactly found himself treated like a potential employee of the month, either. Kevin had warned him about Kirsty Muir and he hadn't been wrong.

She'd been making life difficult in every way she could and probably spent her breaks coming up with new ideas. The snide remarks and the bitching Brett could live with. The gossip, too... but he still had a huge bruise on his foot from where Kirsty had "accidentally" dropped a crate of garden supplies on him.

He said nothing, partly because it wasn't Tommy's fault and mostly because they only had twenty minutes. The detention center had a pretty liberal visitation policy, though it never seemed like that when you were sitting in the cubicle, willing the clocks to stop.

Brett shrugged. "You can't know everything."

"You'll try, though," Tommy said. He rested his hand against the glass and he sounded... proud? "It's so good to see you."

"Glad to be here."

"You speak to my mom yet?"

Brett's stomach lurched, and he wished for all the world he could look Tommy in the face and lie. He dropped his gaze to the bench and knew that he was blinking too fast.

"Uh, I did go over, like I said. Um. She's kinda shaky. She's okay—don't worry—but, I mean, she's not been home that long. She's still taking the pills and stuff. And, y'know, I think everything's just been such a series of shocks...."

All traces of that wonderful smile had gone from Tommy's face.

"She's not coming, is she?"

"She didn't say that."

Tommy curled his lip. "She wouldn't. She'll just let it slide. Do nothin', just sit around and wait for…. God, I—" He exhaled tersely and shook his head. "For once, I just wish she'd meet something head-on."

"Hey, give her time, okay?" Brett tried, desperate not to see Tommy's mood drop. Not now. He'd come here to buoy him up, not depress him. "Scott seemed to think that's what she needs."

"Maybe."

Brett saw Tommy trying to be charitable for his benefit and changed tack. "Okay," he said instead. "Anything else I can do? Ribideaux say when the next prelim is?"

Tommy shook his head and looked away, as if he wanted to mention something but wasn't going to. Brett told himself he'd imagined it.

"Damn lawyers are in and out of here like gophers. I don't know. I'll call you if I hear something."

"Call me anyway? Your list's approved now, right?"

The corner of Tommy's mouth twitched. "How much do those calls cost you?"

"Tommy!"

"All right, all right… I'll call. You know I'll call."

"Good."

Brett couldn't stop the grin that edged over his face. Somewhere, he was lying on a red plaid blanket under an ocean of warm, golden skin that smelled like pine needles and cinnamon. Sunlight bathed the both of them, and time didn't pass except in lazy circles.

"Love you," Tommy murmured.

"I love you too."

Brett supposed it kinda made up for all those times before when they could have said it but hadn't. Now it became almost like a code, their ritual for signing off. And at least he could take that home with him.

TOMMY stared at the familiar scratches on the interview room table. To his left sat Michael Ribideaux, and on his right, Ribideaux's colleague, Carla Nolan, a Blackfoot woman from the same law firm. Opposite them, the prosecutors, Nina Schiffer and Daniel Thomas, were armed with folders of paperwork and incisive arguments.

He didn't understand why he had to be here; most of what they kept talking about went straight over his head, and they weren't bothering to look at him much, anyway.

"Not a chance," Schiffer said. "He took the gun from the house—"

"Unlocked cabinet," Nolan cut in, glancing at her notes. "Readily available, often left lying around."

Schiffer cocked an eyebrow. "Immaterial and you know it. He took the gun, drove to the bar, and lay in wait. Premeditation, pure and simple."

Ribideaux spread out his hands in a conciliatory gesture. "Please, Ms. Schiffer. Prove it. As far as I can see—and I'm sure any jury will agree—my client simply sought to arm himself as a precaution against a violent man."

"Self-defense? I don't think so." Schiffer scoffed. "You take a gun to a knife-fight, proverbially speaking, it's intent. Your client, Mr. Ribideaux, clearly intended to kill his father. Which means, Tommy," she added, addressing him directly for the first time, "you are going to be facing life without parole."

He looked up sharply but didn't get a chance to say anything.

"Ah, I'm surprised you're not trying to scare him with the death penalty," Nolan muttered.

"It ought to scare you, too, Ms. Nolan, seeing as it's a perfectly viable alternative," snapped Thomas.

"In what state, Mr. Thomas? Texas?" Ribideaux's calm tone could either have been a bluff or genuine arrogance. He gave a shark-like smile. "Considering the current moratorium on lethal injection and the extent of the abuse to which Martin Hawks had subjected his entire family, if you really think a jury's going to convict on a death penalty…."

"That's your defense?" Schiffer looked appalled. "Don't tell me you're going to try pleading diminished responsibility. Your client had perfect awareness of his actions and their criminality. A troubled home life is no excuse for a premeditated crime."

Tommy looked numbly between the two of them. Carla Nolan slipped him a brief, small smile. He guessed she meant to be encouraging, but his head was swimming. He couldn't even catch everything that Ribideaux said, though the odd phrase leapt out.

"…having witnessed the systematic physical and sexual abuse of his mother, endured repeated beatings, emotional and verbal abuse, including threats on his life, Counselor. The night of the incident—"

"Oh, come on. Let's be correct about it. The night of the murder?"

Ribideaux looked annoyed. "The night Martin Hawks died, my client was in a state of extreme distress, having witnessed his father violently attack his seven-year-old sister. We have a psychologist's report strongly indicative of a classic dissociative state, and we're all aware of the degree of remorse my client has exhibited over the past couple of days, although," he added, with a pointed look at Schiffer, "he clearly bears little responsibility for any regrettable action in which he may have been involved."

Thomas rolled his eyes. "He doesn't remember? Two shots to the gut and one to the head, and he can't remember doing it? That's convenient."

"Plus he was high," Schiffer put in, glancing at her notes. "Please *do* tell me you're not going for some kind of half-baked attempt to blame it on the pot, Counselor."

Ribideaux narrowed his eyes, and Schiffer's gaze lingered for a moment on Tommy.

"Let's face it," she said briskly. "Any confession or denial on your client's part is irrelevant. The forensic evidence on its own is enough to secure a conviction. There's the DNA, GSR…."

Tommy shut his eyes. The dark inside his head comforted him, private and soothing. He wished he could block out their voices too, and whatever all the goddamn acronyms stood for. He'd missed out on a visit for this… although, and he felt guilty for the sneaking, underhanded little thought, it came almost as a relief to not have to see Brett. Sure, Tommy was grateful for everything he'd done, but things had started to get difficult.

He always tried to be so capable, so strong and yet, somehow, he managed to be a reminder of everything that Tommy had tried to get away from. Everything he'd tried to push away before he turned it to crap... because that's what he'd done, hadn't he? It was what he always did. Touched things and turned them black, wrecked.

He'd done that to Brett's life—how long would it take before he got to med school now?—to his mother's life.... She'd probably never speak to him again. Probably couldn't believe what he'd become. He'd seen that in Scott's face when he'd come to visit, Karen in tow. All those sweaty, nervous comforts through the glass, empty and lost.

He'd had to move back in with Mei because she needed help around the house, and he couldn't meet the rent on the new apartment, so Karen needed to go back to her parents too. They'd decided to put the wedding on hold until... what had Scott said? Until things got more settled. Who knew how long that would take, or what it would mean?

And that wasn't all. Robbie, Lila, and Katie didn't just have to live with what he'd done; they would have to grow up with it. Tommy exhaled slowly, the lawyers' voices filtering slowly, insistently, back into his head.

"...jury would be extremely sympathetic to the circumstances," Nolan was saying. "And, of course, to the defense of the little girl. Because, uh, in so many cases of this kind of domestic abuse, violence is often succeeded by sexual abuse, a statistic all the more common when the child approaches seven, eight, nine... starting to head on up to puberty. Disturbing, but true. I'm sure that—"

What the hell?

"Totally unsubstantiated," Schiffer refuted airily. "And unless you really expect a judge to agree to a warrant for a rape examination on the child—"

"No!" Tommy's head jerked up. "I—God, no!"

"Tommy, it's all right." Ribideaux placed his hand on Tommy's arm. "Nobody's suggesting that's what happened, just that—as Ms.

Nolan says—a lot of cases like yours do escalate into other forms of abuse, and that is something we would want to make a jury aware of."

Tommy looked desperately for some hint in the lawyer's face, some indication that this wasn't anything but a play. They'd talked about statistics before, they'd talked about so much, but not... not raking up the family's business in court. Calling names and making suggestions. He blinked, his eyelids heavy.

He remembered Lila sitting on Martin's lap, him stroking her hair. She had it braided. *Come sit with Daddy.* His hand on her. *You're Daddy's girl, right, baby?* Tommy had felt slightly queasy then, like it somehow wasn't right. But not because his father... he wasn't some kind of pervert, it wasn't that. It was because he had no damn right to confuse her. No damn right to make her think that their family was normal, that everybody lived like that; love and security right up until the monster came out.

He had no damn right to hurt her.

"I don't want that to happen. They can't...!" Tommy took a breath, aware of all four of the lawyers' attention, fixed on him with apparent interest. He spun around to face Ribideaux, frantic and begging. "We can stop that, right? We don't have to do that. Please?"

CHAPTER
SEVENTEEN

BRETT knew something wasn't right from the minute he walked into the detention center's lobby. He exchanged, as he'd been growing used to doing, a few words with some familiar faces. Most of the people waiting for visits were Indian, and—he didn't know, maybe because of some kind of grapevine—by the time he'd come up for his fourth visit, he'd been starting to attract friendly nods and smiles. Mainly from middle-aged women. Brett wasn't sure why; some kind of maternal impulse, maybe. Still, he wasn't about to reject any offer of kindness.

"Hello, Mrs. White Horse," he said, smiling as a woman in a busy floral blouse sidled up to him.

She didn't smile back.

Brett had looked through the photos that Scott had slipped into the bag with Tommy's stuff... and kept back a couple, along with one or two of his shirts. He hadn't thought anyone would mind. A lot of the pictures showed Tommy's paternal grandparents; a short, smiling Assini—no, Nakoda—woman, Brett corrected himself because he'd been trying to learn, and a broad, red-faced white guy with a stubbly beard and a huge smile. They looked happy. So did Tommy in the shots he'd joined them for. Younger... with braces and a nasty case of acne. But happy.

Mrs. White Horse reminded him of Tommy's grandmother. Same kind of blouse, same kind of smile. Only sadder. She worked at the high school on the Rocky Boy rez, she'd told him just last week, as a librarian. She came up Wednesdays through Saturdays to see her son. He'd been waiting to go to trial for six months now.

"What are you going to do?" she asked, touching Brett lightly on the elbow. "It's such a long way."

"I'm sorry?"

"You didn't know?" A look of surprise passed across her eyes. "I heard your friend got on a transfer list... but it could be I'm wrong."

Brett swallowed, then managed to dredge up a sick little smile. Transfer? Why the hell would they trans— *Where* the hell would they transfer him?

"Guess I'll find out," he said, as cheerfully as he knew how.

TOMMY sat down and picked up the phone, barely glancing at Brett. When he did, he wet his lips nervously, not even trying to smile.

"So what's happening?" Brett demanded as he clutched the phone to his ear. "I heard something about you transferring."

"Not just yet," Tommy said gently. "Soon, though."

"Well... transferring? Where? Why?"

Tommy bit his lip. He'd spent the past two days going over this, trying to work out how to tell Brett. He'd wanted to call, ever since Ribideaux had last spoken to him... God, he'd wanted Brett to know. But he couldn't do it in a phone call or a letter. And now he was sitting there, eyes wide, wanting the truth. And he had a perfect right to it. Tommy took a deep breath.

"I'm, uh, I'm goin' to Deer Lodge. I'm takin' a plea bargain."

He could have sworn the temperature dropped by at least ten degrees.

"What?" Disgust etched Brett's mouth.

"It means it won't have to go to trial. You're right, Ribideaux's good. He—"

"He's a goddamned dump truck lawyer is what he is...! I mean, what the *fuck*?"

Tommy sighed. He'd known Brett would take it this way.

Please don't. This is for you... all of you. All the people I love. Can't you see that?

"He didn't rush into it. He explained it to me, we talked it all out…. It's the best option, Brett. Really. I plead guilty to voluntary manslaughter, do ten years, maybe less with good behavior time, take the, uh, the therapy…."

He stopped. Brett did not look happy. A frown settled between his brows and his eyes darkened, his fingers clutching the black plastic phone receiver like it was a poor substitute for Tommy's neck.

"So you're just giving up?"

"No, I…. It's not giving up," Tommy said wearily.

Damn Brett and all his perfect visions of heroic last stands and miraculous acquittals. What the hell did he think? All the DNA evidence and the signed confession would somehow just go away?

That'd be about as incredible as the nightmares stopping.

Tommy pushed a hand though his hair and exhaled. God, Brett could be so fucking naïve. So idealistic. And Tommy couldn't bear the thought of all that getting kicked out of him.

He rubbed the back of his neck and swapped the phone to his other ear.

"Look. If I go to trial, it's a pretty good bet I'm gonna end up with worse. Okay? They got the forensic evidence, the confession—"

"What about the psych report? Huh? Ribideaux said they could move for dissociative whatever-it-is so you weren't responsible, because you—"

"I'm not crazy!"

"No one's sayin' that, Tommy. Just that…. God, can't you let anybody help you?"

Tommy glared at him. He knew Brett regretted saying it by the way he winced as the words left his mouth, but Tommy also knew he'd meant it. Things said in anger often hold the most truth.

"Yeah? And you think I like takin' your fuckin' charity? I might be a lot of things, Brett, but I'm not a damn liar. Way I see it, taking the ten's better than risking life without parole, and it saves putting everybody through all the crap. I don't want that for Mom, the kids, Scott… or you," he added, his voice softening a little. "Can't you understand that?"

"Jesus, Tommy! How important d'you think that is, between a jail sentence and an acquittal?"

Tommy closed his eyes. "I am not gonna *get* an acquittal, Brett. Wake up, will ya?"

"But no jury would…. It was self-defense."

"No, Brett. You can believe that all you want, but—"

Brett sat back, looking like he'd just been punched in the gut. He shook his head dumbly. "So, what? Now you remember? Or you…."

Tommy watched him for a moment, waiting to see if he'd say it. *You always did?* He knew Scott thought that… he'd as good as said it the last time he'd visited. Did Brett take him for a liar too?

Brett stared down at the Formica bench and picked at its scarred surface.

Tommy's irritation evaporated. "I'm so sorry," he whispered, hating to see him look like that. Hating how much worse it made everything. "I never meant to hurt anyone. I just wanted… I wanted to stop it. It's still kinda fuzzy, what happened. But I didn't go there wantin' that. I didn't *plan* to…. You know that, right?"

Brett nodded sulkily.

"I wanted to threaten him, maybe," Tommy went on. He needed to say it, needed to get it out, to make Brett look up. *Look at me.* "I wanted to tell him not to come back to the house. Find somewhere else, someone to…. I-I couldn't let him touch Lila again. Couldn't let him hurt her… any of 'em. We fought, and… I… I remember one shot."

He swallowed, his tongue rough against the roof of his mouth. Slowly, Brett raised his head, a confused frown twisting his brow. He started to speak, but Tommy cut across him, knowing that if he didn't say it now, he might never. If he couldn't give Brett anything else, he wanted to give him all the truth he had.

It would be a goodbye present, maybe.

"The pathologist said the first shot hit in the gut. He might have been drunk, out of control, but it wouldn't have put him down… not for good. I think I panicked. I… I think I got scared." He blinked quickly, his voice almost dropping to a whisper. "I think… I knew if he got up again, he'd kill me. And I was scared of him. Of what he'd done. What he *could* do…"

"Tommy… they mighta bugged these rooms. Don't—"

"That's why I shot him again. And again. That's gotta be what… what happened. Don't you see? In court, it's gonna look bad. I'd have no chance. This is safer. You have to see that."

Brett seemed, briefly, at a loss for words. He sniffed, nodded, and wiped his eyes with the heel of his palm.

"Okay," he said after a moment. "All right. So what happens now? What do we do?"

Tommy just looked at him, in awe and disbelief. *We*. He would, in that moment, have given anything at all to touch Brett. Just a minute. Just to hold him and tell him he was wonderful. He licked his lips. "Brett… this changes things, darlin'."

Brett shook his head, bullish and determined. "No."

"It does. It does…. Ten years. That's a long time. I can't ask you to—"

"You don't have to ask, Tommy. Hell, don't you know that by now?"

"But I don't wanna chain you. I can't—"

Brett pressed his fingers to the glass, cutting across him. "Ten years has got nothin' on us," he whispered fiercely. "You hear me? I promise."

Tommy let out a small, choked breath. Everything he'd planned to say—all his fine words, his noble sentiments, the gentle letdown he'd lain awake on his bunk constructing—was completely lost when he looked at Brett. God, he could be impossible. Tommy tipped the phone closer to his mouth.

Screw goodbye.

"I love you. Love you so much."

"I love you too. Where they sendin' you?"

"Uh…." Tommy swiped at his eyes. *Typical goddamn Brett. Rip me up, then go straight back to base. Asshole.* "Deer Lodge. State pen…. It's about, uh, two hundred fifty miles south. I think."

Brett nodded. "Hm. Well, I guess that's not so bad. Would you do the whole thing there?"

"I guess so, yeah. I won't know more until after the proper hearing. Gotta go before the judge, get the plea bargain ratified, or whatever…. I don't know when, yet," he added, anticipating Brett's next question, "but I'll let you know."

"All right. Is there anything you need? Anything I can do?"

Tommy whistled a breath through his teeth. "Uh…. You can talk to Ribideaux about all the details. He knows more'n me. But, um, I- I'm gonna need to liquidate a few assets, for Mom. Gotta get it all arranged before… you know. So, would… uh, would you sell the truck for me?"

Brett stared. "The Chevy?"

"Yeah. I'm not gonna drive it in here, right? And Mom won't be driving for a while. When she does, she don't like anything bigger'n the Taurus. Scott's got the Pontiac now, so… the money'll come in handy. I thought it'd be better, if she's gotta go, that you handle it."

"I…. Of course. Yeah, sure."

Tommy dredged up a smile. *That's my guy.* Brett might hate the thought—they both knew what that stupid truck had come to represent over the course of this year—but he wasn't going to bitch about it.

They grabbed at the rest of the time, talking about when the hearing—and that transfer—might be. How long they'd have left, here, where at least he wasn't too far away. Brett passed on the news about Karen's latest scans, how she and Scott had said they'd been planning to come by later in the week but now thought they couldn't make it, and Tommy decided he must have been crazy to ever think he could have got rid of Brett so easily.

COUNTING in weeks seemed easier than days. They slipped more fluidly into months, and the rhythms of life crept back in. Brett even started to get used to them again. He quit the job at Thurston's and started work at an old people's home; hardly where he imagined he'd be now, but it did offer some actual medical experience and—better for the pay scale—clerical work. It went a little way to mending fences with his parents too. They found it hard, he knew, to have everything they'd hoped for him and all they'd expected of him thrown back in their faces. To be so torn between disappointment and pride. But, slowly, things were getting better, and Brett found he had what he now thought of almost as a second family to fall back on. Most of his old friends might not speak to him anymore, but these days, Scott treated him like the next best thing to a brother-in-law.

It had felt odd at first, like somehow they expected him to replace Tommy, but as he got used to it, he really appreciated it. It had been Scott who caught him that day at the end of October just standing in the driveway looking at the Chevy. The dying sun glistened on the swells of the truck's dark brown paintwork. He couldn't sell it.

"You gonna come in and eat?"

Brett looked guiltily over his shoulder. He was supposed to just take the details so he could get the ad in the local paper. He'd put it off long enough. *Quick job. Yeah, right....*

"Uh. You're sure your mom won't mind?"

Scott took a last drag on his cigarette and tossed the butt down on the stones. "Nah. She's gettin' used to you, I think."

Brett smiled. Mei did seem less hostile than she had been the first few times he'd met her, but... he could never really feel sure of what she truly felt.

"Listen, Scott? About the truck... would you take an offer? From me, I mean."

Scott frowned. "What d'you want to—"

"I'll buy the Chevy, sell my Bronco. Well, not in that order, but.... You'd get what you'd get for it any other way, of course, just... it'd go to me, not...." Brett faltered, feeling embarrassed. "Forget it. Sorry. Stupid idea."

"Nah." Scott clapped him on the back, hand staying long enough to squeeze Brett's shoulder, a small but powerful gesture. "It's... nice. Tommy'd like that."

Brett exhaled, relieved.

"You're sure?"

"Yeah. Now, c'mon. Pasta in't goin' to eat itself."

BRETT shut the front door behind him. Another three weeks had passed since he'd first put the idea to Scott. Halloween, Turkey Day… all gone by when, somehow, it seemed impossible that they could without Tommy. The days had grown shorter and colder, and Christmas displays festooned the stores. Brett's birthday—December 20th—was approaching ever faster, and he couldn't help but think of how, back in May, he'd been idly dreaming about how they might get to spend both it and Christmas together… whether he'd come home from Washington or if Tommy would be up there with him.

Now, ever having had dreams just seemed stupid.

He tossed the Chevy's keys in his hand, rubbing his thumb over the little red dreamcatcher before putting them in his pocket. Scott had been right; Mei was warming to him, at least a little bit. She'd even gone to see Tommy, just that once before his transfer. Tommy called afterwards but didn't talk about it. He asked about the kids a lot, though.

Brett knew Mei didn't always let them speak to Tommy when he phoned, and, being Tommy, he worried about the cost of the calls. He wasn't alone in that, of course; Brett had thought his father would have a heart attack when he opened the last phone bill and found the detailed little appendix at the back listing all the collect calls from the facility.

Brett, this bill… it's nearly three hundred and twenty-five dollars!

To his surprise, it had been Monica who came to his defense, though she'd needled him afterwards. Asked if he could really be sure he wasn't… what word had she used? Over-invested.

Honey, it's just that you're driving his truck, wearing his shirts….

Brett had tugged guiltily at the crewneck under his flannel shirt, surprised she'd noticed and wishing he'd hidden the holdall Scott had given him a little better. He guessed she'd seen the stack of photos pinned up in his room, too, and wondered just how much snooping his mother had taken it upon herself to do. He'd set his jaw, preparing for her tirade, but it never came. Monica had just sighed softly.

It's going to be harder with him all the way down at Deer Lodge, isn't it?

He'd thought, for a moment, she hoped those two hundred and fifty miles might bring him to his senses, but then she'd hugged him— tight.

If you want someone to keep you company going down for visits... you know I will, don't you, sweetheart?

It meant a lot. And he almost took her up on the offer.

Brett had been bugging Ribideaux for all the information he could get on visiting at the state pen. He followed the advice, got himself on all the right lists, and applied for a contact visit—though he wasn't totally sure what that meant—as soon as Tommy's transfer came through.

It didn't prepare him for how grueling the journey would be.

As IT turned out, "contact visit" meant pretty much the same thing as the regular kind that Brett had been getting used to, but with no glass. The state prison had different hours, allowing much more time, but the rules and regulations were just as stiff and draconian.

The drive was a bitch. Bus services ran north and southbound from the facility, laid on for visitors, but the timetable and coverage were both erratic enough to make the idea pretty useless for Brett.

So, he sucked it up and, tired and gritty-eyed on his eventual arrival, waited like before with the friends and relatives, wives and girlfriends, and submitted to the searches and pat-downs that ensured he had no contraband. He kept his eyes down, stance neutral, trying to ignore the Puerto Rican guy on the other side of the room who—Brett had convinced himself—wanted to knife him.

They trooped into a room painted the same nauseating, pale-green color he'd seen at the detention center, filled with rows of tables and chairs and one correctional officer sitting at the end of every other row to oversee proceedings. The inmates sat, already waiting, and the

sudden lift in the atmosphere caused by all those ecstatic greetings
made Brett feel dizzy. Hugs and kisses were being exchanged, voices
rose in delight... and for a moment he couldn't find Tommy. Then,
Brett spotted him in the far corner, and his feet stumbled as he walked
the length of floor that seemed to go on forever.

Tommy stood up, a queasy smile on his face, looking tired and
thin in yet another set of loose-fitting orange shirt and pants. His hair
was pulled back, though a few strands had escaped and hung over his
face. Nothing mattered to Brett except holding him then. He shut his
eyes against the room, the whole world. Tommy flung his arms around
him, face pressed into his shoulder, breath on his neck, and Brett
hugged him so tight. He still smelled of pine trees and cinnamon, but
also... prison laundry soap?

"All right, champ. Sit down."

They broke reluctantly and took their seats. Brett knew the
rules—one brief hug or embrace on arrival and on leaving, hand-
holding allowed but no passing of objects—but he couldn't help
wishing that the officer who had spoken would drop dead.

He wasn't sure if Tommy wanted to touch him or not. Brett kept
his palms flat on the table, but Tommy sat tucked in on himself, his
shoulders hunched and his body tight.

"You okay?" Brett asked tentatively.

That looked like a fresh bruise on his neck, didn't it?

Tommy's dark eyes flickered, and his hand shot across the table,
gripping Brett's wrist hard, his thumb stroking the soft skin on the
underside of his arm.

"I'm getting along," he said, without much emphasis.

Brett decided not to push it any further. He'd grown used to
correctional officers breathing down his neck, but not like this, all in
with the other visits. It felt kinda claustrophobic.

"So," he said, desperate for something, anything, to break the
way Tommy was looking at him. "You got to see your mom?"

"Uh-huh." Tommy nodded. "And the kids. She brought Lila and
Robbie. I'd started gettin' scared they'd...."

He trailed off. Forget? Brett doubted it. Not two days ago, he'd
seen Scott damn close to tears because Lila had told him about a

nightmare she'd had. How she was scared to go to sleep because a monster with blades for hands came out of the darkness, red-faced and flecked with spittle, roaring and slashing at her. How she'd wake, screaming for Tommy.

"Nah. That's not gonna happen," Brett said. He pulled his wrist gently from Tommy's tense grip, turned his hand over, and took those lean, brown fingers in his. "You know that."

Tommy exhaled tightly. Brett slipped him an encouraging smile, determinedly not thinking of what had him so rattled. Strange, the way this was even harder than talking through the glass. He glanced down at their interlaced fingers. Shit, he hadn't even thought about it... would it be all right, here? Like this?

Tommy squeezed his hand, his voice low and his eyes shiny. "Love you."

Brett took a shaky breath. "Love you too. Are you really all right?"

Tommy blinked and looked down at the table for a moment. "Katie's growing up fast, Mom says. Walking, talking really well now. Had a good first birthday. I heard you sent a present."

Brett forced another smile. That's what you did here. Be cheerful for them. Right?

Oh, God. What's happened?

"She's a cute kid," he said.

Tommy's gaze traced Brett's face slowly, as if committing to memory all the details he must already know. "Yeah," he murmured. "She's gonna practically be in middle school before they even start thinking about lettin' me out of here."

"Tommy...."

"She will. Not to mention the therapy."

The word passed his lips like a curse. Brett guessed the court-ordered sessions weren't going well. He wanted to ask, but Tommy didn't give him the chance.

"And, uh, what about you, huh?"

Brett felt like his chest might split in two. "I'll be here," he insisted. "You know that."

Tommy looked away, his face turning blank. "I never wanted to chain you. I... I don't want that."

Aw, hell... not this again.

"Hey." Brett leaned forward slightly, trying to catch his eye. "Stop it."

"Nah, I mean it. You shouldn't feel like you gotta—"

"I don't plan on makin' five-hundred-mile round-trips from some kinda sense of obligation, Tommy. And," Brett added, seeing his face, "if you say a *word* about gas money, hand to God, I am leaving right now. Okay?"

That got a smile. Just a little one, but a smile all the same. Brett bit his lip, relieved, though still worried.

"So how is it? Compared to Havre?"

Tommy gave a perfunctory shrug. "It's all right. More facilities. There's a ranch... routine's all different, still gettin' into that. I-I'm getting along, okay? How's work?"

If Tommy wanted to play it like that, Brett supposed he had no choice. So, he talked. He told bedpan jokes, and explained how he'd found a correspondence pre-physical therapy degree he planned to start when he'd bankrolled a little bit more. How there'd always be more than one way to do things. He searched Tommy's eyes for some sign he understood that—really understood it—but he looked so blank, so impassive. Like he already had a jail face on.

So, they kept things light. Passed on news. Scott and Karen had tied the knot, finally. Just a simple civil ceremony, with a few drums and a huge blow-out afterwards. The baby would be coming any day now. Brett promised to bring photos when he had them.

He tried to talk small talk, little things about nothing. Tommy didn't make it easy, but being able to touch him, to hear his voice without a phone, and have him almost close enough.... Better than nothing. The time slid by, and the visit ended too soon, though Brett couldn't deny feeling an uneasy, guilty relief that it was all over. He tried to push it from his mind.

He hugged Tommy again before he left, and felt it like the breath would be squeezed out of him.

"Love you, baby," Tommy whispered against his cheek, making Brett's stomach flip.

"Love you too," he assured, knowing he couldn't say it enough. "I love you."

Tommy kissed him then, lips pressing against his briefly, telling him so much more than words could. Brett guessed he'd decided to be honest about himself in prison. He didn't understand it, but he wasn't in a position to complain.

The guard cleared his throat, and they broke apart. Further down the line, a couple got reprimanded for embraces "not kept in good taste." Tommy's hand trailed down the back of Brett's arm as his eyes tried to fit everything he couldn't say into a few inches of airspace. Brett was aware of the looks they were getting. Somebody catcalled. Tommy smiled at him, though, and he seemed better than he had at the beginning of the visit.

"See you, Brett."

Brett nodded. "Yeah. Soon."

"All right."

ON HIS way out of the lobby, Brett noticed the Puerto Rican guy again. He was walking a little way behind, falling in step. Brett hurried up, but he didn't make it out of the door before a voice called out to him.

"Hey!"

Brett wasn't sure what to do. Speed up, slow down, ignore the guy, or turn around. *Shit.* The footsteps behind him sped up, and then the guy jogged through the crowd, overtaking him. They'd got out of the main gates now. The bus had parked a little way down the street, and visitors split off into knots and groups.

The guy stood in front of Brett, tall, muscular, shaven-headed, with a black goatee. Maybe twenty-five? An ornate tattoo, possibly of an eagle, curled up the side of his neck. Battered black low-rise jeans hugged his hips, and his hands were burrowed deep into the pockets of a washed-out and well-worn red fleece. He looked over his shoulder, then pulled one hand free of the fleece, reached out, and tapped Brett on the arm in a familiar kind of way. Brett almost flinched, but he wasn't bleeding and, well, the guy actually seemed friendly.

"A'ight?"

Brett didn't register him speaking at first, still busy trying to catch up. "Uh," he managed. "Hey."

"Javier Tavarez. I, ah, I just wanted to say that, you know, it gets easier, man."

Brett guessed he must have looked confused, because Javier smiled. A very big smile, with a gold tooth in it.

"Uh...?"

"Roberto's three years into ten to twelve, and still they ain't transfer him home to California. I get to come up maybe once a month. At first it's hard, but it gets easier. You know?"

Realization slowly dawned on Brett. His eyes widened even as he felt like a complete idiot. Questions burst inside his head—no, seriously... this guy was gay?—and slowed up his reactions even more. Javier curled his lip, looking at him as if he was a complete moron.

"I, uh.... Thanks," Brett managed. "I didn't realize. Uh."

"Roberto says your boy's name's Tommy, yeah?"

"Yeah."

Javier stuck his hands back into the pockets of his fleece; Brett guessed the Northern climate came as something of a shock to him.

"He'll be fine. You shouldn't worry about it, man." Javier chuckled to himself, and shot Brett a strange sideways glance. "Nobody can suffer as much as someone who's young an' in love, right?"

Brett blushed furiously. This was embarrassing. Far more so than talking about his and Tommy's relationship with their parents, the police, the lawyers... but it was also strangely uplifting.

"Yeah." Javier gave him another shiny, metallic grin. "I'll see you around, kid. And don't worry. My man gonna see to it ain't nobody shit your boy. They on the same floor. Now, I got a bus to catch. Keep strong, uh...?"

"Brett."

"Brett. A'ight."

And, with that he left, jogging away through the knots of people and climbing aboard the southbound bus. Brett watched him go and, after, he hung around for a while in town, bought a cup of coffee, and stared at the sky before contemplating the drive home.

Funny, but just when he thought he'd started to get the world back into focus a little bit, something like that always seemed to happen.

CHAPTER
EIGHTEEN

GETTING the world back into focus did take a long time. Not an effort
to make things the way they'd been; that couldn't happen and probably
wouldn't even have been desirable, but it was important to make a new
bedrock. A fresh ground stable enough to build on, even if somehow,
the best thing about it was knowing it wasn't permanent.

Brett knew better than to talk to Tommy about "one day," but he
still thought about it. They built their routines around letters, phone
calls, those ass-busting round-trips that Brett made, even the time he
knew he was coming down with the flu and ended up having to stay
two days in a motel at Deer Lodge before feeling well enough to drive
home.

Tommy kept up with his therapy, as his plea had demanded, but
he also joined an educational program. With a solid record of good
conduct—excepting a couple of scuffles in the first few weeks that
Brett *knew* must have happened, but which the stubborn bastard
wouldn't say a goddamn word about—he even managed to get work
on the facility's ranch. That brought him out into air that, while too
close to the cattle to really be called fresh, must have felt sort of like
the outdoors. Brett was proud of him. And slowly, Tommy seemed to
get used to the strictures and the routines and the way that society
inside worked.

He changed. Brett saw that.

From the first time he noticed that deadened, withdrawn look in
Tommy's face, it scared him. Over the course of their visits, he'd
loosen up and smile and talk and be almost himself… but Brett had the
feeling it still lingered somewhere inside. That dim lifelessness.

It took Brett almost three years to scrimp together the money for college. His plans had changed a little; physical therapy would take slightly less time and money to establish himself in than full medical training, and being able to do a lot of the preparation through the correspondence course helped. A series of low-paying healthcare jobs provided experience and funds, but for the body of his actual training, Brett would still need to go to Washington State... the Vancouver campus. It put him off.

"It shouldn't," Tommy protested, time after time. "You should go. I want you to. Go. Spread your wings."

Brett relented, like he'd known he would, because he knew he couldn't stay working as a glorified candy-striper forever, but he hated the thought of not being able to get down to see Tommy as often. Tommy seemed less... needy these days, true. And he had friends, Brett knew. Of a kind. There was, for example, Javier's partner, Roberto, who turned out to be six-feet-four and built like a barn. Brett guessed he was a good guy to have on your side, though he privately admitted to a gnawing jealousy of the man, and a certain degree of fear.

They didn't talk about it. Brett didn't want to know..., or, at least, successfully pretended that he didn't. Tommy said it was okay. Tommy said prison wasn't the way people thought, and he was all right because the guys on the unit watched out for each other. He had friends, he said, who made sure he didn't have any more trouble than what he brought on himself.

He explained it in those terms, anyway, and the description made Brett's skin crawl, right up until the day he first found out Tommy had done something stupid.

It being high summer, the days could hit up to the low seventies this far south in the state. When Brett saw Tommy favoring his left shoulder—wincing when his sleeve pulled against the top of his arm— he thought it was the heat, but his face looked a little sweaty and feverish. Icy terror squeezed Brett's chest. Could he be getting sick? Flu, or the start of something worse?

Please, no.

"You okay?" he asked.

Tommy nodded. "Yeah, I'm fine. Just… sore. Itchy. I…." He lowered his voice and glanced briefly at the guard. "I got ink. Can't show you, but—"

"You did *what*?"

"Well, I… Brett, what? Whassa matter?"

The panic didn't even have time to condense into anger; it suddenly flipped, like the tumble of falling masonry, tempting Brett just to get up and walk out. Who cared how long he'd have to wait to get here again, if this kind of crap happened as soon as he left?

"How could— I mean, why would you do that? So stupid!" he hissed, scowling. "What the fuck were you thinking? You could've caught anything. Hep C, HIV… that didn't even cross your mind?"

"Brett…."

"Christ, Tommy! Why?"

Tommy just stared at him for a moment, then his face shut down, a muscle twitched in his jaw, and he looked at the table, nothing else to contribute but a shrug.

That fuckin' jail face again.

Brett said nothing. He didn't trust himself not to yell.

"Can't expect you to get it," Tommy muttered. He glanced up at him again, cool-eyed and disdainful. "You're never gonna know…. Nah, you know what? It's done now. The guy's safe, uses clean needles, cleans his machine… and he's good. Says you can make real green money doin' it."

"Tommy!" Still angry, Brett heard the note of begging spring unbidden into his voice. Heard it, hated it, but hoped it would work.

"All right." Tommy relented with a sigh. "I'll get tested."

"Thank you. And… just don't get anything else done. Please? You want tattoos, you can get 'em when you get out."

Tommy glared at him, and Brett shut up, slouching sullenly in the hard plastic chair.

After that, he didn't feel so bad about Washington.

THE anger wore off, though. And, although what Brett now thought of as his whole family—Monica and Stephen, but also Scott, Karen, and their son, Atian (born a little under two weeks after their wedding), Mei, Lila, Robbie, and even Katie—thoroughly supported him, proud and full of love, he hated leaving.

I could never leave Montana... my feet are frozen to the ground.

Stupid line, but he and Tommy had laughed about it—once. Seemed like a lifetime ago.

Brett was paralyzed with homesickness for the first two weeks solid, and being older than most of the other students, even if not by much, didn't help. But it passed, and as he settled into campus life, Brett thought of the irony of it all. He'd once imagined this as the awakening, the threshold of his life; that he would somehow find here the space, the time, and the acceptance to learn who he could become. He'd fantasized about meeting his Mr. Right at college, or at least his first Mr. Right Now, because he'd never really thought that he believed in love either being perfect or lasting forever.

He'd thought, somehow, that he'd taste everything and he'd have every opportunity. As it turned out, there really wasn't anyone who caught his eye for a second glance and—even if there had been, and whatever Tommy had said—that whole idea still seemed like forbidden fruit.

Besides, Brett was busy.

He worked hard, learned a lot. He joined the GLBT students' association, used the gym, and took up running. He made friends: Emma, who could be a little blonde but, despite the green nail polish, could also actually be both really sweet and really smart; Tori, the bi-femme goth chemistry grad; and Nick. Hardworking, talented, confident Nick, who took Brett aback twice at the Spring Ball, first by trying to kiss him and second by taking it so easily, so comfortably, when Brett pulled away and ran.

"So, you're spoken for?"

They sat in a coffee bar not far from the biology school. Emma had just left to get to her class, leaving them alone—albeit in a crowd—for the first time since that night. Brett shifted in his tubular steel chair and prodded at his cappuccino with a spoon.

"Yeah, there is somebody."

"Lucky guy. In Montana?"

"Mm."

Nick watched him for a while, his green eyes soft behind his glasses. He didn't demand, didn't ask questions... just drummed his fingers quietly against the side of his iced coffee.

They didn't talk about it for a while after that.

MAINLY, Brett managed to keep his relationship with Tommy from his friends. He'd still go back to Montana as often as he could, pulling extra bar work to cover the costs, and he paid to have the correctional facility calls routed to the house he shared with Emma and two of her friends.

The calls eventually got him busted.

"Oh, and there's a weird message on the answering machine," Emma said, taking a low-fat yogurt out of the refrigerator.

"Yeah?" Brett dumped his books on the kitchen table. Could his mother not go one day without worrying? Maybe it'd be something about the upcoming seminar on muscle atrophy he'd been planning to go to.

Bound to be one of the two.

"Uh-huh." Emma peered at him over the yogurt, wide-eyed and curious. "Like a creepy call or something. Just part of a recorded message... probably one of those sales things, huh? Said something about a facility or—"

"Shit!"

"What's the matter?"

"Shit, shit, *shit*! Fuck!"

"Brett? What?"

He stared at her in all her blue-eyed, bouncy-curled idiocy.

"No, I'm sorry, Emma.... It's just a friend of mine. I didn't know he'd call, but I should be here to take the calls if.... They're collect. If

you don't select to take it when you get the recorded message, they....
God!"

Brett exhaled deeply. Three years, and he hadn't missed one
fucking call. Not one. But Tommy had always said when he planned to
call and, this time, he hadn't mentioned it.

Oh, shit, what if something's wrong?

Something must have happened. Brett had spun out a dozen
catastrophes in his head before realizing Emma was staring at him.

"Your friend calls you collect? All the time? Is this the guy
you... *the* guy?"

He made a face. He really didn't want to talk about this now. She
knew he had somebody back home, after what had happened with
Nick, but no more than that.

Emma frowned. "How come? What is he, in prison? Or is he just
cheap?"

His gaze flickered briefly and she gasped. Brett's heart sank as
Emma gawped at him in a combination of awe, fear, and excitement.

"Emma...."

"Oh my gosh, he *is*, isn't he? Really? What'd he do? Oh! I'm
sorry." One green-tipped hand clamped over Emma's mouth, and her
eyes grew even wider. "You're not s'posed to ask that, are you? I just
never knew anyone who... uh. Wow."

Brett smiled weakly. "Yeah. I'd, uh, be really, really grateful if
you didn't mention it. Not that it's a secret or anything, but there's
really no reason anybody needs to know. Okay?"

She nodded fervently, and he knew she meant it. He just didn't
believe she could possibly be capable of keeping anything quiet.

"You wanna go get some coffee?" he asked, partly because she
was still looking at him like he had two heads, and partly because he
couldn't bear the thought of Tommy, left hanging on an empty phone
line.

THE fact that Emma tried not to spill it humbled Brett. She really
tried... for all of about three days. Even so, he found it a relief to have

his friends know. He told himself he didn't mind. After all, it wasn't like he could ever be ashamed of Tommy. Sure, it would have been nice to have a part of his life left totally untouched by the penal system and its grim, arid grip. Equally, it would have been nice not to wake up every morning and wonder what Tommy would be doing, if he was okay, what had happened in the night, whether today would be the day he got told he'd got a transfer to Shelby or Great Falls—or worse, out of state—due to overcrowding. It was easy to feel far too familiar with all the rules and regulations, the visits and the privileges, until they started to change the way you thought.

Up until Montana actually instituted proper drink-and-drive laws, it hadn't been uncommon to hear slightly idiosyncratic measurements of distance; Brett remembered, years ago, his father referring to Glacier National Park as "a six-pack drive" away. These days, he found himself thinking in terms of how far he could drive in a round-trip without having to stop over at a motel. The visits ran from two until seven, and he hated to miss a minute, even if it meant not getting home until the early hours of the morning.

So, yeah… Brett had to admit that having people to bitch to could be invaluable. Especially the times life seemed so unfair that he couldn't stand it, like if he made the trip only to find there'd been a lockdown, or Tommy had been sent to the clinic and wasn't accorded a visitation privilege that day. It felt good to have people who knew, though he hated that the knowledge raised questions for them.

Questions Brett *really* didn't want to answer.

"It must be so tough, though. Physically. I mean…." Nick popped open another beer. "You only get to see him for supervised visits? No—"

"Nick," Tori warned from her seat on the floor by the couch.

Thursday nights had become a regular kind of refuge for them. Mindless action movie on the tube, popcorn, pretzels, and beer on the coffee table: the students' essential relaxation equipment.

Nick held up his hands innocently. "I'm just saying," he protested. "I don't know how you stand it. I think I'd explode."

He shut up as Tori hit him in the thigh, and Brett managed to laugh it off.

Later, when the girls had gone to bed, Nick apologized.

"I didn't mean... I'm sorry if I offended you. I'm not, like, totally sexually obsessed, I just... I'm actually kinda awestruck. You must really have something special with this guy."

Brett laid his head back against the couch. Tired and buzzed from a long week, he got a little bit raw just talking about it. "Yeah," he said. "Guess so."

"You two together a long time?"

"Uh-uh." He shook his head. "Well... comin' on four, four and a half years, I guess, but he's been—I mean, we haven't... y'know. That's what's crazy. We had maybe six months, sneaking around, before everything went all... uh, before it got complicated, right? I wanna say I knew he— that I knew we had somethin' special," Brett corrected himself, taking another swig of his beer. "But I didn't. Before Tommy, I'd never been with a guy before. I had no idea what to expect, but he made it all so easy.... He's incredible."

Brett stopped, embarrassed. It felt weird, talking to Nick like this, knowing he could understand and—more than that—that he understood not just falling in love, but falling in love with another man. And for all his feeling that— gay, straight, or bi—love was love, Brett knew that the differences still mattered.

"He better be." Nick took off his glasses and polished them on the hem of his sweater. "You deserve that."

Brett looked away quickly, an uncomfortable smile wreathing his mouth. He knew Nick found him attractive. It excited him, but he also found it kind of unsettling. He stifled a belch, wondering if, just maybe, he might be slightly drunk.

"So, what did he actually do?" Nick asked.

Brett knew he had to be drunk when he told him. To his credit, although Nick froze, his glasses still half-polished in the folds of his sweater, he didn't say anything except "oh."

"He got ten years. Voluntary manslaughter," Brett explained. "He wouldn't go to trial... took a plea bargain. He coulda been acquitted, with the right jury. I mean, his—the guy... he was violent. It was self-defense. Practically."

"Right." Nick nodded and put his glasses back on. He reached for his beer. "S'a hell of a long time, though. For you too. Prob'ly more for you... isn't it?"

Brett blinked, tried to shrug it off. He didn't want to admit it, but Nick had a point. He curled his lip.

"Mmnn. It's.... I mean, I can see him. He can call me. I can't call him, but.... And we write. I visit. It's hard, bein' up here, 'cause I can't go as much as—"

"Yeah, but you're really gonna say you don't miss holding him? That you're gonna go ten years without some lovin'? Hell, guy! It's one thing to say you got some pure, spiritual connection, but my balls'd burst."

Brett looked at him, wondering whether to be mad or not. Nick gazed back lazily and after a beat, they both laughed. Nick got up to get another couple of beers and instead of going back to his chair he flopped down on the couch next to Brett.

"I mean," he said, very solemnly, holding up his bottle as if to make a toast, "I think it's beautiful. I couldn't do it. They musta been some crazy six months."

Brett laughed softly. "Yeah, kinda. I-I don't know. Guess I gambled on what we could be."

"See? That's what I think's beautiful," Nick said, clapping him on the thigh as he swigged his beer. "He think the same?"

Brett frowned. Nick hadn't taken his hand away. That wasn't the strange thing, though. He shifted, suddenly aware of the heat rising to his face and the blood rushing to his crotch.

"Y-yeah," he managed. "We'... solid. I'm not saying it isn't har—it isn't difficult, I mean. Uh. Yeah."

Nick squeezed his leg, and Brett swallowed heavily. He tried not to think of Tommy telling him to get on and live his damn life; that it didn't matter. It *did* matter. It mattered to Brett. Only it had been so long. Such a long time. Nick seemed a hell of a lot closer than he'd been two minutes ago. Brett felt his breath, warm on his ear, his neck. Nick... neck. Huh. His hand, making the switch from thigh to groin, like the most natural thing in the world, groping Brett through his jeans.

"Oh," Brett murmured, half-expecting to find Tommy's name on his lips.

But it wasn't there. No words passed between them at all as Nick unbuttoned his fly, touching him so slowly, giving him all the time in the world to say no. Brett closed his eyes, his mouth dry, letting it happen. He knew there might be the vague possibility that someone could walk in, but even that didn't worry him. Not now.

The breath sang in his throat as Nick leaned forward, taking Brett's cock in his mouth, sucking him off twice without stopping. Brett spread his arms out along the back of the couch, the beer bottle still clasped tightly in his fingers. Nothing existed but the pleasure. The feel of him. Nick's short brown hair under his fingers as Brett held his head, insisting, instructing, in a way he'd never done—never had to do—with Tommy. The sound of Nick, jerking his own cock inside his jeans.

It seemed like it took him forever to finish.

"Feel better?"

Nick sat up, his chin still glossy. He licked his lips, his eyes and cheeks bright. It threw Brett off center.

"I.... Yeah. Um...."

"It's all right." Nick stood and zipped up his fly. "No strings, 'K? If you want. If... if you need it."

BRETT'S first thought when he sobered up concerned kicking Nick's ass. The second... well, wasn't exactly about kicking it. He was still furious with him, though, and furious with himself for letting it happen.

The whole incident made him dread Tommy's next call. Brett wanted to tell him about Nick, but not in a letter, and the next visit seemed so far away. They'd agreed—well, Tommy had said—that it wasn't a problem if he wanted to play. Brett'd had to admit it seemed like a sensible, rational plan... though he'd made it clear he didn't intend to and that, if Tommy did, he didn't want to know about it.

They'd segued into another one of those not-quite-fights that they'd started getting so good at. Brett loathed those. Not just for the time they spent circling, sniping at, and irritating each other, but because for days after, he'd think maybe he'd been persuading himself to believe in something he shouldn't. That maybe he'd bound himself to Tommy before he'd really understood what it meant.

Monica had tried to warn him of that right from the start, back when she was still so shocked and angry, her spite an ineffective weapon. He was too young to do this, she'd wailed, too young to know what he was letting himself in for. Brett remembered yelling at his mother, his childish anger probably, in her mind, proving her point, but he'd refused to back down.

He loved Tommy, he'd protested, and that was almost all of the truth.

The guilt was always there, though, and now it was just winding out into new ways of needling him. He hadn't helped Tommy that summer, when he should have, and now maybe they were destined to pay for that together, everything that had been so bright and wonderful tarnishing into resentment and contempt.

I can't even wait for him like I said I would. Fuck....

Brett hated being so powerless. Unable to confess, to ask for Tommy's absolution; always waiting for his calls, his letters. Always subjugated to the constant routines, strictures, the waiting... focusing on the little moments, the pretences of normality they could snatch.

Tommy would be thirty-one, almost, by his release.

Until then, what could there be for them?

They'd already changed. Brett knew that. Both of them. He'd never expected to stay the same person he'd been that summer—he hadn't expected it of Tommy either—but on the darker days, it mattered. In the blackest throes of it, Brett could almost convince himself that he'd only been clinging on to something he'd invented in his own head, that they'd never really had anything more than some stupid adolescent fling.

Then, Tommy would send him the visiting order he'd been waiting for, and he'd make the long, long trip to Deer Lodge, and in those few precious hours it would all change again.

The phone calls were almost as bad.

"But...."

Brett sat at the kitchen table, eyes stinging, not sure whether he hated the anger or the humiliation more. The phone felt hot and cramped against his ear, and Tommy's voice was infuriatingly calm, echoey with static and understanding.

"It's all right to need your itches scratched, hon. I told you."

It wasn't the reaction Brett had pictured from him. He swallowed. *Damn it.* He'd worked himself up into fits of incredible angst over coming clean about Nick, and this was what he got? He didn't know what to say. The silence seemed craggy and insurmountable... and it cost over three bucks a minute.

"Yeah, but—" He swiped at his eyes with the heel of his palm and glanced at the clock. "A-Are you?"

Tommy laughed, sending the line crackling. "We don't have itches. We have flea powder."

Brett smiled wetly. He didn't care if Tommy was telling the truth or not right now.

"I'm sorry. I just.... Are you mad at me? Truly?"

"Not mad. Never mad at you. Jealous, maybe. A little bit. It hasn't fallen off, ya know. And you know I miss you. But I never wanted you to feel bad, remember? I never wanted—"

"Chains. I know, I know. I love you."

"You too, babe. You still okay if I send a VO for the fourteenth?"

"You know it," Brett murmured, and that made it easier, knowing that, for them, things remained as near normal as they ever got.

Still, it wasn't the only time over the next three years that he resorted to Nick.

In amongst all the stuff Brett learned at college, Nick taught him that sex needn't involve the soul or the mind, or even that much attraction between the participants. They arrived at ground rules that helped Brett keep his sense of detachment—no kissing, no anal, no touching in public—and then worked on slowly eroding them away.

Nick treated him as a friend rather than a lover, yet through him Brett gained a wider experience of his own body and its capabilities. It almost matched up to the fantasy he'd had of college life, though Nick never came close to Tommy in any number of ways, and that scared Brett almost as much as the fact he'd already known he wouldn't.

Nick had great qualities: he could be gentle, sympathetic, giving, and open-minded. He didn't bitch about the restrictions Brett put on them, complain about his refusals or his inevitable low days. He took every bad mood without protest or criticism, and Brett supposed that explained why he didn't want him.

It sucked. He wished he did; Nick was everything he'd hoped to find in a college boyfriend, the epitome of that long-held dream. Even worse than that, he was actually a nice guy.

And yet, he only made Brett miss Tommy more.

CHAPTER NINETEEN

"REALLY? You really mean it?"

Tommy nodded, trying to keep the grin off his face. "Yeah. I mean, it's not… nothing's certain, and a lot of guys don't make it on their first and even their second hearings, but—"

Brett shook his head, still reeling from even the idea of it. Tommy had said he had news in his last letter, but this…! He couldn't have hoped for this.

"How long?"

"I make the petition, it's maybe four, six months 'til the hearing, then waiting for the decision…. Eligibility isn't gonna make it automatically happen. Listen. Brett, listen… will you do some stuff for me?"

It was a pretty quiet day, the visiting room only about half-full. When he'd arrived, Brett had found it mildly depressing that he knew at least eight of the wives and girlfriends waiting to visit. Not that the way they treated him wasn't… nice, in lieu of a better word.

Visiting as Tommy's openly gay partner hadn't always been easy, but Brett had been surprised, the first time he got real hassle, to find a slew of women standing up for him. Like he represented some kind of cuddly mascot. Yeah, it felt… nice. Emasculating and kind of humiliating, but nice. He'd wondered if Javier got the same treatment but found it kinda hard to picture anyone giving him grief in the first place, plus he didn't seem to visit so much these days.

Brett kind of wondered if something had happened, but asking felt stupidly like bad manners, or as if maybe he shouldn't risk jinxing him and Tommy by raising the specter of someone else's failure. For all he knew, Javier could have caught time himself.

Right now, though, Brett didn't want to waste a minute thinking about anybody, any*thing* else. All the petty troubles and the limitations and even the goddamn five-hour drives didn't matter, and he was floating on air. Parole. It could mean, in theory, that Tommy would be a free man in as little as, what? Ten months? He'd served six years. Long, long years, but…. Brett blinked, trying to focus on what Tommy was asking of him, what he needed.

"…letters. Y'know. In support of, uh, how great I am. I don't know… family, clergy, bank managers. Everybody we can get. And I need…."

Tommy paused, tucked his hair behind his ear. Brett watched that familiar mannerism, watched the hair brushing Tommy's jaw. He wished he hadn't cut it shorter.

"A housing plan?" he prompted, quirking an eyebrow. "I read up on this too, you know."

Tommy smiled and, for a moment, Brett thought he'd reach for his hand, but he didn't.

"I called Mom this morning to tell her. She says there's room for me at the new house," he said, still calling it that though Mei and the three kids had been living there for more than two years now. "So—"

"You could come to me," Brett said, a little reproachful.

He regretted it, because he knew he should give Tommy time and anyway, Mei was his mother. There had been a time when it hadn't seemed like it would ever happen, but she did want him home. Or so she said.

"I mean, it's not like I don't have enough room in the apartment. Guess it's just which would look better on the report, huh?"

Tommy shot him a look of gratitude, and Brett understood it.

"All right," he said. "I-I'll get the letters started. Your old boss, in Burnham… he'd be worth checking out, right?"

"Guess so, yeah. That'd be a bit of continuity too, maybe."

Brett nodded. Tommy had finished a vocational degree in carpentry in the summer; he probably had better qualifications than his former employer by now. The tribal council, in addition to the programs that—if you dug deep enough, for long enough—could be found to help prisoners, had been great for him.

Not only that, he'd completed all the violent-offender classes and all the therapy they'd made him do. He'd got six years' good conduct, more or less… he'd taken part in sweat-lodge ceremonies, for crying out loud. What did you call it? Wa inipi, Brett thought. He'd tried to keep up. Karen had been really sweet and tried to explain it all to him. She'd invited him up to the Milk River Indian Days thing in July, and it had been pretty incredible to go to a pow wow as something different, even if only slightly, than just another white guy with a camera.

So, Brett crammed his head with all the stuff he'd have to do, ready for the petition. Letters to send, testimonials to request, plans to make… but Tommy looked happier than he'd been in so long, and that filled Brett up so much that nothing else mattered. Not even the thought that a parole application didn't mean a parole request granted, or the thought that, if Tommy did get out, it would only be the start of what they had to face.

"YOU oughta stop worrying about it," Scott said as they sat on his deck knocking back a beer later that weekend.

Brett shrugged. Half past eight on a September evening, the nights still pretty mild. Indoors, Karen was trying to convince Atian to at least stay in his room, even if he wouldn't go to sleep. Scott glanced over his shoulder and swore as sounds of a scuffle broke out.

"Ah, screw it. Back in a minute, Brett."

"Sure."

With a grunt, Scott got up and went in the back door, muttering about kids and the trials of his existence. Brett listened to the five-year-old's inevitable wailing yell of temper and the pounding of his feet on the floor. He looked around in time to see Scott carrying his son, upside down, back to bed, threatening him with stories about how bears came down to eat unruly children in the night. Atian squealed, wriggling in his father's arms. He'd not long ago started kindergarten, and already his teachers had begun making noises about ADHD.

Over the scene of domestic chaos, Karen caught Brett's eye and shot him a grin. He smiled back. Scott was right; he shouldn't worry. If the board granted parole first time around, great. No, more than great: amazing, fantastic, incredible, but… if not, it didn't matter. They'd still made it more than halfway through Tommy's time, and they'd stayed strong.

Yeah, right.

That would be like letting a high-stakes poker game roll as if the outcome meant nothing… and it did feel a little bit like poker. They took their time over building a really good hand: letters of support from everybody that Brett could beg, bully, or bribe into writing, detailed plans for how and where Tommy would live… even a letter from his old firm in Burnham, saying they would possibly be interested in taking him on, parolee or not.

Brett had sweated blood over that one.

After that, they couldn't do anything but wait. Ironic that the waiting seemed so busy—so full of nerve-racking, gut-churning worry and so much nit-picking from Tommy. As the decision got nearer, he got worse. He was grumpy, permanently stressed out… bitchy, even. Brett threatened to quit visiting and put a block on his phone calls at one point, only half joking.

"I'm sorry, baby," Tommy murmured and squeezed his hand across the table. "I don't mean it. I'm an asshole."

"It'll be over soon," Brett said, holding onto his fingers, not wanting to let go of the comforting weight of his hand. It wasn't enough—it wasn't ever going to be enough—but he needed something. "One way or the other."

Tommy snorted. "Yeah. I just hate the fuckin' waiting."

"I know. I know."

Brett tried to smile, but it turned to ashes in his mouth. They'd done nothing but wait for years and, hell, he'd got so tired of it.

BRETT focused on work, like he'd grown used to doing. He found it easy enough. He'd started a new position at the hospital's physiotherapy clinic, lived in a cheap apartment down by Rotary Park, and he had plenty to keep him busy, because he'd spent years making sure that he did.

Slowly, the months inched past, and from time to time, he even forgot about the impending hearing. Then, of course, Tommy would call, and they'd go back into that circle of reassuring, wondering, and panicking over all the details. Sometimes, there were tears.

"Baby, don't…."

Brett sat on his kitchen floor, the phone pressed to his ear, his back resting against the second-hand refrigerator. It had a picture of a clown—or possibly Karen—that Atian had drawn, fastened to the door with a plastic magnet next to a photo of Katie in her first-grade Christmas pageant, apparently dressed as a cranberry. They'd all started growing up so fast.

"I'm sorry, I just…. I wanna come home."

"I know. Believe me, I know. You just hold on a little longer, all right?"

"I don't know if I can."

Brett bit his lip. Not now. Not after all of this. He searched for some intense, motivational little speech, something—anything—he could say, but came up blank. A horrible, hollow feeling. Tommy sniffed, the line choking up with static.

He hadn't had a downer like this in a long while. They happened, sometimes, and it didn't even need to be any single thing that set it off. Just the weight of it all, maybe. He'd call and cry, and Brett was supposed to make it better.

"You can," Brett said softly. "You just hold on. You've been doin' it for long enough. You can do it. Okay?"

The words sounded worthless, even to him. He banged the back of his head slowly against the refrigerator a couple of times, but it didn't make him feel any better. Eventually, Tommy pulled himself together, and they went through their rituals, talking about the kids, Brett's work… swapping I love yous just before the thirty-minute cut-out.

Brett stayed sitting on the floor for a while, the phone still in his hand. He felt useless and dirty, like he should have had the right words, should have been able to find them instead of just being so fucking empty, and so damn tired.

That night, not for the first time, he dreamed about the parole decision.

Brett dreamed that they waited and waited, only to be told it had been denied and the process would have to begin again. The waiting, the cold, hard, indeterminate waiting went on and on, and it happened in the kind of time that exists in dreams, viscous and endless. He dreamed that they ended up hating each other for everything that they'd been, everything that still kept them bound together.

Brett woke suddenly, his breath short and the alarm clock by his bed flashing 3:32 a.m.; it had only been a dream, right? Fumbling somewhere between waking and sleeping, he leaned down to the drawer in his nightstand and snagged one of Tommy's shirts, pulling it on before he burrowed back under the covers. Dreams weren't premonitions.

He tugged at the sleeve of the crewneck and tried to get comfortable again. Tommy's shirts had never been that great a fit to start with, but Brett had broadened more since he'd started wearing them. He turned his pillow over and pressed his cheek into the cool cotton. What if, when Tommy did get out—on this hearing or not—his freedom wasn't enough? What if what they'd had couldn't be brought back, couldn't be saved? It might be too different, too… damaged.

No. No, that's not…. It won't happen like that.

They'd wait, and if they had to, they'd do it all again because they'd come too damn far to give up now, and because, yeah, it had been tough, but if this hadn't broken them, nothing could.

He lay awake for a while, telling himself that over and over. That the things in his life he could never have foreseen—the differences between where he found himself and where he'd thought he'd be as he headed up to his twenty-fifth birthday—had been his choices.

You coulda walked away, Brett mouthed in the dark.

And he'd thought about it. He hated to admit it, but he had, and he'd been tempted to do it. It would have been… well, not *easy*, but he could have done it, so many times. At the beginning, when he was still so swirled up in guilt and anger and still able to believe that maybe he'd just stuck with Tommy out of some sense of blame. As if feeling guilty for not helping him explained it all. He could have walked then. He could have walked when Tommy made the plea bargain, backed away from this thing before it got a hold of him, burrowing through him like some vicious, twining fungus.

He could have, but he hadn't.

Brett had believed in Tommy, and he believed in the two of them enough to have faith in them both. Sure, blind, optimistic faith had given way to the roots and tendrils that grew with time, binding him to Tommy in new ways—his dependency, his gratitude, the routines and realities of what everyday life had come to be—and binding him to Scott, Karen, Atian, Mei, Robbie, Lila, and Katie too…. Like a really dysfunctional version of the Waltons.

He knew he could never replace their brother but, slowly, he had taken on part of Tommy's role. He'd represented him, been the part of him that showed his place in the family wasn't forgotten. The truest kind of acceptance Brett guessed he could have hoped for.

And now it would all change. He wasn't sure he'd be ready for it.

Restless, he turned over again and kicked back the covers. *Bullshit.* There would be time to adjust. Time to work up to it. It didn't necessarily mean everything would fail, break under some sudden strain.

We're tougher than that. We have to be.

CHAPTER TWENTY

TOMMY stood in the parking lot, looking up at the small, plain condo. Light rain pattered on his shoulders. He should have called. He had called, but maybe Brett wasn't home yet, and anyway, he kept his cell off at work and… and, well, what did you say?

Seven hours ago, the only thing Tommy had been looking forward to was lumpy mac and cheese and maybe the possibility of checking out a new book from the reading program in his rec hour. Then Tommy's PO had come by, said to his celly, "Grant, you're paroled," and, in the time it had taken Tommy to turn to the guy and say "Damn, you lucky bastard!" he'd heard six tiny words: "You too, Hawks. Get your stuff."

And that had been it. He didn't understand how when he'd expected so many long days, so much drawn-out anticipation. There had been no nail-chewing, gut-twisting wait, no dressing out box, and no time to think. Just… out. The air felt different. Everything looked different too. Colors, shapes, everything just that little bit more defined.

He realized his palms were sweating. Maybe he shoulda gone to his mother's house. That had been put down as his registered address, after all, but what could he do? Sit on the porch 'til she got home from work? Just wait for Lila or Robbie to let him in, all that awkward silence and clearing of throats?

No, he couldn't do that.

Tommy started to climb the stairs. They'd been to see him, about two weeks ago, all four of them. Hell, kids grew up fast. They… well, they weren't kids any more. Only Katie, and damn if she didn't look just like Lila had at that age. And Robbie! Robbie was turning into the image of Scott. Lila just looked beautiful. He'd wanted to hug her, but he'd been scared.

She'd seemed strained, distant. They all had, and that hardly surprised him… he didn't feel like he belonged to them anymore. Not really. She'd kissed his cheek with all the quick gracelessness of a teenager and looked at the floor for the rest of the time.

Tommy swallowed nervously. He'd found Brett's apartment easily, no need to write down the number. He knocked on the door and stepped back, waiting to see if there'd be an answer, scoping out somewhere he could sit and wait if not, but just as he moved to hunker down, a movement from behind the door caught his attention. The moment stretched out, taut but empty, and Tommy tried not to shake as he heard the bolt slide back. What the hell should he say?

"Oh my God!"

The words trailed off in a yelp as Brett launched at him. Tommy wanted so much to look at him, but he couldn't; his eyes closed, his face buried in Brett's neck, in the soft cotton of a shirt that smelled of home. Brett's arms enfolded him, and he wasn't sure that any of it could be real.

Neither of them spoke anymore except in a series of gulping breaths too dry to be tears and too harsh to be sighs. Tommy, holdall forgotten at his feet, held on to him, willing both his tears and his hard-on to go away. It seemed as if, before today, he'd never been touched, never been held.

"Oh, God," Brett whispered again, breath warm on Tommy's ear.

They'd talked about the possibility of this; release dates sometimes did get changed at the last minute, bumped up or down according to the complex timetabling demands of the system. Brett had said that on the online support forum he'd joined for prisoners' families they called it an "oh my God moment." Tommy saw why, and he smiled at that. Just another of the things he'd never thought for a second would happen to him.

To *them*.

He tried to pull away, to look at Brett; it was like trying to come up for air in a rough sea heavy with waves. Brett pushed the hair off Tommy's forehead, tucked it behind his ear. Such a small, intimate gesture. His touch meant a great deal more than Tommy could put words to.

"What the hell…?"

Tommy shook his head wordlessly and just stared at him. Brett had aged. They both had, he knew that, but somehow he'd not noticed those subtle changes: the beginnings of lines around his mouth and eyes, the last broadenings of his shoulders, the final thickening of legs, arms, waist…. It was as if, in all those visits, he'd never really looked at him, so busy trying to memorize everything, cling to it tight enough to last, that he hadn't really seen the time pass.

But he liked it. Brett looked like he'd finally grown into himself. Tommy laughed. They both did, a damp little explosion of relief, of awe. Brett hugged him tight again.

"Come in. Just… come on."

The room wasn't large, and the furniture didn't match, but everything from the physio books butting up to the spy thrillers on the bookshelf to the white-petaled coffee plant on the end table seemed to say "Brett." It felt like walking into him. Intoxicating. The door shut behind him. Tommy took a deep breath, telling himself that it didn't matter.

"I like your place," he said, feeling Brett fill the air behind him.

He had no idea how it could be possible to be so aware of depth and space but it seemed he knew, down to the last molecule, where Brett would fit in the world. His world. He felt Brett touch him, felt him move, ending beside him, waiting to see if he'd take off his coat. Suddenly, every second stuck to his skin like wet sand. As if he could hear every speck of dust falling to earth, and he almost wanted to turn and run.

Tommy had thought so often of how this would be. Fantasies had filled the darkest parts of his nights. When he'd been frustrated and hard, they would strip clothes and souls, make fierce love in the hallway. When he'd been lonely and lost, he'd dreamed of long embraces and tenderness. Sometimes, bruised and low, he'd just tried to picture it, whether it would be awkward, desperate, tearful.... Now, the absurd terror that it wasn't real gripped him.

"Tommy?" Brett stepped in front of him, concerned. "You okay?"

"Yeah. Yeah, better than that. It's just so good to...."

The first kiss silenced him. Tentatively, they held each other—uncensored, unwatched—rediscovering the taste and texture of kisses, the hardness of cheekbones, the yielding places and corded muscles of necks and jaws, the softness of lips and cheeks.

Again, Tommy wished he could get rid of the diamond cutter in his pants. Brett chuckled as he ran his hand over it, dragging a gasp from Tommy even through the thick denim.

"Ah.... Shit!"

"It's all right. Came prepared, huh?"

Tommy frowned. "Didn't come here for that. Well... not.... I mean—"

"Shh." Brett rubbed his nose alongside Tommy's. "It's okay. Plenty of time. You hungry? I have food. It's not meatloaf."

Tommy didn't feel able to argue with a statement like that. "Really?"

"Sure. What do you want?"

Tommy took a minute to think of an answer... questions like that hadn't happened to him for a while.

"Uh...."

"How about grilled cheese? That sound good?"

"Mm. Thanks."

Brett gave him one last squeeze and moved off to the kitchen. Adoration welled up in Tommy—had Brett known how to make that easier?—tinged with only a little worry. He could take most things, but not Brett being careful with him, managing him.

Nah. It's gonna be fine.

"All right. Go on, go sit down. Relax. Have you called your mom yet? Or d'you want me to?"

Tommy shrugged and shook his head, wordless and overwhelmed. He let Brett see to things and drifted over to look out of the window. It overlooked the road outside, the hospital just visible beyond that and, further back, the purple-blue haze of mountains standing against the sky. So much space out there, Tommy realized. It had been easy to forget the Big Country went on for so far.

He flopped gratefully onto the faded green couch and listened to Brett clattering about in the kitchen.

So, bam, here's your life back, sew up the holes and get on with it.

Tommy bit his lip, barely noticing Brett set the grilled cheese sandwich down in front of him. Brett frowned, watching him carefully.

"You coulda called me. I'd'a come got you."

Tommy shook his head, reaching out for the sandwich. Doing so felt odd, and he still seemed to be gliding through a world that wasn't quite the same as he remembered it being—brighter colors, more sounds, sharper air—but his stomach rumbled and quieted the shreds of panic. Warm, crispy, gooey… he bit into a little piece of heaven, eyes closing and a small, satisfied grunt escaping him.

He hadn't wanted to call anybody. The journey had been his time. A slice of hours in which he could just breathe, just let himself get used to it all.

Freedom? Not yet. Liberty, maybe. For now, that was probably enough.

"Want a beer?"

Tommy nodded fervently around the sandwich, and Brett smiled.

"'K."

He snagged two from the fridge and sat down next to Tommy, giving him all the space the couch would allow.

Tommy snuck a sidelong look at him, marveling at how his presence changed things. Brett, who had been his rock for so many fucking years: his constant, his sensible, motivating helpmeet. Sitting here with him, cheese grease running down the side of his palm, all Tommy wanted to do was hold him, and yet he'd never felt so awkward.

It was almost like it had been, that summer a lifetime ago, when he didn't know what Brett wanted, didn't know whether to touch him or not.

Tommy glanced at him once more and met complete trust in those hazel eyes. He swallowed, bread and cheese balling in his throat. It seemed like a hell of a lot to live up to.

BRETT kidded himself he'd known what to expect, even if he hadn't expected it yet. He'd read up on the kind of things he might see in Tommy—the ways guys could get institutionalized, find it hard to adjust back to life—but none of it had prepared him for this. He wanted to touch Tommy, wanted to fall off the ledge and prove his reality, his presence and... and that they could still do that. That they still meant more to each other than just something to focus on, something to hold on to.

He needn't have worried.

Tommy ate his sandwich, drank his beer, and belched happily. He grinned lopsidedly at Brett and, for a moment, it looked like he'd never changed.

"Thanks," he said, his smile softening.

Brett shook his head. "Just... glad you're home."

Home. A simple word, but loaded with a lot of baggage. He wished he hadn't said it—this wasn't Tommy's home, after all. Not technically. Tommy didn't seem to react, though. He just kept looking at Brett, the way he hadn't looked in a very long time.

God. Does he want it as bad as me? Or should I not push it?

It was a distinctly odd feeling, Brett decided. Being alone together after so long, wanting desperately to touch him, and yet tainted by the lingering fear that it somehow wasn't the right time, that he shouldn't—

"Brett?"

Tommy reached out. Such a simple thing to do, though there had never seemed to be so much space between them. Brett couldn't ignore the way it felt—just the gentlest brush of fingertips against his knuckles, but it turned the whole world silent.

"Uh-huh?"

He wanted to grab Tommy, hard, cling onto him and work out all those years of pent-up frustration. Six years of not being able to touch him. Six years of long, meaningful looks across Formica tables, hands pressed close where bodies couldn't follow. Six years of truncated kisses and yearning phone calls. A whole wall of time that stood between them still, the changes it had wrought littering the floor.

"Can I… I mean, you're not…."

"Stay as long as you want," Brett murmured. "I can call your mom later, let her know what's—"

"Yeah."

He pulled Tommy close, gently but purposefully. It was awkward at first, like they'd both forgotten how to hold each other, but that didn't last. The embrace came back like a memory, warmth and tentative breaths locking them together. Everything somehow felt better with those arms around him, and as he moved in to claim Tommy's mouth, the strange dichotomy of it struck Brett. All at once so familiar, and comforting because of it, yet also colored with that electric brilliance that had glimmered between them at the start. So new, so exciting… he guessed they had this honeymoon period to look forward to.

Brett's stomach knotted in anticipation, quivering even tighter as Tommy deepened the kiss, fingers sliding under the hem of his shirt.

"Don't call her yet, though," Tommy purred as they parted. "Little later?"

"Mnn," Brett agreed, blissfully tangled up in him. "Lots later. Consider yourself in hiding."

"Hmm… funny. Hey, I just realized. Are you wearing my shirt?"

Brett grinned sheepishly. "If I said yeah, would you think it's weird?"

"I knew you had 'em. Scott said." Tommy smiled. "He thinks it's sweet."

Brett pulled a face. "Aw, hell."

"No… it's nice. *You're* nice. I…." Tommy stopped, stumbling a little on the words as his thumb traced Brett's neck. "I—"

"I know. Look, this can go slower if you want. It doesn't have to be now."

Tommy frowned doubtfully. "Nn-nn," he said after a moment, tugging at Brett's fly. "Now."

"Okay," Brett consented, trying to keep the shake out of his voice. He cleared his throat. "Uh, bedroom, then. To the left. I'd'a cleaned up if I knew you'd be dropping by," he added as they lurched through the door.

"Don't care," Tommy murmured, "don't care 'bout anythin' except you."

The bed, clothed in warm, soft colors, seemed to wash over them. Hands shook, breath caught, and buttons snagged in the process of undressing. Brett pulled away a little as he slipped Tommy's shirt off, pausing to take a close-up look at that tattoo.

It showed a dragon, or at least part of one. Half-folded wings, coiled neck, and fang-filled, open mouth picked out in dark blue ink, rake shaded to a blurry gray in the shadows. The dragon's front legs held up as if in battle, its whole forward section was made to look as if it had burst through a tear in the skin, a jagged, tooth-like incision.

Brett knew what it meant. He'd done his homework right after Tommy had told him about the tattoo. He hadn't been sure which made him feel sicker: the fact that he'd read how most prison ink got applied with jerry-rigged machines made out of things like nine-volt batteries, old guitar strings, and plastic pen casings, or what the dragon represented. It stood for the darkness within, the pain and the temptation and the rash moment of doing something terrible breaking out onto the surface, no care for what it destroyed along the way.

He shivered. Tommy's hand stroked through his hair.

"You still don't like it, do you?"

Brett glanced up at him and smiled. "It'll grow on me," he lied.

"Oh. Well," Tommy said, his voice thinning as Brett leaned in to kiss the tattoo, moving down across his chest in firm, swift bites. "I figured I could always get cover-up work, or… mmm… something.

Huge portrait of you inked all over my back, so you can look at yourself when we—"

"Not funny," Brett said indistinctly, giving him a warning nip on the stomach that nearly ended in disaster. "Another crack like that, I will let you come in your pants. I swear."

"Oh! Okay, kidding. Just kidding… I'll behave. Promise."

"Good."

TOMMY gritted his teeth and shut his eyes as, carefully, Brett knelt over him and unzipped his fly. He held his breath, tilting his hips up to help his jeans on their gradual, agonizing descent, barely hearing them hit the floor when Brett tossed them away.

He muttered shapeless, lost words left half-formed as Brett's hot breath grazed him. After that, just the hot wetness of his mouth. Incredible, dark, needling pleasure, choking and pushing him until he lost himself in it, giving in to that final freedom. It didn't take long until he felt Brett going over the edge too, groaning out his release without even touching himself, and it seemed to last forever.

Afterwards, just lying back among the pillows, relishing their softness and abundance, and feeling the heaviness of Brett's head resting on his stomach soothed him. Just as well, because Tommy couldn't have moved even if he'd wanted to. He felt… turned inside out, he supposed. Not just from what they'd done. He'd shaken, sweated—even cried—given so much more than he had in so long.

Now, he reached up and swiped away more silent, unwanted tears. Brett rubbed his side, comforting him.

"Hey. Wanna take a shower? Or are you sick of sharin' by now?"

Tommy grinned. He loved Brett most of all, right now, for letting his weaknesses stay unspoken.

"Mainly, yeah. Could make an exception for you, though."

Brett sat up laboriously and stretched. Tommy let his gaze trail slowly over every softly sculptured muscle in Brett's torso, reading the changes, the differences in his body. The sticky smears and that slutty, impish smile….

Brett winked at him. "That's good. 'Cause you did what you always do. You always get the hair, y'know? It's like you aim on purpose."

Tommy raised one leg and gave him a halfhearted kick. "I'll show you on purpose."

Brett laughed. "Come on. Shower first."

"Mm. Sounds good."

They used up most of the hot water. Brett—despite complaining about his own hair—took time to wash Tommy's. He soaped, massaged, and rinsed, seeming to revel in the new sensations. Tommy relaxed, melting against him under the spray. It wasn't something he'd ever thought he'd list as a turn-on, but it felt great. He smiled, thinking of how a few months back, Brett had shyly mentioned he preferred Tommy's hair longer. He'd started growing it again, of course—ready in case the parole did come through, stupid though it had seemed at the time—and this definitely made it worthwhile.

"That all right?" Brett murmured.

"Mm."

Tommy tipped his face up to the spray, letting the water run over his closed eyes. After a moment, he turned to face Brett, shaking the water off himself like old memories.

"Wanna make you feel good too," he whispered, reaching for him in the blur of steam, need cracking open in his voice. "I... I want everything. Wasted so long, baby."

"Not wasted," Brett muttered. He reached past Tommy's kisses to turn off the shower. "I've always been here."

Tommy sighed, his face still pressed against Brett's, wet skin warmed with the breath trapped between them. That wasn't the point, and Brett knew it. Didn't he? He found it so hard to tell what Brett understood and what he didn't. Sometimes he was right inside Tommy's head; when he'd thought nobody could ever figure out what he was going through, Brett would step right up to the plate. Other times, he could be so wide of the mark it wasn't even funny.

He tugged at Tommy's wrist. "Come on."

Reluctantly, they stepped out of the shower and toweled off. Tommy padded back into the bedroom—slowly, unused to all these

different rooms, no matter how hard he tried to keep calm about it—
and flopped down on the bed. He quirked an eyebrow at Brett.

"You staying there?"

Brett blinked. He was still propping up the doorframe. "Oh… no.
Um. I, uh, remembered…. I-I don't have any protection." He winced.
"Sorry. Don't keep 'em in the house, 'cause, well…."

Tommy smiled sleepily. God, Brett looked sexy when he
blushed.

"Never?"

Brett shook his head. "You know. Only with Nick. And that
never felt… well, he wasn't you. It, uh, just didn't end up being
something we did."

Tommy looked away. Not embarrassment, not exactly. Just the
feeling his chest might burst. Brett came and sat on the edge of the
bed, watching him. Tommy could tell how badly he wanted it—his
hand shook a little as he traced it over Tommy's chest—but he knew
that, however much the air crackled, they weren't about to take any
chances. He'd requested a whole panel of tests after the parole
hearing… HIV, hepatitis, everything the medical center could screen
for. He'd been careful—apart from the tattoo, maybe, and even he
acknowledged now that perhaps that hadn't been the greatest idea
ever—but infection rates among the inmate population ran so high that
he'd wanted to be sure. To know, before he got out, if there could be
any problems in store.

He'd told Brett, just so he knew, and the memory of his face—
pallid and appalled as he tried desperately to take it in his stride, and
failed—had haunted Tommy. Everything came back negative, but he
still felt like a leper.

Brett patted his leg.

"Look, I better call Mei. She's gonna want to know you're back.
You wanna go over there? If she asks, I mean? What d'you want me to
say?"

Tommy shrugged against the pillows. "Whatever."

He didn't mean it as indifference, but Brett looked at him a
moment too long before he left the room.

WHEN she heard, of course Mei wanted them over for dinner. Tommy's homecoming had to be celebrated in style, and the meal at his mother's—no, *his* house, Brett corrected—ended up being a long, rowdy affair. Scott and Karen brought Atian, who ran riot for most of the time, skidding on the laminate floors in his socks and wearing his shoes on his hands, while Lila preened loudly in the way of teenage girls showing everybody that they're absolutely not feeling overwhelmed at all, and Robbie did his man-of-the-house act. He got more like Scott every day, Brett thought.

The hard part wasn't being there. It felt right, it felt... like home. Mei sat them side by side at dinner, and no one blinked an eye when, adjourning to the sitting room with coffee after the meal, Tommy sat close to Brett, looping an arm around his shoulders and, once, nuzzling his cheek.

Brett realized, with a glowing kernel of excitement, that he'd have to get used to this. Learn how to be with Tommy all over again.

Properly, this time.

The thing that sucked was leaving him there. Brett knew he had to, but it seemed so cruel. They'd had barely a few hours together, and he'd been so tempted to ask Tommy to stay the night.

It wouldn't have been a good idea, he supposed. He needed—no, they both needed—time to adjust, and Tommy probably a whole lot more than him. He'd looked tired earlier, when they got out of the shower, and not just from the quick tumble. A horrible weariness lingered in his face, like this was all too much for him.

Best that he has some time to himself.

Hard though it was, Brett guessed he'd have more luck finding that at Mei's place. Besides, though the homecoming itself didn't seem to be too difficult, he knew Tommy had plenty to work through with his family. It rankled, but even now, Brett still felt like that didn't include him. Stupid, he knew, but true.

All the same, it ached, knowing he'd have to go back to the apartment without Tommy. But, his mother's house had been registered as his home, after all. And—although he didn't like to admit it—Brett knew it would never have been a good idea to put the extra pressure of moving in with him on Tommy's shoulders.

Not yet.

"I'll come by tomorrow," Tommy promised as they said goodbye at the door. "When you get off work. Six?"

Brett nodded, feeling childishly, jealously, irritated by it all. He could see Lila over Tommy's shoulder, peering at them without quite spying, exactly, from the dining room doorway.

Tommy leaned in and kissed him softly. His breath tickled Brett's upper lip, and he pushed forward into the kiss, not willing to let him go. Not again. Tommy didn't resist him, and Brett deepened the kiss, sought out the warm fire of his tongue.

"Mmn...." Tommy pulled back first, hand on Brett's cheek. "I love you."

"Love you too, baby."

"Tomorrow, right?"

"You never have to ask. You know that."

Tommy smiled, his eyes dark and hazy. "Stop by the drugstore on your way home?"

"Sure." Brett winked at him. "Sleep well, darlin'."

"Hah. Yeah, right!"

HE FOLLOWED Brett out onto the porch, leaned on the rail, and watched him walk slowly down to the Chevy, dawdling with every step. Tommy fought down the feeling he had every time he watched Brett leave, that cold, slightly itchy, slimy uncertainty. *Hate to see you go. Love to watch you walking away.* He curled one hand in a wave as Brett pulled away and listened to the familiar sound of that engine fading into the night.

Slowly, Tommy realized he wasn't alone. He was about to turn around when, from the corner of his eye, he saw Lila's smooth brown arms come to rest on the rail beside him.

"Hey," he said.

"Hi."

He looked over at her, watched her stare out into the street. The lights blazed in one of the houses opposite, a warm yellow glow pooling out into the yard. Lila leaned her head against his arm, and Tommy wondered what he should say to her. He took a breath, the air suddenly cool on his face. She glanced up at him, her eye makeup too heavy and her brows plucked too thin. A smile pulled on her mouth.

"Y'know," Lila said, nudging her brother affectionately, "if you two turn any sweeter, you'll melt in the rain."

Tommy chuckled and shook his head. "Shut up, Bear Bait."

She pressed closer, filling up his world when he bent to kiss her hair.

"I'm glad you're home, though."

Tommy closed his eyes, just letting the night wash over him. Somewhere a dog barked, the sound echoing off the traffic noise and the distant, passing lilt of a siren.

CHAPTER TWENTY-ONE

TOMMY tugged ineffectually at the edge of the comforter, resigning himself to having about a third of it. Brett hadn't changed; he still hogged the covers. It didn't matter, though. Even after nearly three weeks, this seemed new enough for his annoying habits to be kinda cute. Almost. He listened to Brett's gentle snoring, and the sound soothed him.

He'd come home.

He'd been realizing that from the first day after he got out. They'd never waited for six o'clock; he'd been sitting outside Brett's door by five fifteen. At 5:29, Brett had barely parked the Chevy before they'd been all over each other. It was fierce, clutching stuff, the bed heaving and slamming against the wall, Tommy reciting multiplication tables and old Super Bowl scores under his breath, trying to hold off. Something about it scared him a little, something about the desperate way they touched, him still in his T-shirt and one sock, blue boxers tangled around Brett's ankles. Their cries mixed like the depths and lifts of an ocean, the sounds of hoarse voices and wet flesh rippling and echoing over each other. Tommy remembered giving in some time after nine times seven and the New England Patriots.

It felt like he hadn't left Brett's apartment since, though that wasn't true. Sure, Tommy was spending more and more time here, though he technically resided at his mother's, but plenty got him out of the house. There'd been that horribly awkward, tense dinner with Brett's parents, for one thing. He suppressed a shudder at the memory. It wasn't that they weren't nice people, because they did seem to be, but they'd only ever met him as an inmate before. He recalled that Christmas they'd come to Deer Lodge with Brett and been so determinedly nonjudgmental about everything, and how Brett had made a point of holding his hand.

Then, of course, he'd had to schlep all over town on job interviews that always followed the same pattern. At first they seemed so promising, but then they always disintegrated... even his old boss in Burnham. Fine on paper but, all of a sudden, the economy wasn't so good; he turned out to be over-qualified or didn't have enough practical experience or some other reason cropped up, some other excuse. Endless meetings with his parole officer had demanded his attention, too, and then Katie's school orchestra recital.... Tommy couldn't help the feeling that everybody kept thinking purposely of things to do with him, ways to reintroduce him to the world. And after it all, he'd find himself stopping by his mother's house for a while but always coming back here. *Back home?*

He wondered. Maybe.

Brett had left space for his things in the closet, stocked up on spare razorblades, socks, underwear.... Tommy had even found a few new shirts, still in their wrappings, stuffed in a drawer. An extra toothbrush had miraculously appeared in the bathroom. He hadn't had to ask for a thing. And it.... No, it didn't piss him off. Not really. Not exactly that.

Tommy blinked, shaking those snippy, ungrateful thoughts. He wrestled a little bit more of the covers back from Brett's sleeping grasp. Only, he'd nearly turned twenty-seven years old and, apart from those few weeks just after Scott had moved out, he'd never even had his own room. He'd always shared with Scott because of the twin thing; you did get used to it, blanking out the noises and the rhythms of someone else's presence, but you never had any privacy. The joint seemed pretty similar, in a way. You might try to retain your space, but you always had another guy there.

Tommy had never had a bad cellmate—sheer blind luck, he guessed—and he'd found it easier, knowing someone else was sleeping there. Someone between him and the night, between him and all the other guys out on the floor, the yelling and the secrets in the dark. Now, Tommy wondered if he could ever manage being alone. He used to think it would be nice to have his own place, some little apartment somewhere. But maybe not. Maybe, Tommy thought, as Brett shifted beside him, he'd finished with isolation and loneliness.

He turned over, rested his head on his arm, and burrowed his free hand beneath the covers, seeking out Brett's warm skin, letting his fingers trail down his side and come to rest on his hip. Brett mumbled in his sleep and pressed back against Tommy; the body responded, even if the brain was asleep, and Tommy thought immediately and incongruously of that Nick guy.

The jealousy came suddenly, unexpected and hard, like a punch to the face. Oh, Tommy had always known about him, Brett insisting like he had on being so completely honest. Far too honest. Frankly, it would have been easier not to know. But back then, the anger, the hurt, had seemed easy to hide away, easy to keep from him. Tommy had been able to stick to his sensible response: itches need scratching. Okay, so he'd lived with the fear that Brett would fall for someone else, choose something easier, but he'd managed to deal with it.

Why should it be tougher to cope with now? It was over. Long over. And, anyway, Brett might have spread his wings a few times, but he'd come home to roost. That meant something, didn't it?

Tommy kissed the back of Brett's shoulder, waiting for a moment to see if he'd wake, and knowing that he wouldn't. He sighed and slipped out of bed, wishing he had a cigarette.

He'd always hated smoking. The smell, the taste, the gritty staleness of it was somehow an indelible part of the blackest days he could remember. He'd never thought he'd start, but it had helped… especially after he gave up using weed. Too many random piss tests and cell checks. Brett would never have forgiven him if he'd wrecked his good conduct with a drug infraction. He hadn't exactly approved of the cigarettes, but….

Tommy wondered, as he padded to the window, whether Brett would have asked him to quit, if he hadn't already stopped.

BRETT woke, dimly aware of movement in the room. He sat up in bed and blinked. It was still dark outside, and the drapes hoarded moonlight except for a pale, narrow band spilling through.

Tommy stood by the window, half-turned away from him, holding the drape back slightly, looking out at... what? The stars? The soft light threw his body into shrouded relief against the dark. His arms, his shoulders, back, legs, his beautiful ass... and that fucking tattoo curling over the top of his left arm like a shadow. All of him, perfectly imperfect, drawn as if with some strange airbrush palette of blues and grays.

Brett choked down his first impulse: to speak. *What's the matter, baby?* That attempt to bridge the gulf; the irresistible desire to communicate, to try to share. He said nothing, just watched. Waited.

After a moment that seemed to last such a long time, Tommy turned. He smiled, and Brett raised a hand, scrubbed at his hair, and stifled a not entirely pretended yawn.

"Can't sleep?"

Tommy gave a little one-shouldered shrug.

"You want anything?" Brett asked.

Another shrug.

The silence stretched out between them, thick and unyielding. Things would get better, Brett told himself. You had to expect rough patches. Only, Tommy seemed so damn hard to read, now more than ever.

He licked his lips nervously. "Come back to bed?"

Tommy looked at him for a while, his features blurred in the half-light. The silence lapped around them. Brett knew this mattered, this moment. He looked at Tommy, praying the question he hadn't asked had been heard and understood.

Come back to me?

After an eternity, Tommy pushed away from the window, padded across the floor, and slipped back under the covers.

"You're cold," Brett muttered.

He wrapped himself around Tommy and tucked the covers around them, pretending to ignore the strange relief rushing through him, as if holding Tommy now was as good as holding him forever.

"It starts here, right?"

Tommy frowned. "What?" he asked, Brett's hair prickling against his mouth, warmed by his breath.

"Everything," Brett murmured. "Here on out, it's a new start."

He shut his eyes, needing Tommy to agree, to just nod and hold him and say, yeah, this would be their life from now on. Snug, warm and… safe.

Only that would make it a blanket fort, not a relationship.

Tommy pulled back, and Brett cranked his eyes open just enough to see his solemn look, clouded in the dimness. Tommy's chest rose and fell to the rhythm of his own, the steady beat of his heart echoing where their bodies touched.

Yeah, maybe it would be difficult. But life tended to be like that. Brett shifted against the mattress, determined to take back what he'd said, to tell Tommy that, actually, maybe it didn't all need to be new. Maybe they'd be fine, just building up where they'd left off, just… getting along.

Only, Tommy seemed to have other ideas. He smiled, his kiss a whisper on Brett's mouth.

"You're right," he said softly. "It is. Everything's gonna be different, darlin'. And we're gonna make it count."

Brett let his words sink in, lips still pressed together, bodies still cleaving tight to each other. Nothing else felt like it would matter now, and so maybe it could be true. Couldn't it? They could make it work with just a little optimism, some luck, and some blind faith.

He hoped so.

It was at least worth trying.

M. KING resides in a damp, verdant corner of southwest England, where she may usually be found behind a keyboard and a vat of coffee. A former Arvon Foundation Award winner, she is an inveterate scribbler and teller of tales and has never yet met a genre she didn't like.

Her work features flawed and fascinating characters, vibrant storytelling, and worlds to lose yourself in time and again, with titles ranging from horror to fantasy, humor to romance, erotica to tear-jerking drama… and more.

On the very rare occasions she isn't writing, M. King enjoys taking long, muddy walks with her dogs—otherwise known as the hairy chaos monkeys—reading, dabbling in her herb garden, and falling off horses. Just not all at the same time.

Visit her web site at http://www.thenakednib.com. You can contact her at lavengra@yahoo.com.

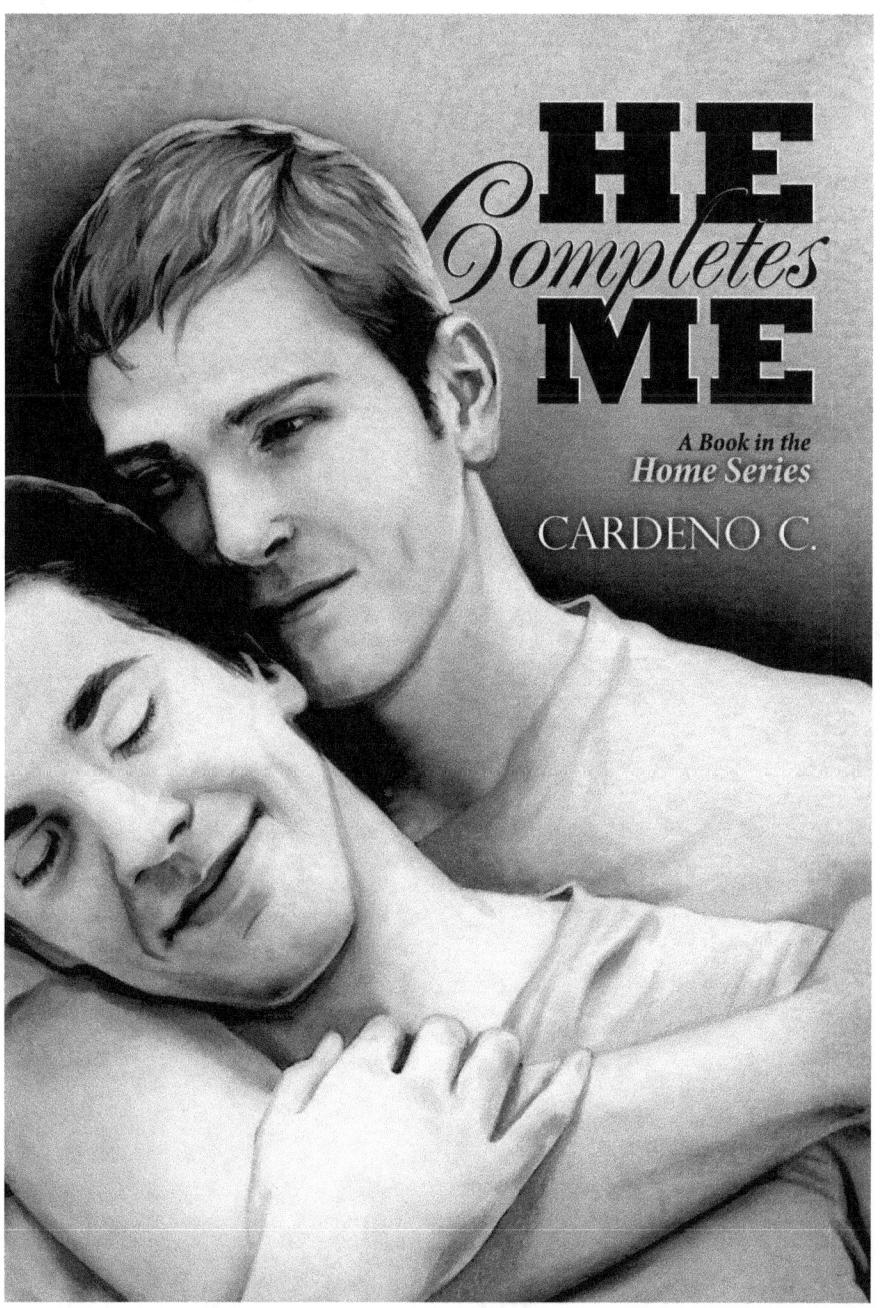